PRAISE

ASSASSIN'S

G000115816

"A heart-pounding and breath-holding thriller."

—**Galen D. Peterson, Author of *Strike Hard and Expect No Mercy***

"If you found Samuel G. Tooma's first novel, *The SOOF*, riveting, its sequel, *Assassin's Revenge*, will have you on the edge of your seat throughout. In *Assassin's Revenge*, Tooma pushes his protagonist, Samantha Stone, to new heights as she pursues a villain as vile as the world has ever seen. Anton Yulov, AKA the Ghost, soon learns what it's like to be the object of a woman scorned."

—**Joseph C. Pinto, Educator**

"A swirling vortex of action is the only way to describe *Assassin's Revenge* by Samuel G. Tooma. It's the perfect follow-up to his excellent novel *The SOOF*. Full of twists, surprises, mayhem, and even a traitor, this sequel doesn't disappoint. Buy it. Read it."

—**James A. Davison, Author of *Trinity 3.11*, *I Am Lazarus, and Bottom Feeder***

"The clever and talented Samantha Stone is back and pitting her skills against a depraved and ruthless international assassin in this exciting sequel to *The SOOF*. I really enjoyed Tooma's engaging and often witty storytelling in this intriguing action-thriller."

—Robert Smoot, Senior Software Architect for a major international corporation

"I live an ordinary life. But *Assassin's Revenge* took me for an exciting ride with extraordinary characters ranging from the depraved to the sublime. And Tooma somehow weaves them into a riveting plot with a female protagonist, Samantha Stone, who carries the show. I can't wait for the next Samantha Stone novel."

—Kathleen Sturm, Book Lover

"*Assassin's Revenge* is an action-packed thriller that kept my attention during the entire book. There were many surprises as the plot unfolded and came to an unexpected and happy ending. It was a quick read that can be enjoyed by any reader. Samuel G. Tooma has come up with a complementary sequel to his previous book, *The SOOF*."

—Jonathan Rubin, Air Force Veteran

"I thoroughly enjoyed Samuel G. Tooma's first novel, *The SOOF*. In fact, I didn't want it to end. It's sequel, *Assassin's Revenge*, thrilled me to the max. It is full of action and suspense with many twists and turns along the way. The protagonist, Dr. Samantha Stone, is a breath of fresh air and remains either a real human superhero or a humble female James Bond. I anxiously awaited every scene she was in. The story culminates in an eyebrow and pulse-raising ending that I didn't see coming. I certainly hope there are future Samantha Stone adventures on the horizon. Loved this book."

—Dr. Larry C. Gunn, MD

"I found *Assassin's Revenge* exciting and suspenseful. I read it in one sitting. Just couldn't put it down. The Christian undertone woven throughout the story was uplifting to me. I recommend Tooma's book to all who love to read."

—Timothy Scharold, MD

"*Assassin's Revenge* is the fast paced, can't put down sequel to *The SOOF*. An amazing protagonist in a non-stop chess match with an evil foe accelerates the tension to the thrilling conclusion."

—Richard D Groves, Author of *The Hidden Game*

Assassin's Revenge

by Samuel G. Tooma

ISBN 978-1-64663-799-7

Published by

 köehlerbooks™

3705 Shore Drive
Virginia Beach, VA 23455
800-435-4811
www.koehlerbooks.com

ASSASSIN'S
REVENGE

SAMUEL G. TOOMA

VIRGINIA BEACH
CAPE CHARLES

BE SURE TO READ
DR. SAMANTHA STONE'S
FIRST ADVENTURE

The SOOF by Samuel G. Tooma

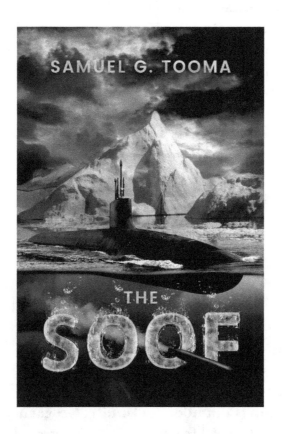

CAST OF CHARACTERS

- **Dr. Samantha Stone**—Environmental scientist, Naval Research Laboratory
- **Captain Ira Coen**—Commanding officer, USS *Hawkbill* (SSN-999)
- **Commander Fred Boone**—Executive officer, USS *Hawkbill* (SSN-999)
- **Harlan Bradbury**—Director, Central Intelligence Agency
- **Admiral Roger Flaxon**—Chief of Naval Operations
- **James Milsap**—President of the United States
- **Lieutenant Odd Bergstrom**—Norwegian Navy
- **Lieutenant Commander Lars Sarsgaard**—Commanding officer, Norwegian Outpost OP-247
- **Ragnar Solberg**—Head, Norwegian Security Agency
- **Captain Forrest Jenkins**—Lead officer, Team Bravo
- **Commander Jared Townsend**—Lead officer, DEVGRU SEAL Platoon
- **Lieutenant Josh Freeman**—Junior officer, DEVGRU SEAL Platoon
- **Master Chief Bryan Boxer**—Chief of the boat (COB), USS *Hawkbill*
- Sonar Tech 1st class **"Twigs" Twigerton**
- **Anton Yulov**—Russian Minister of Finance; AKA The Ghost
- **Anna Yulov**—Daughter of Anton Yulov
- **Rhetta Yulov**—Wife of Anton Yulov
- **Mr. and Mrs. Smith**—CIA spies
- **Mary Graham**—Department head, CIA
- **Captain (Commodore) Dimitri Gregarin**—Commodore of three Russian ASW frigates
- **Jean Barlow**—Secretary to CIA Director Harlan Bradbury

- ◇ **Frank Bilger**—CIA Witness Relocation chief
- ◇ **Bill Williams**—CIA Witness Relocation deputy
- ◇ **Bartholomew (Bart) Frampton**—Samantha's junior bodyguard in Telluride
- ◇ **James Breland**—Samantha's senior bodyguard in Telluride
- ◇ **Guy Andrews**—Ira Coen's bodyguard
- ◇ **Henry Biggsbie**—CIA agent in Telluride
- ◇ **Dr. Jenkins**—Hospital doctor in Telluride
- ◇ **Jack and Jill Hill**—CIA surrogate parents for Samantha's twins
- ◇ **Matthias Roberts**—Chief CIA agent assigned to protect Samantha
- ◇ **Nathanial Breakstone**—Samantha's junior bodyguard in Gulfport
- ◇ **Gilbert Stewart**—Samantha's Oregon State University boyfriend and bush pilot
- ◇ **Big John**—Secret Service agent for President Milsap
- ◇ **Wanda Bedford**—Nurse, Norfolk Hospital
- ◇ **Dr. Larry "Gunner" Gunn**—Samantha's doctor in Norfolk
- ◇ **Simon Prather**—Samantha's junior bodyguard in Norfolk
- ◇ **Irena Rossova**—Anna Yulov's friend in Grindelwald, Switzerland
- ◇ **Gunther Kemp**—Anna Yulov's German friend in Grindelwald
- ◇ **Heinrich Schlosser**—Anna Yulov's German friend in Grindelwald
- ◇ **Rodrigo Ortiz**—CIA agent in Grindelwald
- ◇ **Carrie Sheffield**—Samantha's name in Grindelwald
- ◇ **Joe Pinto**—Samantha's bodyguard and martial arts teacher in Virginia Beach

PROLOGUE

A RUSSIAN MILITARY COUP THAT was ten years in the planning threatened the very existence of the world order as we know it. The coup's objective was to topple the existing Russian government by replacing the incumbent political leaders with carefully selected military generals and admirals. Concomitant with this political coup, a blitzkrieg of conventional forces was to be carried out to overrun western Europe, and the United States was to be rendered powerless by a barrage of tactical nuclear missiles launched by five specially designed nuclear submarines stationed under the Arctic Ocean ice pack just north of Canada. Fortunately, a young Norwegian naval officer stationed at a remote observation outpost on the highest elevation in northernmost Norway observed suspicious Russian naval activity being conducted in the Barents Sea north of Russia.

This unusual activity was brought to the attention of the Norwegian Intelligence Service and to the Norwegian Security Agency. By comparing this new information with seemingly unrelated intelligence data, a picture began to form of a possible Russian effort to establish world domination.

The Norwegians quickly decided to bring this potential threat to the attention of the US Central Intelligence Agency. When the director of the CIA was briefed on the Russian activity, he presented the Norwegian information to key CIA department heads. It was clear that the CIA had not picked up on what the Russians were up to. The director quickly set up a briefing to the president, the chairman of the Joint Chiefs of Staff, and the Chief of Naval Operations.

When the briefing to the president was over, he was extremely angry that his extensive intelligence service and his military leaders had not picked up on the Russian military coup. He immediately initiated a plan to thwart the Russian attempt for world domination. Key to the president's plan was the destruction of the Russian secret command and control facility which was built under the waves and ice pack of the Sea of Okhotsk. This facility, called the SOOF, for Sea of Okhotsk Facility, was essential for the Russians if their plan was to succeed. It was believed that without central command and control, their evil objective would fail. With this in mind, a suicide mission was designed to send a nuclear submarine into the Sea of Okhotsk with an embedded platoon of Navy SEALs to destroy the SOOF the day before the surprise Russian plan was to be initiated.

To accomplish this mission, the commanding officer of the USS *Hawkbill* SSN 999, Captain Ira Coen, had to remain undetected until the SOOF was destroyed. At any time, if this secrecy was compromised, Captain Coen was prepared to ram the SOOF with the *Hawkbill* at the cost of the 140-plus people on board. Failure to destroy the SOOF was not an option.

The most serious threat to the *Hawkbill* was two of Russia's most deadly attack submarines commanded by two of its most senior naval officers. Their mission was to protect the SOOF at all times. Of equal importance to the success of the mission was to deal with the harsh and unknown environment of the Sea of Okhotsk. To overcome this deficiency, the most knowledgeable American environmental scientist on the Sea of Okhotsk, Dr. Samantha Stone, was asked by the president to help plan and carry out this mission.

Captain Coen's submarine tactical skills and Dr. Stone's environmental knowledge were fully put to the test during this extremely important and dangerous mission designed to save the world.

Although Ira initially rejected Samantha to be on the mission because of her lack of military experience, it soon became clear to him how valuable her knowledge was if the personnel on the *Hawkbill* had any chance of returning alive. As preparation of the mission was proceeding in Pearl Harbor, an attraction between Ira and Samantha began to grow. Even though the attraction was mutual and strong, they realized that it had to remain in check in order to not jeopardize the mission. However, once their duty had been discharged, Ira proclaimed his deep love for Samantha, and she did the same by telling him to call her "Sam." Even before their death, she had never allowed anyone else other than her parents to call her that. But now, she realized that she loved Ira just as dearly as she had them, and she wanted to build a life with him.

PART ONE

IDYLLIC

Hero of the Russian Federation Medal with Gold Star

CHAPTER 1
HOMECOMING

AS THE NUCLEAR SUBMARINE USS *Hawkbill* SSN 999, neared her home port of Pearl Harbor, Hawaii, the commanding officer, Captain Ira Coen, made an announcement to the crew.

"This is the captain. We are about one hour from port. I want the on-deck detail dressed in whites and ready to man your mooring stations. Quartermaster, have the Jolly Roger ensign ready to hoist. I want everyone to know that our mission was a success. We will be coming to the surface shortly. I understand that the seas are calm, and our ride into the harbor should be smooth. Once again, I want to thank everyone on board for a job well done."

Ira handed the mic back to his executive officer, Lieutenant Commander Fred Boone. "Well, it's almost over, Fred. To be honest, I never really thought we'd make it back alive."

"I tried not to think about it, Ira. It was always in the back of my mind, but I was able to keep it there." Fred thought for a few seconds then said in a whisper, "The truth is, if it weren't for Samantha, we probably wouldn't be talking here right now."

"I tried to tell her that very thing when the mission was over, but she passed the credit back to me."

"Hmph. That's Samantha."

"Sure is." Ira turned to the petty officer manning the pilot's station. "Pilot, bring us to the surface slowly. Officer of the Deck, check for surface ships."

"Aye, sir. To the surface slowly," the pilot repeated.

"Aye, sir. Checking for surface traffic," repeated the OOD.

Once on the surface, the mooring detail was set and the Jolly Roger ensign was hoisted, signifying *Mission Accomplished.* It was a beautiful sight to see with the boat's black deck lined with brave submariners, all dressed in white and standing at attention.

However, as the assigned mooring pier came into sight, an even more amazing sight was seen. The pier was filled with hundreds of people. A military band began playing "Anchors Aweigh." As *Hawkbill* neared the pier, the men on the deck could see numerous admirals and generals standing at attention saluting the returning heroes. They also saw that families of the crew had been flown to Pearl to welcome them home. And most surprising of all was that the president of the United States, James Milsap, was there as well. Numerous media vans were parked nearby, and television crews were recording the event of the returning submarine.

When the gangway was secured connecting *Hawkbill* with the pier, the band began playing "Hail To The Chief," and President Milsap went across the gangway to greet Captain Coen on the quarterdeck.

President Milsap came up to Ira, shook his hand, hugged him, and said in his ear, "Well done, Ira. Well done."

"Thank you, Mr. President. But to be honest, all this hoopla on the pier is a surprise. You could have warned me."

"I wanted it to be a surprise. Welcome back."

The president began shaking the hands of the XO Fred Boone, the Navy SEAL officers, and the other officers on the deck. When he reached Samantha, he took both her hands in his and took a step backward stretching out their arms. Milsap then smiled and shook his head. He then pulled her toward him and gave her a long, hard hug. When he did this, everyone on the submarine's deck erupted into cheers and clapping. He said to her, "God, Samantha. I am so proud of you. I thank you from the bottom of my heart."

"Thank you, Mr. President. But it was Captain Coen, Commander Townsend, and Lieutenant Freeman that did all the work. I was just an advisor."

Milsap looked at her, smiled, and shook his head. He then said, "There's a certain admiral on the pier that can't wait to give you a hug. I won't tell you who it is, but his initials are Roger Flaxon."

"Roger is on the pier?" she said excitedly, craning her neck to see if she could pick him out.

"Yes, he is."

Captain Coen then announced to the crew that they were free to disembark the boat and meet their families. The crew on deck again erupted into loud cheers. And the band began playing "Anchors Aweigh" once again.

On the pier, joyous family reunions took place, television crews conducted interviews with officers and men of the *Hawkbill*, the governor of Hawaii talked with President Milsap, and the band kept playing rousing military songs.

Then, for Samantha and Admiral Flaxon, the action around them seemed to stop as their eyes met on the pier. They approached one another, said nothing, then hugged. After at least a minute of this embrace, Flaxon said, "Samantha, you are like a daughter to me, and I honestly thought I would never see you again. Thank you for coming back."

"Roger, you are making me cry." She hugged the admiral again.

A voice behind them said, "What are you two lovebirds doing? And why are there tears in your eyes?"

"Forrest!" Samantha yelled out. She immediately threw her arms around Captain Forrest Jenkins, the leader of the team that planned the mission to destroy the SOOF. "It's so good to see you.

Are you still going to church?"

Forrest ignored Samantha's remark and kissed her on the cheek. He then said, "Unlike the admiral here, I never had any doubts that you'd make it back. My only regret is that I couldn't sail with you to see you in action. From what I hear, you were magnificent."

"What's going on here with you guys. All I did was stand around and make some suggestions."

The admiral and Captain Jenkins looked at each other and laughed. Forrest said, "Samantha. There is somebody standing right behind you that is waiting very patiently for his chance to get his welcome home hug."

Samantha turned around and there stood the young Norwegian navy lieutenant, Odd Bergstrom. Lieutenant Bergstrom was the Norwegian navy officer who had initially detected the sinister Russian naval activity in the Barents Sea. "My God, Odd. I see that you are a lieutenant commander now. Congratulations!"

"Thanks, Samantha. The promotion came through just last week. Well, enough of this. When do I get my hug?"

They embraced warmly for a long time. Odd said, "It's been one hell of a year for us, hasn't it?"

"Now that you mention it, Odd, it certainly has."

Meanwhile, Captain Jenkins and Captain Coen's eyes met through the crowd. They immediately walked quickly toward each other and embraced. The two naval men had a serious falling out as junior officers that plagued them throughout their naval careers. Just before the Okhotsk Sea mission, they both admitted to each other the poor decisions they made that led to the fracturing of their relationship. With heartfelt conviction, they forgave one another for their childish actions.

Ira said, "God, Forrest, I wish you had been with us in the Sea of O. It was very scary but exciting at the same time."

"I felt so depressed watching the *Hawkbill* leave the pier. I wanted to be on it with you and the others."

Ira looked at Forrest with tears in his eyes. "Well, we have to get together soon over a few beers, and I'll fill you in on all the details. As I said, it was quite exciting."

"I'll bet, especially with Samantha involved."

"Forrest, she was a gift from heaven."

CHAPTER 2
HOME SWEET HOME

EVENTUALLY, THE JUBILANT ACTIVITY ON the pier began to die down. The returning submariners and the SEALs united with their families and began leaving to spend time with one another. The band packed their instruments and left in a bus, and the media vans drove off. The governor's entourage departed. Left standing on the pier was the original Team Bravo—Captain Forrest Jenkins, Captain Ira Coen, Commander Jared Townsend, Lieutenant Josh Freeman, Lieutenant Commander Fred Boone, and Dr. Samantha Stone. With them was the president of the United States, Admiral Roger Flaxon, and Lieutenant Commander Odd Bergstrom.

Admiral Flaxon finally announced, "Well, here we are. Mission accomplished. Let's celebrate. If that's okay with you, Mr. President?"

President Milsap nodded his head and said, "I've already arranged to have a buffet set up at Carter House on the base housing facility. Open bar." Milsap gave his ever-present entourage of military aides and secret service agents a wave of his hand, and limos began approaching the group. The president began walking toward the approaching vehicles. He turned around and said, "Are you coming, Samantha?"

She responded, "I thought you'd never ask."

Ira smiled broadly knowing that this was her favorite line.

Thirty minutes later, the group was comfortably settled in the elegant Carter House, which had been Samantha's and Odd's home during the planning of Project IDES, the classified code name for the mission to destroy the SOOF.

"Home sweet home. Right, Odd?"

"Well, I've been here about five days now since we got back from the Arctic Ocean."

"You'll have to tell me all about your encounter with the Russian Borei subs."

"Likewise." He said, "I'm sure it was far more exciting for you than it was for me."

Samantha just smiled and nodded.

They looked at one another in admiration for several seconds. Then Samantha said, "Odd, you should be so proud. If it weren't for you, we'd probably all be dead now. You saved us—and the world."

Odd shook his head and said, "All I did was notice something out of the ordinary was happening, and I reported it to my superior officer." He looked at Samantha with a serious smile. "Besides, if I asked everyone here who they think is the one person most responsible for the success of IDES, from what I've heard, the vote would be unanimously in favor of you."

Samantha shook her head in disbelief. "Odd, you need to get some sleep. You are delirious and talking nonsense."

After everyone had enjoyed the buffet and drank a couple of glasses of wine, the president announced, "Let's get comfortable in the living room. I want to bring the *Hawkbill* people up to speed on what's been happening since the Ides of March a couple of weeks ago. I just got word from the CIA director, Harlan Bradbury, that he has landed at Joint Base Hickam and should be here with us in about twenty minutes. Hopefully, he can update me on what I was told earlier today during my morning brief."

When they were comfortably seated in the living room and their wine glasses refilled, President Milsap began.

"As you know, the Russian coup was contained before it even began. On fifteen March, the day before their planned D-Day, in a coordinated preemptive strike, we caught their ground and air forces in Europe during their final mobilization, totally unaware. We destroyed a high percentage of their forces. And without command and control that would have been provided by the SOOF, they willingly hoisted the white flag of surrender. In the Arctic Ocean, thanks to Lieutenant Commander Bergstrom here, we sank the five Borei subs before they fired a single missile. At sea, our attack subs sank many of their subs, essentially rendering the remaining ones harmless against our surface naval forces. And, thanks to you people on the *Hawkbill*, their command-and-control facility, the SOOF, was destroyed. The coup was over before it ever started, and millions of lives were saved."

The president relaxed in his chair and took a sip of wine. He again leaned forward in his chair. "All right. The coup is over. What's next? During the three months of planning before IDES, we began to identify very secretly who the military and civilian leaders were that were behind the coup. As they were identified, we began to develop dossiers on each of them. Once we had them all identified, the plan was to round them up so we could put them on trial for crimes against humanity. For security reasons, we could not seek Russian help in this process. But once the coup was contained, Russian help was available to us in locating and capturing the rebels. There were one hundred and thirteen people involved in the planning of the coup on our list. With Russian help, this number increased to a hundred and twenty-eight. During the military actions of IDES, sixty-eight of the rebels on the list were killed, thirty-six in the SOOF alone. This left sixty unaccounted for. Since IDES two weeks ago, we have captured forty-two of the sixty, and they are now in custody at our prison at Guantanamo Bay in Cuba. So, as of this morning, eighteen were still at large. Hopefully, when Director Bradbury gets here, he will have an update."

Just at that time, the director of the CIA, Harlan Bradbury was escorted into the room by a secret service agent. "Hi, everyone. Mr. President. I got here as soon as I could."

Immediately, Odd and Samantha stood up to greet Harlan. "Odd. Samantha." Harlan greeted them with a smile. He went over to Odd, shook his hand, touched the gold oak leaf on his shoulder and said, "Congratulations, Lieutenant Commander. Well deserved."

"Thank you, Mr. Bradbury."

"Well, here's a sight for sore eyes. Come here Samantha and give me a squeeze." They both approached each other and embraced.

"Good to see you, Harlan."

"Mutual." He looked at her up and down and said, "I have to admit, I wasn't sure if I would see you again. You can't imagine how happy this makes me. You can't imagine." He repeated.

Harlan turned his attention to the president. "Mr. President, have you brought everyone up to speed on where we stand?"

"Essentially. Your timing is perfect. Where do we stand on the eighteen criminals still at large?"

"We picked up fifteen of them today. In the last three hours, in fact. Two more should be in hand by tomorrow. We have eyes on them, and it is just a matter of time."

"What about the last one?" asked the president.

Harlan shook his head and said, "I don't know, Mr. President. Three times we thought we had him, but each time he somehow disappeared. Vanished. Like a ghost."

Samantha asked, "Who is it? Does this ghost have a name?"

"It's Anton Yulov."

"Yulov? Wasn't he the minister of finance that was stealing

money from the Russian people to finance the coup?" she asked.

"One and the same."

"What do we know about him?" asked Ira.

Harlan answered, "Look. Carter House here is considered a secure area and I had it swept for bugs earlier today. But I still don't trust it. Before I say any more, I want to be in a designated, controlled secure area. Let's meet at the commander of the Pacific Fleet's headquarters tomorrow morning at 0900. I'll give more information then."

No more business was discussed that afternoon. The president had to return to Washington, DC. The others agreed to meet for dinner at the Pearl Harbor Officer's Club at eight o'clock. It had been a very tiring day, and they all wanted an hour or two of rest.

CHAPTER 3
HEROES

A LARGE ROUND TABLE HAD been set up for the group at the O' Club. With the highest-ranking officer in the navy at the table, Admiral Flaxon, the Chief of Naval Operations, the other patrons in the O' Club dining room took notice very quickly. And it wasn't another five minutes before word got around that also at the table were the commanding officer and executive officer of the *Hawkbill*, the two DEVGRU Navy SEAL officers assigned to the *Hawkbill*, and the military head of Team Bravo. Oh, and by the way, there sat the director of the CIA. Also, they noticed within this august group was the female environmental scientist that had been on the mission in the Sea of Okhotsk. With all these notable people at this one table, no one was quite sure who the low-ranking foreign officer was. But he had to be important if he was with this group.

When the salad was placed before them, Samantha said, "I would like to ask the Lord to bless this food we are about to enjoy."

Several of the others said, "Amen to that, Samantha." Samantha said the blessing, and they began to dig into their salads.

When they had all finished their entrees and were waiting for their after-dinner coffee, a line began to form at their table with autograph seekers and those just wanting to thank the *Hawkbill* people for their heroism and wish them well. And, as it almost always happened, Samantha seemed to get most of the attention. For almost an hour, the line of well-wishers remained long. It was clear that everyone wanted to thank Samantha and the others for what they did. Finally, the last autograph was signed, and the dining room was empty except for the O' Club staff who had patiently waited for the well-deserved homage to end.

Outside the O' Club, Ira and Samantha held back until the others had left. Finally alone, Ira took her hands in his and said, "Sam, I'd like nothing better than spending the rest of the night with you. But I am so tired that I'm about to drop right here on the spot."

"Me too. It has been one heck of a day."

"Well, maybe tomorrow we can get some time alone together."

She smiled and said, "If you are asking me for a date, I thought—"

"—you'd never ask." He finished the sentence for her.

She laughed. "Ira, you are getting to know me too well."

"I've got a long way to go before I know you too well."

Samantha stood on her toes and kissed Ira passionately. A couple coming out of the O' Club saw them kissing. The woman said, "Come on you two. Get a room."

A little after nine the next morning, everyone sat in the secure briefing room drinking their coffee. "Okay," Harlan said, "Let's begin. Samantha, Ira, yesterday you started asking me questions about Anton Yulov, and I cut you off. We started getting into an area that is highly classified, and I didn't think it was appropriate to discuss this at Carter House. The bottom line is this: we now have captured all the coup war criminals but one. We took into custody two more last night leaving only the ex-minister of finance,

Anton Yulov, still at large. As I said yesterday, we thought we had him several times before, but somehow, he slipped through our fingers. I don't know how, but he did. We have our agents all over the world looking for him. We are working with Russia's KGB as well as INTERPOL. He has, essentially, disappeared from the face of the earth. But rest assured. We will get him. He seems to have an uncanny ability to show up somehow. Then simply disappear. But he will make a mistake. Everyone does. Then we will get him."

"Why the secrecy, Harlan?"

"Well, we want him to think that we have forgotten about him. We don't want him to know that we are conducting a world-wide search for him. We believe this will increase his chances of getting sloppy and making a crucial mistake."

"Flaxon asked, "What do you want us to do, Harlan?"

"Just don't talk about Yulov at all. Forget about him. He will slip up, then he is ours. Let us do our job."

A long silence followed. Then Admiral Flaxon said, "If it's alright with everyone, I'd like to change the subject."

"Yeah, I'm done. What do you have in mind?"

"This thing at the O' Club last night was a surprise to me. You guys are not only heroes in the United States. You are heroes all over the world, especially in Russia. President Milsap has authorized me to tell you this. The Russian presidential election is next Tuesday. As you know, the incumbent president is in an advanced stage of Alzheimer's. He will be replaced by one of the two candidates running for the office of the presidency. Right now, the race is too close to call. But Milsap told me just before he left for DC yesterday, that both candidates have approached him and want Ira and Samantha to visit Moscow to receive the Hero Of The Russian Federation Medal. This is a very prestigious medal in Russia. You two are wildly popular there. The Russian people are in love with you."

"God, Roger. Why is this happening?"

"Samantha, you and Ira and all the men on the *Hawkbill* saved their country from very evil men. They greatly appreciate your significant act of valor. They want to reward and thank you in the best way they can, which is by giving you both a medal."

"I don't know, Ira. What do you think?"

"It doesn't matter what I think. It's what the president wants that really matters. Looks like we are going to Moscow."

"Are our plane tickets going to be paid for?" Samantha asked.

Everybody in the room snickered.

CHAPTER 4
FUTURE PLANS

THE NEXT EVENING, SAMANTHA AND Ira were alone at a small dinner table at the O' Club. No sooner did they sit down before people started approaching their table to thank them. Ira finally said, "Look, Sam, this is all very flattering, but I would like to spend some time alone with you. This will never happen here. Let's get a taxi and go to Waikiki where no one will recognize us."

"Sounds like a good plan to me. Let's go."

As soon as there was a break with the well-wishers, Ira and Samantha got up to leave. As they walked out the door, they met Jared and Josh coming in. They exchanged a few words and went on their way.

Josh leaned over to Jared. "I told you, Jared. I told you. You are the only one who hasn't seen that Captain Coen and Samantha are an item."

"Maybe you are right, Josh. Maybe you're right."

Ira and Samantha found a small out-of-the-way restaurant primarily frequented by locals. "Nobody should recognize us here, Ira."

"Let's hope not."

When they ordered their wine, they sat in silence for several minutes. They looked into each other's eyes intently. Samantha asked, "What are you thinking?"

Ira didn't answer right away. Finally, he said, "Samantha, I was just thinking that in my whole thirty-eight plus years of life, I have never thought about anyone like I do about you."

"Uh oh. This sounds serious. I hope this is going where I think it's going."

"I hope so too. Well, here it is. Like I said in my stateroom on the *Hawkbill*, I love you, Sam. That feeling has not changed since then ten or eleven days ago. In fact, I'm choked up with emotion over the love I have for you. I can't even describe it. You are all I can think about."

Samantha smiled widely. "Those are the most wonderful words I have ever heard. I meant what I said to you in your stateroom that day. The only other people I have ever allowed to call me Sam were my parents. They have been the only two people that I have ever really loved. Until now."

Their hands met at the center of the table, and they clasped them tightly. They looked at each other steadily. Finally, Samantha said, "Ira, suddenly I'm not hungry. I want to get somewhere alone with you, make love, and then plan our future together. We have so much to talk about—marriage, our careers, our future, kids. Heck, I'm thirty-five and you're thirty-eight. My biological clock is ticking away. We need to talk. What do you think?"

"I haven't gotten past the *let's make love part*."

"I guess you noticed that was the first thing I listed. Let's get out of here and scratch that off our to do list."

"I thought you'd never ask."

She laughed and said, "Pink. My underwear is pink."

Ira grinned and said, "A new favorite color, I'm sure. Let's go."

Ira began to stand up, then he noticed that Samantha remained seated, and her smile had suddenly disappeared. A great look of apprehension appeared on her face. Ira said, "What's wrong, Sam? You really look concerned."

"Ira, I am. Please sit down. This is hard for me to say, but before we let this relationship go any further, there's something that I must tell you about me. It's only fair to you."

"My God, Sam. This sounds serious. What is it?"

Samantha looked down at the table, closed her eyes, and took a deep breath. After she slowly exhaled, she looked at Ira for almost ten seconds. She began, "I've told you about my mother."

"Yes. She died of cancer at a very young age."

"That's right. She was only thirty-eight. Your age. She had a very aggressive form of cancer called Triple-Negative Breast Cancer. TNBC. TNBC gets its name from the fact that the cancer cells produced in the body test negative for three different hormones. In other words, it is hard to detect early on using standard hormone tests. Once it is detected, however, survival time is usually less than five years. Also, it seems to target women under forty."

"I don't care, Sam. It might not happen to you, and if it does, we can fight it together."

"That's wonderful to hear, but I haven't finished, Ira. The very scary part is this. My grandmother, my mother's mother, may have died of the same type of cancer also before she turned forty. Genetically speaking, I'm a strong candidate to contract TNBC. I'm aware of this ticking time bomb that may be inside of me, and I'm staying on top of it with yearly mammograms and MRIs looking for possible manifestations of the disease like brain lesions and heart associated aneurisms. Ira, I could die in just a few years. And it won't be an easy death. So, before we go any further with our relationship, I feel that this is something you need to know."

"Like I just said, Sam. I love you, and we can deal with this together. This doesn't change how I feel about you and what I want our future to be."

"Oh, Ira. You are such a breath of fresh air in my life. You know that I have been engaged to be married twice before. I told you that I broke off the engagements because I admitted to myself that I really did not want to spend the rest of my life with them. That was true. But, both these guys, when they heard about my medical situation, dropped me like a hot potato."

"They were uncaring creeps."

"Yes, they were. And because of their reactions to my medical situation, I gave up the idea of ever getting married and having children. I have devoted my life to my career. However, when I met you in Pearl Harbor, I changed. Suddenly I felt alive again, and I tossed caution to the wind. I wanted you. I wanted to be married to you. I wanted to have children with you. I love you so much, Ira.

Suddenly, Samantha's smile returned to her face. She took another deep breath and said, "Come on, my love. I've got a new color to show you."

Over the next week, Samantha and Ira began planning their future together. It was two days later, March 31, when they announced to everyone that they were in love and set a wedding date of May 18. They had decided that they would have a full military wedding ceremony, site yet to be determined. It was at this time that Admiral Flaxon announced that Captain Ira Coen was now one of the youngest naval officers ever to be addressed as Rear Admiral Ira Coen and that he had been assigned to be the new commander of the Submarine Forces in the Atlantic, COMSUBLANT. During the ensuing celebration of Ira's promotion, the wedding site was set for Norfolk, Virginia.

No one was really surprised about the proclamation of their mutual love. Most noticed how they looked at each other when the SOOF mission was being planned, how they would bump hands and discretely intertwine fingers, and how they teased each other playfully. What did amaze everyone that suspected their attraction to one another was how they kept their feelings in check during the mission. They were serious and business-like at all times.

During the first week of April, Samantha and Ira began forming the wedding guest list. Samantha said, "Ira, certainly all of Team Bravo should be there."

"I agree. We went through so much in planning the mission. They are family to us. What about Flaxon?"

"Ira, on the pier when we returned to Pearl, Roger said he thought of me as his daughter. My dad is no longer with us. Would you mind if I asked Roger to give me away?"

"The only thing about that is I still think he has a crush on you. He might try to bump me off at the altar and take my place."

"Ira. You are the silliest man I ever met. What do you say? Can I ask him?"

"Of course. I know that he'll be delighted."

"And I would love to have Odd Bergstrom at our wedding."

"That's another one that has a crush on you. It'll be tough on him, but absolutely. He should be invited. One guy I would really like to invite is my chief of the boat, Master Chief Boxer."

"Bryan? That's a great idea. How about Twigs?"

"Sonar tech Twigerton? You've always had a soft spot for Twigs. You just made me think. He's another one in love with you. So is Boxer. My God, Samantha. What did you do to my crew? They are all in love with you."

"Come on, Ira. Let's get serious about this."

"I am serious. I don't know how I won out over all those guys."

"I'm going to ignore all of this. What about Harlan Bradbury?"

The wedding list preparation went on for some time. Eventually, President Milsap was added as well despite all the distractions caused by having the president of the United States in attendance.

That evening, Ira and Samantha were in Ira's stateroom on the *Hawkbill*. Ira said, "As you know, this is my last night as

CO of the *Hawkbill*. Commander Rodriguez assumes command tomorrow. I'll find out tomorrow the date I have to report as COMSUBLANT. In any event, I will still have to meet with my new boss before that date for briefings. Would you be able to come with me?"

"I should be able to. I've resumed my work at the Naval Research Laboratory online. It really doesn't matter where I work from. How will you be getting to Norfolk?"

"Being an admiral has its perks. I'm pretty sure they will fly me first class commercial. I'll probably be getting details and my orders tomorrow. Then I'll know for sure."

"I'll check with my boss tomorrow to see what NRL can do for getting me home to DC."

After a short pause, Samantha changed the subject. "Kids. Kids, Ira. I want to have a baby with you."

"I want nothing more. Maybe two or three."

"Well, we'd better get started. Like I said, my biological clock is ticking away. At thirty-five, it might already be too late."

"I hope and pray that's not true."

"Well, right now, everything seems to be functioning in the right way. I'll pray that we can conceive quickly."

"Sam, let's pray together on that right now."

"Ira, you continually blow me away."

They both got on their knees and began to pray.

CHAPTER 5
PRE-WEDDING HONEYMOON

THE NEXT DAY, ADMIRAL FLAXON informed Ira that he had been granted administrative leave until the last week of May, after Samantha's and Ira's honeymoon. Housing for the newlyweds would be provided on Admiral's Row at the Norfolk Naval Base. Flaxon also informed him and Samantha that they both needed to report to the White House for a meeting with President Milsap as soon as they got to DC. They were given airline tickets for Friday, the day after the change of command ceremony on the *Hawkbill*.

"I wonder what this is all about?" Samantha said.

Ira said, "Probably the trip to Moscow. With Ilya Versilly winning the presidential election in Russia, he probably has asked Milsap to have us over. Probably a public relations thing to make Versilly look good."

"Wow, Ira. This is a whirlwind for me. I've got a military wedding to set up—which I know nothing about, by the way. I've got a house to set up. A honeymoon to arrange. A job to keep. And now, a PR trip to Russia? How can I do all this in only a month?"

"I don't know, Sam. You always seem to figure things out. I have faith in you."

Samantha shook her head and sat down to think. Ira knew that she needed a little peace and quiet, so he left the room for her to be alone.

An hour later, she left the room and found Ira talking with his executive officer, Fred Boone. When she approached the two men, Ira saw her and said, "Samantha. I've got some great news. Fred's been promoted to commander and has been assigned as the commanding officer of a Virginia-class boat that will be commissioned in a few months."

"Wow, Fred! Congratulations. This is good news."

"Thanks, Samantha. This all took me by surprise. I'm really in shock."

Samantha gave Fred a long hug and said, "Commander Boone. Has a nice ring to it. CO Commander Boone. Sounds even better."

Thank you, Samantha. This wouldn't have happened if it weren't for you."

"Why do you guys keep insisting that it is me? It's not about me. It's about us. Team Bravo. The last time I looked, I didn't see any 'I' in the word team."

"If you insist, Samantha. If you insist."

"Well, congratulations, Fred."

She then looked at Ira and said, "Ira, I've got an idea I'd like to drop on you. Got a minute?"

"Sure. What's your idea, Sam?"

"If we can somehow talk Milsap into scheduling our trip to Russia after our wedding, we can stay over in Europe somewhere for our honeymoon. We can schedule our return for a few days before you take over your new command. What do you think?"

"Sounds good to me. All we can do is ask. But be prepared for a no. Politics often override sound judgment."

On Friday, Samantha and Ira flew to Washington, DC for a meeting with the president at the White House.

When they were seated in the Oval Office, Milsap informed

them of the trip to Russia. No date was given for the trip. Samantha then presented her request.

"Samantha, I saw what you were up against with your wedding and all. When President Versilly made his request, I told him about your wedding date. He was very gracious and agreed for you to come after the wedding. He also offered his personal dacha on the North Sea for you to stay on your honeymoon. He said that he could assign a planner to you to help with organizing your honeymoon in Russia."

My God, James. You have just taken a huge load off my chest. I can't believe all this."

"If it's all right with you, I can assign a small team to you for helping with arranging the wedding and setting up your new home."

"You will do all this, James?"

"Hey. I'm president of the United States. This is a lot easier and more fun for me than dealing with those clowns in congress. Trust me. It's my pleasure."

"Thank you, James. Thank you so much."

Ira added, "Thank you, Mr. President."

By the end of April, almost all the arrangements had been completed. The itinerary in Russia was locked in concrete, the wedding details were set, and the honeymoon plans were all arranged.

"Only two weeks to go. Getting nervous?" asked Samantha.

"A little. I've never been married before."

"Hey, we're essentially married now. You won't even notice a difference."

"Well, like you just said, only two weeks to go before the wedding. What do we do until then?"

"I've still got some small details to deal with, but nothing that would be a showstopper. Look. I've got an idea. Want to hear it?"

"Sam, you never seem to run out of ideas. What is it?"

"I know this isn't a tradition, and it will probably be frowned upon by many people I know, but why don't we take a pre-wedding honeymoon?"

"A what? I've never heard of such a thing."

"Yeah! Let's fly down to a resort in the Caribbean, drink margaritas on the beach, and go snorkeling and scuba diving on the reefs down there."

"I know how to drink margaritas, but I don't know a thing about scuba diving."

"I'll teach you. It'll be fun. Come on, say yes."

"You can scuba dive?"

"Duh! I'm an oceanographer. Of course, I know how. What do you say?"

"I am on leave. I guess I'll go with you."

"If you didn't say yes, I would have called off the wedding."

CHAPTER 6
TO RUSSIA WITH LOVE

THE IDYLLIC LIVES OF SAMANTHA and Ira continued over the next several weeks. They thoroughly enjoyed their pre-wedding honeymoon. Ira struggled with his scuba diving at first, but under the expert tutelage of Samantha—and a great deal of patience on her part—Ira eventually got the hang of it, and they enjoyed swimming among the wildlife of the many reefs that were available there.

Their military wedding went off without any major hitches. The bridge of swords went as planned, Fred Boone's children were adorable as the flower girl and the ring bearer, and Admiral Flaxon played his role of giving away Samantha with dignity and grace. But the cutting of the cake with Ira's sword did not go so well. Before the cake was half cut, it was mutilated by Ira so badly that it was unrecognizable as a wedding cake. Samantha, in her inimitable way, turned this disaster into an event that had everybody, even those in their dress white uniforms, rolling on the floor in laughter.

Samantha was now officially named Samantha Stone Coen.

On the twentieth of May, two days after the wedding, the newly married couple were in the air on their way to Moscow. Upon landing in Russia, they were quickly escorted to a waiting limousine and driven to a five-star hotel, the Metropol, in the center of Moscow. At the hotel, numerous personnel were waiting for them and showered them with courtesy and concern for their needs. Most of the hotel's staff spoke English, but an interpreter was assigned to them to assist when Russian was spoken to them. However, Ira soon found out that his new bride was very knowledgeable in the Russian language.

"My God," Ira said. "You know more Russian than our interpreter knows English. How did this happen?"

"When I was at Oregon State University, I took Russian as a minor. I actually got pretty good at it. But I haven't used it for eight or nine years, and I'm a little rusty."

"You are always surprising me. What's the next surprise?"

"I'm wearing a new color underwear today. I'll surprise you tonight."

Ira looked at her, shook his head, and smiled.

The four-day visit in Russia was a whirlwind of constant activity that included television interviews, elaborate dinner affairs, and speaking engagements to various crowds and groups. The command of the Russian language by Samantha amazed the crowds. Everywhere they went, they were showered with cheers, hugs, and words of thanks. They were truly heroes of the state. On the last day, over an international television broadcast, Russian President Ilya Versilly personally awarded Ira and Samantha Russia's most prestigious honor, the Hero Of The Russian Federation Gold Star medal.

Following the award ceremony, Samantha and Ira were resting in their hotel room. Samantha said, "We've been so busy on this whirlwind tour, I haven't had a chance to appreciate the beautiful suite of rooms they put us up in here at the Metropol. Look, Ira. It even has a beautiful Steinway piano."

Ira went up to the piano and began playing "Chop Stix" with his two index fingers. He turned around to Samantha and said,

"Come here, Samantha. I'll show you the keys, and we can play it together."

Samantha sat by Ira on the piano bench. He showed her the high note keys to play, and they played together laughing the whole time.

"That was fun, Sam."

"It was, Ira. You know, I used to play the piano when I was younger."

"You play the piano, too?"

"Actually, I do. Want me to play something for you?

Ira shook his head and gave up the seat to Samantha. She extended her arms, intertwined the fingers of both hands, and exercised them. She then looked at the keyboard for a moment and began playing "Rhapsody on a Theme of Paganini" by Sergei Rachmaninoff. Ira's jaw dropped almost to the floor as the beautiful melody filled the room. He walked up to her and put his hands on her shoulders.

"Where and how did you learn to play like that, Sam?"

Samantha stopped playing, looked over her shoulder, and smiled at Ira. She turned around on the piano bench and said, "My mother was a concert pianist for the Bangor, Maine Symphony Orchestra. That's how she made her living. That, and giving piano lessons to young students in my hometown of Jonesport, Maine. She started teaching me to play when I was about three years old. I'm a little rusty now, but when I was sixteen, I was quite accomplished. In fact, I was scheduled to compete at the Tchaikovsky Piano Competition in Moscow when I was sixteen. That's when my mother was diagnosed with her breast cancer. I had to cancel my trip and drop out of the competition because her health deteriorated rapidly. She died only a year and a half later. I was only eighteen when she died."

"You've told me about the tragic loss of both your parents, Sam. But your ability to play the piano like that amazes me. You amaze me. And to think that I just showed you how to play 'Chop Stix.'"

"You are so sweet, Ira. Let me finish the piece for you. I'm really enjoying playing again."

Samantha finished playing the Rachmaninoff, and when she was done, Ira applauded vigorously. Right then, there was a knock on their door. Ira opened the door and the concierge assigned to them entered the room and said, "Excuse me Admiral Coen, I hate to bother you because I know that you are tired, but there are six gentlemen in naval uniforms that wish to meet you. Should I send them away?"

"No, Yuri. Bring them in."

Before Yuri turned around to get the six waiting navy men, he saw Samantha sitting at the piano, and he said, "When we reached your door, we heard you playing Ms. Coen. We were all mesmerized by what we heard. We just stood there outside your door and listened. That's the most beautiful rendition of the Rachmaninoff rhapsody that I've ever heard."

"Thank you, Yuri. It's one of my favorite pieces. I used to play it often."

Yuri bowed to her, went to the door, and escorted a Russian naval officer and five enlisted sailors into the room. The officer said, "Thank you Admiral Coen for allowing us to disturb you. I know that you and your wife must be extremely tired."

"No. That's quite all right. What can I do for you?"

"I am Captain Dimitri Gregarin. We have never met, but not long ago, we were once about three miles apart, and you spared my life."

"What do you mean?" asked Ira.

Captain Gregarin proceeded to relate that he was the commodore of the three Russian ASW frigates guarding the exit from the Sea of Okhotsk through the Kurile Islands to the Pacific. Ira immediately recalled his decision not to destroy the three ships.

"Captain Gregarin. You were no threat to us. By gathering

your ships together and staying dead in the water, I concluded that was your way of flying a white flag. How could I have taken action against you?"

Captain Gregarin answered, "Admiral Coen, that is not an internationally recognized signal. I just hoped and prayed that you would interpret my actions correctly. My prayers were answered, and me and my men want to thank you from the bottom of our hearts."

Samantha immediately went up to the five smiling enlisted sailors, spoke to them in Russian, and gave them all hugs. They were giddy with excitement for the chance to hug Samantha. She then turned to Captain Gregarin and said in English, "You don't know how wonderful this makes me feel to know that you and your men are alive and with your families. When Admiral Coen gave the order not to shoot, I was so proud of him then. But your personal visit here to thank him makes my heart swell with pride."

Ira was speechless at all this. The six Russian navy men thanked Ira numerous times, bowed to him, and left.

When they had left, the concierge who had been watching all this came up to Ira and hugged him. Then looking at Ira and then Samantha, he said, "Admiral Coen, I had no idea. I thank you for all the Russian people."

When Yuri had left the room, Samantha said, "That was a surprise."

Ira responded, "What's all the fuss? It was an obvious decision to make."

"Ira. I was there in the control room when all this was happening. Everyone there but you wanted to take those frigates out. Everyone but you."

The next day, Samantha and Ira were flown to Jumala Beach, Latvia, near Riga, and driven to Versilly's dacha on the North Sea coast. Over the next week, they were flown to several beautiful vacation spots in Russia and in some of the neighboring countries.

It was a very exciting and tiring week. But it was a honeymoon to remember.

After their return from Russia on the first of June, the couple took advantage of Ira's remaining administrative leave. Ira's change of command ceremony was scheduled for the fourth of June. This gave them three days with no obligations except to rest and to try to make a baby.

The change of command was filled with pomp and circumstance. A band, numerous flag officers, and civilian dignitaries all were in attendance, including the director of the CIA, the Chief of Naval Operations, the chairman of the Joint Chief of Staff, the Team Bravo officers, and the president of the United States. It was rousing and televised nationally. After all, no one had ever risen in the ranks as fast as Ira Coen. The heroes of the Sea of Okhotsk mission were all there, including Dr. Samantha Stone Coen.

At the end of July, Samantha announced to everyone that she was pregnant. Not only pregnant, but pregnant with twins, genders not yet determined. The projected birth date was mid-February.

Ira and Samantha's idyllic life continued through the summer and fall, and the birth of the twins, a boy and a girl, took place on Valentine's Day. The boy was given the name of Roman, after the book of Romans, and the girl was given the name of Paula, after the name of the apostle Paul, who penned the book of Romans.

PART 2

ANTON YULOV, THE GHOST

A Cessna Citation

CHAPTER 7
FIRST ANNIVERSARY BBQ

THE FIRST YEAR OF IRA and Samantha's marriage could not have gone better. Ira settled in as COMSUBLANT, and Samantha did double duty writing an updated version of the environment of the Sea of Okhotsk and raising her twin babies, Roman and Paula. In February, just after the twins were born, Samantha suggested to Ira that they plan on throwing a first anniversary party at their home for all their friends. Something simple like a barbecue in their backyard and swimming in their heated pool. Ira thought that this was a great idea, and he highly endorsed it. In fact, he even took the lead on some of the planning. Samantha greatly appreciated Ira's help because she could spend more time with the infant twins.

"Ira, to help us out here, let's ask Harlan to handle the invitations. He knows everyone and has their addresses, especially the Norwegians, Odd, Lars, and Ragnar."

"Good idea, Sam. Harlan did volunteer to help us with the anniversary planning. I know he would be delighted to help. I'll call him."

Invitations were sent out in late February, and by early March, everyone who had been invited responded, and there were no refusals. Not even from the Norwegians who were eager to make the trip to the United States.

On the morning of their first wedding anniversary, May 18, Samantha was scurrying around frantically. She wanted everything to be perfect before the people she loved so much arrived. Ira was in the backyard cleaning the pool, putting away baby toys, and making sure the barbecue pit was ready to go. At ten, the babysitter came to pick up the twins. By eleven, all was in order and Samantha and Ira had a chance to relax.

"Ira, I'm so excited about seeing everyone again. I haven't seen Lars or Ragnar in a couple of years."

"Lars is now the deputy director of the Norwegian Intelligence Service in Oslo, and his job is keeping him very busy. Ragnar is still the NIS director, and they both have a lot of interactions with Harlan, but almost always by phone and secure telephone conferences. Since both Lars and Ragnar will be here today, I'm wondering who is running the show at NIS?"

Samantha added, "Odd will be here as well. I'm so excited to see our Norwegian friends again."

"Hey, I'm not an excitable guy, but I am excited about seeing everyone again myself."

Precisely at noon, the doorbell rang. Samantha opened the door and there stood a very large secret service agent. The very one that guarded the door at Carter House when Team Bravo was planning the SOOF mission. When Samantha recognized him, she shouted out, "Big John!" She immediately stood on her tiptoes and threw her arms around him and buried her head in his rather large neck. Her arms were not long enough to completely encircle his extra wide body, but she squeezed him as best she could. "Why are you here?" She asked excitedly.

"I'm now part of President Milsap's protection team."

Samantha took a step to the side so she could see the street from around him, and there was President James Milsap standing by his limo waving at her.

"If you don't mind, Samantha, me and a few of the guys have

to check out your house to see if it is safe."

"No, no, go right ahead. Can I go to the street to see the president?"

"It's okay, but I'll have to frisk you first."

"Touch me, and I will kill you where you stand."

"Yes, Ma'am. Go right ahead. He's waiting for you."

Samantha smiled at Big John and went to greet the president.

The guests arrived steadily, and by 12:30, everyone was there. A good hour of fellowship took place as many of the men had not seen each other in a long time.

At two o'clock, Samantha announced that it was time to open the anniversary gifts everyone had brought. By 2:45, the gifts, most of them funny gifts, had been opened. Ira announced that the pool was open, and the steaks were fully marinated and ready to be cooked. Everybody cheered, got a fresh bottle of beer, and went out to the backyard.

When Ira started putting the charcoal into the barbecue pit, Twigs Twigerton came up to him and said, "Need any help, Admiral?"

"No thanks, Twigs. I've got everything under control. Get in the pool and have fun with the others."

"Okay, sir. But the president of the United States is in the pool. How should I act? Suppose I splash water in his face, and he gets mad?"

"Hey Twigs. Today, he is not the president of the United States. He's just a friend of all of us trying to have a good time and to escape from his stressful job. If he gives you a hard time, sic Samantha on him."

"If you say so, sir."

As Twigs was walking away, he turned around and asked, "Admiral Coen, I see that you have a big bucket of golf balls here. Do you play golf?"

"Yes, I do, Twigs. The Ocean View Golf Club is about thirty to forty yards past those trees over there. These golf balls are stray shots that go over those trees. I've found them in our pool, and I even found one in my barbecue pit here this morning."

"Golly, Admiral. You probably don't ever have to buy a golf ball."

"Twigs, get in the pool and have some fun with Samantha and the president."

"Yes, sir. Right away, sir."

Twigs joined the others horsing around in the pool. And, as expected, Samantha was the center of attention. Of course, she was the only female there and the only one wearing a tiny bikini.

Ira cooked the steaks to perfection. Almost everyone said he had missed his calling and that he should have been a chef instead of an admiral.

Around six o'clock, Samantha announced that they should go inside for a special dessert she had chilling in the refrigerator. The mood was very festive, and a lot of playful teasing was going on as they went back into the house.

They all convened in the kitchen and watched as Samantha took a huge ice cream cake out of the refrigerator. Remembering the cutting of the cake disaster at their wedding a year ago, she told Ira to not come near the cake. Everyone laughed at the memory and supported her directive to Ira. Ira defended himself and said, "I fail to see the humor in all this. It wasn't my fault. The cake was lopsided to begin with. That's why I couldn't cut it cleanly."

As they were going into the living room to eat their ice cream cake, Odd Bergstrom looked into the dining room and asked, "What's that?"

Samantha asked, "What are you talking about, Odd?"

"When we finished opening your gifts in the dining room, the table was bare. Now there is a gift on it."

"What?" exclaimed Samantha. She went into the dining room followed by the others. On the table sat a new gift. It was exquisitely wrapped in bright purple foil with a large yellow bow on top.

Samantha asked, "Alright. Who put this gift here?"

Everyone looked around to the others, but no one took responsibility.

Ira asked, "How did it get here? We were all swimming in the pool except for me. I was cooking. Did anyone see someone else?"

No one responded. Finally, Ragnar said, "Open it up, Samantha. Maybe there's a card inside with a name on it."

Samantha went over to the well-wrapped box and nervously pulled it toward her. "It's surprisingly light, like there's not much in it."

She took off the bow and carefully cut the gift's tape with her fingernail.

When the box was opened, she looked down into it and then looked at her friends.

"What is it, Samantha?" asked Twigs.

With a puzzled look, Samantha reached into the box and pulled out a stack of envelopes tied together with a yellow bow. She untied the bow to loosen the envelopes. Each envelope had a name on it, one for each of the guests. Samantha passed out the envelopes to everyone.

"What's going on here?" asked Ira. He then looked at the envelope in his hand and said, "I'll open mine first."

Ira opened his envelope and pulled out a three-by-five index card upon which was handwritten the number twelve.

Everybody then began opening their envelopes, and each one had index card with a different number on it.

6. Bryan Boxer

7. Ragnar Solberg

8. Fred Boone

9. Lars Skarsgaard

10. Josh Freeman

11. Odd Bergstrom

12. Ira Coen
13. Harlan Bradbury
14. Twigs Twigerton
15. Roger Flaxon
16. Forrest Jenkins
17. Jared Townsend
18. James Milsap

The president said, "I don't get it. Who put the box here?" He then turned to one of his agents and said, "Didn't any of you guys see someone come in and put the box on the table?"

"No, sir. We were all by the pool watching you."

Josh Freeman asked Samantha, "Is there anything else in the box?"

Samantha reached into the box and pulled out another box that was wrapped exactly as the outer box. It had 'Dr. Samantha Stone' written on the outside. Samantha untied the yellow bow and took off the purple foil wrapping. She opened the box and pulled out an envelope just like the others. In the envelope was a note. Samantha read the note out loud.

> Samantha, I hope you enjoyed your first wedding anniversary very much. I hope it was one to remember because you will never have another. You are next, **BITCH**!

She paused, then said, "The word bitch is in uppercase and is in bold typeface. I know what that word means, but what is meant by 'you are next?'" She thought for a moment then said, "Is this a joke you guys are playing on me? If you are, it isn't the least bit funny. It must be one of you guys, because no one knew exactly what our guest list was, yet everyone here got a number."

Harlan then spoke up and said with urgency, "Mr. President, I request that you assign two of your bodyguards to stay here tonight to protect Samantha. I think I know what might be going on here. But I need a little more information to be sure. I want us all to meet tomorrow morning at 0900 in a secure room at Ira's headquarters, and I'll tell you what I think is going on. Mr. President, be sure your men carefully protect Samantha tonight."

CHAPTER 8
ANTON YULOV

THE MOOD OF EVERYONE CHANGED from festive to gloomy. They ate their dessert in silence. The president talked to two of his secret service bodyguards, one of which was Big John. He stressed the importance and seriousness of their assignment to protect Samantha. Soon thereafter, the guests began to leave.

When all were gone, Samantha and Ira sat in the living room with the two guards close by. "What's going on, Ira?"

"Sam, I honestly don't know. What I do know is that I am worried."

"I don't like the look Harlan had on his face when he was leaving. It was a look of real concern. And why did he ask Milsap to give up two of his guards to protect me? That has to be highly unusual."

"I don't know. But it has something to do with that gift and the note in it. Harlan got very serious when you read the note."

Samantha asked, "How did that gift get in here?" The agents made sure all the doors were locked. I saw them do it. Who is the gift from? Ira, this is crazy. I'm not sure if I'll be able to sleep tonight. Even with the guards here."

"Me too, Sam. But we have to try. We need to be very alert tomorrow."

Samantha told the guards that she and Ira were going to go to bed early. She then called the babysitter and asked if Roman and Paula could spend the night with her. When the sitter agreed, Samantha told her to lock all her doors and windows and to not open the door for anyone.

The next morning, a car with armed agents arrived to take Ira and Samantha to the scheduled meeting.

When they walked into the secure briefing room, Samantha noted that the room was exactly like the small room used to plan the SOOF mission in Hawaii. "Boy. This sure looks familiar."

There were ten chairs around the conference table and three chairs placed against a side wall. The twelve guests took seats, and Harlan stood at the end of the table near the back wall.

When everyone was comfortably seated, Harlan began the meeting. "I was almost sure that I knew who was responsible for the gift box and its contents. But there was one bit of information that I needed to get to be absolutely sure. I now feel certain that the box was put in your house yesterday by our still missing coup leader, Anton Yulov."

"The Ghost?" exclaimed Samantha.

"Yes, the Ghost. Yesterday, we had what we thought was a good lead on him in Toronto. But, once again, he slipped away. That was the information I needed. If we captured Yulov in Toronto, the box wasn't from him. If he got away again, the box was almost certainly from him.

The president then moaned, "Good Lord, Harlan. You told me you were sure you had him. What happened?"

"I don't know, Mr. President. I haven't got all the details from my team. In fact, Mr. President, he may not have been in Toronto at all. It probably was a ruse to throw us off, and he may have been here in Norfolk. That's what I think, anyway."

"Well, what about the gift yesterday? And the numbers we all got? What does that mean?" the president asked.

Harlan frowned and took a deep breath. He finally said, "Let me start from the beginning. I think this will all make more sense if I do. Here's what we know about Yulov. He was born in Kiev, Ukraine. Nothing about his early childhood made it into his dossier. The first unusual account occurred when he was a senior in high school. He tried out for the Soviet Olympic archery team, but he fell a little short on making the team and was named the second alternate. Well, about a month before the summer Olympics started, two of the Soviet archery team members tragically died when a ski resort funicular cable snapped, and the car fell 300 feet to the ground. Four other people were killed in the accident with the two archery team members. As a result, the first and second team alternates were added to the team. One, of course, was our Mr. Yulov, the Ghost, as we are calling him now."

Jared Townsend then said, "Are you saying that Yulov killed those people?"

"We really don't know. It was never proven that the cable was tampered with. But this type of incident is not an isolated event in Yulov's life. Let me go on. After he graduated from high school, he joined the Soviet air force and applied for their special forces, the spetsnaz. He wore their blue beret signifying him as associated with their ground and air forces special warfare units. He eventually became the most decorated man in the spetsnaz. He was an assassin and was credited with at least twenty-eight successful kills. According to his records we obtained, thanks to the KGB, he was a legend as an assassin. He never failed to get his assigned prey. He was also known for the variety of ways he snuffed out his victims. He hardly ever used a gun. Poison. Accidents. He even killed several of his victims with a bow and arrow. He used his Olympic skills. He rose through the ranks in the Soviet air force and attained the rank of general. He has always been outspoken as being anti-West, even well after the fall of the Berlin Wall and the collapse of the Soviet Union. Eight years ago, he ran for the office of the Russian minister of finance even though he had little experience in financial matters. He was clearly behind in the polls in the race for that office. Then his opponent inexplicitly committed murder two weeks before the election. His opponent maintained his innocence, but just as unbelievable as him committing murder was, he committed suicide. Both these cases, the murder and the suicide, have never been conclusively closed. But, as a result, our Ghost won the election since he was unopposed. Sound familiar?"

Lars Skarsgaard said, "Harlan, you think that Yulov killed his political opponent by faking his suicide?"

"I do. I also think that his opponent did not murder anyone. The Ghost did, and he framed his opponent with the crime."

"Good God," said Samantha. "This man is a monster."

"Wait," said Harlan, "there's more. Let's go back to when he was twenty-five. He was courting his future wife, Rhetta. When he entered the picture, Rhetta was engaged to marry someone else. Well, you've probably guessed it. Rhetta's fiancé drowned in a boating accident. So, our Ghost married his high school sweetheart less than a year later."

Flaxon said, "Don't tell me that the reason for this drowning was never determined. Yulov got away with another one."

"That's what we think, Admiral."

Ira said, "How bad can this guy be?"

"It gets worse, Ira. Much worse. And I'll tell you why I am so scared about this whole thing. Ten days after your marriage last May," Harlan looked at both Ira and Samantha, "Rhetta Yulov was found dead in her bed by her husband, the Ghost. The autopsy report said that she had died of a heart attack. But this was suspicious because she appeared extremely healthy and there was no history of cardiac problems in Rhetta's family. So, the authorities decided to investigate the death. They found that the doctor who filed the autopsy report could not be found. He had disappeared. My thought is that if he were in cahoots with Yulov, he has a new identity somewhere in the world. If the Ghost thought the doctor was a loose end, he is probably dead. In fact, he might be dead in either case."

"Next." Harlan continued, "Our husband-and-wife sleeper team in Russia, who we've called Mr. and Mrs. Smith, were found dead three weeks after the death of Rhetta Yulov. They were poisoned. You'll remember that they were our spies who ferreted out most of our classified information on the SOOF. It was this critical information that allowed us to determine how to destroy that facility."

Milsap asked, "Yulov poisoned them?"

"I believe so, Mr. President. It fits. That brings me to the one that hurts me personally the most. One of my key department heads, Mary Graham, died last month when a gas line in her home ruptured at night. The gas ignited, and the house burned down taking Mary and her husband with it. If you remember, Mary was my key analyst and department head that pieced together most of the intel detailing what the Russians were up to with the coup. She figured out that the Russian's D-Day date was sixteen March, for example. At first, we thought that the explosion was an accident, but now I am sure that it was the Ghost's doing."

Samantha said, "I think I know where you are going with this, Harlan. And I truly hope that I am wrong."

"Tell me what you think, Samantha."

"I think that our monster assassin, the Ghost, is getting revenge on those he thinks were responsible for the failure of the Russian military coup. He murdered his own wife for revealing critical classified information on the SOOF. He murdered Mr. and Mrs. Smith for ferreting out this classified information. And he murdered Mary Graham for figuring out what was going on."

"Go on." Said Harlan.

"Up to this point, not counting Mary's husband who was collateral damage, he has murdered four people, and that's what the numbers indicate that were in the gift. Four have been killed, and my number is five. I'm the 'bitch' that's next and then Bryan Boxer will be after me."

The president said, "God, Harlan. Tell me this isn't true."

"I'm afraid it is, Mr. President. Samantha summed up exactly what I think. And, if you think it can't get worse, listen to this. Working with the Russians, we have figured out that when Yulov was the minister of finance, he not only was funding the coup with the Russian people's money, but he absconded with over two hundred and forty million dollars, which he has hidden in several secret accounts in banks around the world. In other words, he has an unlimited budget, and he can come and go and do as he pleases."

Milsap said, "We've got to catch this madman. But the first order of business is to protect Samantha here."

Everyone looked at Samantha with deep concern on their faces, and all nodded yes.

Samantha then raised her hand.

"Yes, Samantha?" asked Harlan.

"After listening to all this about Yulov, I think I know how he put the gift in our house, and I think I'm going to be sick just thinking about it."

Ira asked, "What is it, Samantha? How did he do it?"

Samantha took a deep breath, held it a few seconds, and exhaled slowly through her mouth. "Ira, when we went out to do our final shopping for the barbecue the night before, we had the twins with us. The house was empty. I believe the Ghost somehow got into our house with the gift while we were gone. He hid somewhere and remained there through the night and the next morning. When we were all in the backyard during the barbecue, he came out of hiding, put the gift on the dining room table, and left, relocking the door as he went out. If I'm right, this means that he could have killed me, Ira, and the twins any time he wanted to during the night as we slept. The thought is horrifying."

"But the president's secret service guys checked the house over before Milsap entered. They should have found him," said Harlan. Then he added, "Also, how the hell did he get around the base security?"

"I think the Ghost was counting on them being careless because we were gathering in our house. Most likely a safe house. He could have been hiding in the attic space over the garage. Even if the garage door to the kitchen was locked, that would have been easy pickings for someone like the Ghost. He set up a ruse in Toronto. He knew the names of everyone at our party. He gets around base security, and he hides patiently in our home for eighteen or so hours, not making a sound. Who are we dealing with here?"

CHAPTER 9
TELLURIDE

MILSAP STOOD UP FROM HIS chair and said, "It is clear that we have to make Samantha disappear from the face of the earth. A new name, a new location, and a new background. Harlan, see that this happens by yesterday."

"Yes, sir."

"Also, I want you to double your efforts to capture this psychopath. You've got the entire CIA at your disposal. Just get the job done."

Again, Harlan said, "Yes, sir."

Samantha chimed in. "But what about the twins? I also am worried about Bryan Boxer. He's number six. What if the Ghost can't find me and decides to go after Bryan?"

"Harlan?" asked the president.

"We will have agents assigned to protect Samantha and the twins. We should be okay there. But Samantha makes a good point about Bryan. We should put an agent on him as well."

Bryan said, "No way, Mr. Bradbury! I can take care of myself."

"Bryan. Didn't you listen to what I said earlier? Yulov is an experienced spy and assassin. He can get to you wherever and whenever he wants.

Ira said, "Bryan, take the protection. Harlan's right."

Bryan said to his commanding officer of many years, "Yes, sir."

Harlan continued. "Samantha, pick an out-of-the-way place that you would like to live until we catch this psychopath. We will get you a house, a job, a new identity, and anything else you need to be comfortable. Do this quickly so we can start getting you set up."

"Okay, will do. What about Ira? Is he in danger from the Ghost? I mean, we don't know what he'll do if he can't find me."

Ira said, "I have to stay on as COMSUBLANT. I can arrange to be driven to work and back by armed guards."

Harlan added, "And we can have a twenty-four-hour guard on your house." He continued, "Look, I may be wrong here, but I think that Yulov is so egotistical that he will follow his original agenda. It's a game to him. Why else did he put the gift in the house with the order of the assassinations clearly spelled out? I think he is having fun and toying with us. Can you imagine how big his ego is if he believes that he can sneak the gift into a locked house guarded by the US Secret Service? Like I said, I may be wrong, so I would like to assign guards to everyone in this room, including me. I am on the list. Lucky thirteen."

The president said, "Let's get busy and start on this right away."

The meeting was adjourned, and work on protecting Samantha began.

Samantha, Ira, and the twins were whisked away to a CIA safe house, and agents were posted outside and inside. A team of agents were sent to Ira's house to inspect it for bugs and explosives. Harlan made the quick helicopter flight back to his office in Langley, Virginia. The president and Flaxon left to resume their normal busy schedules in Washington, DC. The three Norwegians began cancelling their vacation plans for their week in the US and arranging flights back to Oslo. All the other military people arranged travel back to their respective duty stations. Harlan informed them all that CIA agents would be contacting them shortly. Life had suddenly changed for every one of them.

In the safe house, Ira said, "Well, Sam. This has been a turn of events for us. Quite frankly, I'm scared to death over the situation you are in. The Ghost is pure evil. From what Harlan told us, this guy can't be stopped."

"I'm scared too. I sure hate to change my life, but if it will save my life, our babies, and the man I love, I guess I will have to."

"Sam, it'll only be for a short time. We have agents all over the world looking for him. We'll get him soon."

"I hope you are right. I want my wonderful life back."

"So do I, Sam. I love you so much. This is going to be tough for us—being apart and all."

"I love you too, Ira. I pray to God that they catch this monster very quickly."

"Do you have any idea of where you would like to be relocated to?"

"I do have a place picked out. Telluride, Colorado."

"That's interesting. Why Telluride?"

"It's out of the way, and I like to ski."

"You know how to ski?"

"Duh! I'm from Maine, remember? Everybody there knows how to ski."

"Sam, is there anything you can't do?"

"Command a nuclear submarine, for one."

"I wouldn't be surprised if you could do that."

"Well, if I could, it would because I had the best teacher in the world."

"Sam. Let's go to bed. I have something else I want to teach you."

"I thought you'd never ask."

The next morning, they were awakened by the smell of bacon, eggs, and freshly brewed coffee that one of the guards had whipped up. Soon, a black car with armed guards picked up

Samantha and Ira and drove them to a waiting helicopter. Within an hour, they were walking into CIA headquarters in Langley. They were escorted into Harlan's office.

"Gee!" Samantha said. "First the Oval Office and now the office of the director of the CIA."

Ira added, "Don't forget the president of Russia's office and his private dacha. And most important of all, the control room of the USS *Hawkbill*."

Harlan interjected, "Will you two stop babbling. We've got important things to discuss here."

Samantha said, "Yes, sir." Then she swiped her pinched thumb and index finger across her lips signifying that she would be quiet.

"Have you given any thought to where you want to relocate?"

"I have. Telluride, Colorado."

Harlan pushed a button on his intercom and called his secretary in. When she entered, he said, "Jean, get together with Frank Bilger and start getting Samantha set up in Telluride, Colorado. He knows what to do. Job, house, that kind of stuff. Also, see Bill Williams about a new identity and background for her. I want this done quickly. But no mistakes."

"Yes, Harlan. Right away."

"Samantha. Do you know how to use a gun? A handgun?"

"As a matter of fact, I do. I belonged to a gun club in high school. My dad's idea."

Ira looked at her in surprise and shook his head.

"Good," said Harlan. "We will issue you a revolver and give you instructions on how to use the one we give you. Also, we will give you a new phone with a new number. It will also have a burner app on it. Do you know anything about a burner app?"

"No, Harlan. Never had the need for one. What is it?"

"It will allow you to use your normal phone, but you can change the number as often as you like. No one will be able to track you that way. You can call Ira, me, anyone and feel confident that no one knows about it. I'm going to give you a list of different numbers for you to use and when to change them. It's important that you do this religiously. Also, we are going to issue you a little pamphlet with the do's and don'ts you should follow as a relocated person. One other thing. I'm assigning two security guards to protect you at all times. If they ask you to do something, do it without question. Exactly as they say. Understand?"

"Yes, sir," she responded.

"Also, one of the guards will be an expert in hand-to-hand self-defense. His name is Bartholomew Frampton, but he goes by Bart. Every day, I want you to spend time with Bart, and he will teach you how to physically defend yourself. Do you have a problem with that?"

"No, Harlan. I was the president of the karate club in high school. I'll enjoy working with Bart."

Again, Ira crinkled up his eyebrows and stared at Samantha.

"The second agent's name is James Breland. He is the senior agent guarding you." Harlan called Jean once more on the intercom. "Jean, if James and Bart are here, ask them to come in and meet Samantha."

"They are walking through the doorway as we speak. I'll send them right in."

Samantha and Ira met the two agents, and Harlan brought them up to speed on their assignment in Telluride and especially on the importance and danger of their mission.

After lunch, Samantha was issued her new identity papers, a history of her new identity, her pamphlet, and a small revolver. She was given a half-hour lesson on its use.

That evening, she and Ira lingered over their bath and bedtime ritual with the babies, then spent their night wrapped in each other's arms, knowing it could be a long time before they could be together again. The next day, she, the twins, and her two bodyguards boarded a CIA jet to Telluride.

CHAPTER 10
ROCKY MOUNTAIN NATIONAL PARK

OVER THE NEXT SEVERAL WEEKS, Samantha settled into her new home in Telluride. She had been there once before as a tourist. She had stayed in Vail, skiing with a couple of friends, and they had decided to take a few day trips to several of the other ski resorts in the area. She and her friends all agreed that their next skiing vacation would be in Telluride—less expensive, less commercial, less traffic, and far quainter than any of the other vacation towns nearby.

Samantha quickly became friends with some of her neighbors living near her, found a good babysitter and hairdresser, and settled into her new job working at a propane gas company, which she could do from her home if she desired. As Harlan requested, she had daily self-defense lessons with Bart Frampton. He was a good teacher, and her skills steadily improved. Using her phone with its burner app, she stayed in nightly contact with Ira.

After a month, however, she wanted to see Ira in person. She ached for his warm touch. Ira not only wanted to see Samantha, but he missed the twins fiercely. Daily photos and videos were just not enough. They discussed a possible long weekend together in Rocky Mountain National Park. They presented this idea to Harlan Bradbury, and after much debate, he reluctantly agreed.

Harlan said, "Samantha, I'm not too wild about this idea. The Ghost is still out there, and I know he is looking for you. I know that you and Ira want some alone time, but please stay close to James and Bart. And I repeat, if they sense anything wrong, do exactly as they say. Got that?"

"Yes, I do, Mr. Bradbury."

Samantha made reservations at the Grand Lake Lodge, a quaint inn near the west entrance to Rocky Mountain National Park. She booked two adjacent cabins for herself, Ira, and the twins and the second for James and Bart. Samantha and the twins made the drive from Telluride to Grand Lake in just under six hours. James and Bart followed closely behind her, ever watchful for anything unusual.

When she reached the Lodge, Ira was standing on the front steps of their cabin. Next to Ira was the agent assigned to protect him, Guy Andrews. They all met and introduced themselves. When Samantha and Ira finished their minute-long embrace, he said, "Okay, guys. Samantha and I haven't seen each other in a month, and we've got a lot to talk about. Let's plan on dinner here at the Lodge at seven tonight."

"You got it, sir. We'll be in the restaurant a little before then to check it out. We won't know you. We'll just be other guests here." The guards went into their two cabins, one cabin on either side of Samantha and Ira's.

When they brought in Roman and Paula and their luggage, Samantha said, "I've missed you so much, Ira." Then she added, "You look good in civilian clothes."

"I didn't want to attract any attention by wearing an admiral's costume. And I've missed you, too. So much."

"Ira, the twins are asleep. You know what that means?"

"I do. Let's get to it."

The next four days were a wonderful time for them both with a 'Let's get to it' every chance they had. On the last day, they stood at the highest point on the Park's road at a scenic overlook.

"Ira, we are looking at one of the most beautiful sights in the United States. It's breathtaking."

"It sure is beautiful. Right now, I am looking at one of the most beautiful sights in the whole world."

"Why, Ira, you are looking right at me. How sweet."

At that very time, Ira's phone rang. Ira listened intently for about thirty seconds, then he said, "I'll be ready."

"What's going on, Ira?"

"Sam, I'm sorry, but I have to go. There has been a serious submarine accident, and I have to return to Norfolk immediately. Our last night together is gone. They have dispatched a helicopter for me, and it will be here in about twenty minutes. Guy Andrews will be going with me."

James came running up to Samantha and Ira and said with concern, "Ira, Bart is really sick. They are tending to him in the visitor's center."

"What's wrong?" asked Samantha with great concern.

"I don't know. He started feeling bad after breakfast, and it has been getting worse since then. He collapsed about ten minutes ago."

"Look, James. Me and Guy have been called back to Norfolk for an emergency. Samantha is all yours now. I'll have some people get here to tend to Bart. I want you and Samantha to get back to the Lodge, pack up, and return to Telluride. Got that?"

"Yes, sir. Right away."

Samantha took the twins to her car and strapped them into their car seats in the back. James went into the visitor's center to tell Bart that he had to leave and that a medical team was on its way to tend to him. When James returned to Samantha to begin the return trip back down to the Lodge, they saw a military helicopter approaching a landing pad near the visitor's center.

James said to Samantha, "Drive slowly and carefully down the road. As you know, there are a lot of cutbacks and razor-sharp turns going back. The outer edge of the road is mostly lined with sheer cliffs. Be very careful. I'll be right behind you. I'm sure you'll do fine. Are you ready?"

"Yes, James. I'm ready."

In tandem, they began the trip down the road.

Fortunately, it was Sunday afternoon, and traffic on the road was light both ways. Samantha was worried about Ira and what kind of submarine emergency he was going to have to deal with. She was talking to the twins, but soon realized that they were both fast asleep. She started following James's advice and began paying more attention to the road because it was becoming more and more steep as she descended.

Even while paying more attention to her driving, she was still trying to take in the amazing vistas that seemed to pop up after every turn. She was checking her rearview mirror to see if James was still close behind her, and she heard a loud *pop*. She wondered what the noise was. Suddenly, when she had to brake for a turn, she realized that her brake pedal went to the floor. She pumped her foot frantically on the pedal, but it remained on the floor.

The car began accelerating down the road. Samantha did not panic, and she thought of the emergency brake. She quickly pulled up the emergency brake lever, and she felt the car vibrate violently, but it did not slow down. The emergency brake was useless. She was now going eighty miles an hour when she should have been at thirty-five. She saw a curve ahead, and she tried to make the turn. But she was going too fast, and two wheels lifted off the road. She barely kept control, and the car somehow righted itself and stayed on the road. She had slowed to about seventy-five with this maneuver, but she was accelerating once again. She was speeding toward another sharp turn, and she knew that she would not be able to keep the car on the road.

She applied all the strength she had to try to turn the wheel. The car once again went on two wheels, but the angle was steeper than before. She could see that she was going to go over the cliff's edge. All she could think of in this moment of imminent death was her two infant babies. But miraculously, there was a guard rail there, and it somehow held and deflected the car from the cliff's edge and back toward the road. Samantha's car doors slid along the steel rail sending sparks shooting everywhere. The car once again violently righted itself and was heading down a straight stretch of road.

Oncoming cars were veering to the side of the road as Samantha's car was now going about one hundred miles per hour. Samantha knew that sure death was only a few horror-filled seconds away. As she looked down the road to see her next, and probably last cut-back turn, she saw a possible way out—a runaway truck gravel pit. If she could only keep control of the car and steer herself into the loose gravel, she may have a chance to save Roman and Paula, who were now awake and screaming.

Samantha grabbed the wheel even tighter and tried desperately to steer the car toward the gravel. There was a steel guard rail on the roadside of the pit. It looked like she was going to hit the edge of the rail head on. She knew that if this happened, she would be impaled by the rail. But maybe the twins would survive. This was her only thought as she fought the wheel to steer the car off the road and into the loose gravel. As she headed directly toward the rail, she screamed knowing this was surely her last breath. The car hit the rail's edge with its left front fender. The whole left side of the car was ripped off, including both the front and rear passenger doors and the left rear fender. The remainder of the car flew into the gravel. When the car hit, it came to a jarring halt, and the remaining four air bags deployed, pinning Samantha to the back of her seat. She could hear the sweet sound of Roman and Paula screaming at the top of their lungs.

Meanwhile, James, who could not keep up with Samantha's runaway car, had caught up with her at the gravel pit. He flew out of his car and ran toward Samantha. He found her trying desperately to free herself from the now deflated air bag and the twisted frame of the car. When she saw James, she yelled, "Get the twins out of the car."

James ran to the right side of the car and struggled with the door, which was partially buried in gravel. Samantha finally freed herself and, with unbelievable strength, helped James open the door. Once they had the two babies out of the car, they began running toward James's car, which was very difficult to do because of the loose gravel. When they were almost to his car, there was a loud explosion as Samantha's car blew up and was engulfed in flames. The force of the explosion knocked Samantha, James, and the twins to the ground with James on top of Samantha and the twins between them. When they were able to get up from the ground, James helped Samantha and her children into the back seat of his car. When he got behind the steering wheel, he asked Samantha how badly she was hurt. There was no answer. When he turned around, he saw that she had passed out, probably from exhaustion. He saw that she also had a serious abrasion to her head with blood running down her cheek, and he thought that she may have been knocked out as well.

James headed back down to Grand Lake and made several calls on the way. Within minutes, Harlan Bradbury was on a CIA jet to Colorado, and a medical team was dispatched to Grand Lake Lodge.

✮✮✮

As soon as Harlan's jet landed, he hopped into a waiting car and drove to the Telluride Regional Medical Center. A waiting agent, Henry Biggsbie, met Harlan's car as he drove up and began briefing him.

"We had a dispatched medical copter waiting at the Lodge, and we flew her here to the Telluride Hospital. We got her here only about an hour ago. She's in the ER right now. She got a severe blow to her head and was knocked unconscious. She was still unconscious when we got her here, but I believe she was coming to when we got her into the ER."

"Where's James and Bart?"

"James is in the ER waiting room. But I am afraid I have bad news about Bart."

"What is it?" asked Harlan with concern.

"Bart has died. We are not sure how until we have an autopsy done. But it looks like he was poisoned."

"Good God, no. Take me to James. I have to talk to him."

"Yes, sir. Follow me."

Harlan and Henry ran into the ER waiting room and saw James leaning forward in his chair with his head in both hands.

"A report, James." Harlan said with great urgency. "Give me a report on Samantha."

"I haven't heard from the doctor yet, and it's been about an hour since they took her back."

"Was she conscious?" Harlan asked.

"She came to just as they were starting to wheel her away. She asked about the twins, looked at me with concern, then passed out again. I told her the twins were fine, but I don't know if she heard me."

"How are the twins? Where are they now?"

"They are fine. They took them to the hospital nursery, and doctors are examining them."

"Well, all we can do is wait. Henry, go to the nursery and get a report on Roman and Paula."

"Right away, Mr. Bradbury."

Twenty minutes later, a doctor came out of Samantha's room. He walked up to Harlan and James with a serious look on his face.

"Doctor?" Harlan asked nervously.

The doctor shook his head and said, "She will be fine, but she took a vicious blow to the head and suffered a serious concussion. She must have hit her head on the windshield because there were pieces of safety glass in her head wound. She was most likely knocked unconscious when she hit her head. But overall, she was lucky. I believe the air bag kept her from going through the windshield."

"That's not what I saw, doctor." When I ran to her car, she was struggling to free herself from behind the steering wheel and yelling at me to get her twins out of the car. I couldn't get the door open because gravel was keeping it shut. I was about to panic when Samantha got to me, pushed me away, pulled on the door handle, and pulled the door open. Gravel went everywhere. I don't know how she had the strength to do that. I couldn't budge the door."

The doctor said, "That's an incredible story because the blow to her head was so severe that she should have been unconscious."

"Let me finish what happened. She got the twins out of their car seat, picked them both up, and ran about thirty yards through softly packed gravel to my car carrying both the kids. Her car exploded, knocking us all to the ground. We got up, and she got the twins into the back seat of my car. That's when she passed out."

"Strange. Very strange, Unbelievable, actually," said the doctor.

"Well, how is she now?" asked Harlan.

"She's still unconscious, but her vital signs are all good, and she's breathing normally. I believe that she is sleeping normally, and that's good. When she wakes up, we will try to assess the seriousness of her concussion."

At that time, Henry returned from the nursery and said, "The twins are both fine."

"Great news, Henry." Harlan then turned to James and said, "Tell me about Bart. What happened?"

"I'm not sure, Mr. Bradbury. We got up in the morning at the Lodge and had our normal breakfast. We both had the same thing—eggs, bacon, toast, and coffee. When we were driving behind Samantha and Ira, Bart started to complain about stomach cramps and nausea. He kept feeling worse and worse as we drove. We were walking to the visitor's center, and he just collapsed. I got him inside, and the employees began ministering to him. I reported that he needed medical attention, and I was told that help was on the way. Then I went to tell Ira and Samantha what had happened to Bart. I didn't find out he had died until Henry told me when I got Samantha to the hospital. The EMTs reported that they saw that Bart was foaming at the mouth. They suspect that he was poisoned. But Mr. Bradbury, we both ate the same food at breakfast, and neither one of us ate or drank anything else after that. How come I'm not dead too?"

"I don't know, James. When you made it back to the Lodge, did you notice or ask if there were any other problems with the guests?"

"I was too busy tending to Samantha and the kids, and I didn't ask. But everything seemed normal there."

"It's a mystery, James. But this could be the work of the Ghost. I'm just not sure yet." Harlan then instructed Henry, "Henry, make arrangements to have Samantha's car recovered. I want it thoroughly examined to find out what happened. Also, I want the autopsy on Bart done right away. Fly in our own doctor if you have to."

"Yes, sir. I've already arranged to have the car recovered and taken to Denver. We will examine it there. I'll get on the autopsy first thing."

That night, Harlan's phone rang at three o'clock in the morning. He bolted awake hoping it was good news about Samantha. "Hello?"

"Mr. Bradbury, this is Dr. Jenkins. We talked earlier about Samantha Coen."

"Yes, doctor. I hope you have good news for me."

"I do. Samantha woke up a little over and hour ago. She wanted to know about her twins. We assured her that they were fine, and that we would let her hold them in the morning. We ran her through a series of concussion protocols and did an MRI of her brain. I just looked at the MRI results a few minutes ago, and I've found no brain damage. That's when I made the call to you."

"Thank you, Dr. Jenkins. That is good news. What's next?"

"I'd like to keep her here for a day or two just to be sure she is okay. That was a nasty blow to her head. It could have been much worse for her. She's a very lucky woman."

"Doctor, she would tell you that she is blessed. She doesn't believe in luck. Thank you, Dr. Jenkins. Thank you for all you've done."

"You're quite welcome, Mr. Bradbury. For some reason, I was just taken by her and didn't want to leave her side."

"I can understand that doctor. She seems to have that effect on people."

Samantha insisted on being released the next day. She was relieved that Roman and Paula had experienced no trauma during the car ride from hell. She also felt no after affects from the accident other than the nasty bruise on her right temple. She didn't even have a headache.

Harlan wanted to have Samantha and James meet at CIA headquarters in Denver the very next day, Wednesday. Ira was being flown to Denver for the meeting as well. Harlan wanted to assess the situation with all who were involved.

When Ira walked into the CIA meeting room, Harlan, James, and Samantha were already there drinking coffee. When Samantha saw Ira, she immediately got up and ran toward him. Before she got to Ira, however, she got dizzy, stopped, fell to one knee, and grabbed ahold of a chair. Ira ran to her and put his arms around her and helped her up.

"Sam. Are you okay?"

"Yes. I'm okay. I got up too quickly, and I got really dizzy."

"Sit down. Take it easy for a few minutes and take a few deep breaths."

Harlan and James looked at Samantha with great concern, but she assured them that she was fine.

After a few minutes, Harlan began. "Okay then. If you are up to it, Samantha, let's get started, and I will tell you what I know so far."

Samantha nodded for Harlan to go ahead.

"First of all, Bart. He did, in fact, die of poisoning. Apparently, the poison was put in his coffee."

"But why his coffee and not mine too?" asked James.

"That I can't tell you right now, James. Second, Samantha's runaway car. The car was rigged to explode by a timer linked to the brake failure. It was there for two possible reasons that I can think of. If the device to disable the brakes did not work, the explosion would have most surely killed Samantha."

"And my babies," she interjected with venom in her voice.

"And your babies," Harlan agreed. "Another possible reason for the explosion was to completely destroy the car so we wouldn't be able to determine why the brakes failed. However, since the car was partially buried in gravel, the part of the car buried in the gravel was not affected by the resulting fire. Because of this, we were able to determine how the brakes were disabled."

Samantha said, "This I want to hear."

"The brake hydraulic line was cut by a device that was

activated by a pressure sensor. The device turned on when you rose up the mountain road."

"How?" asked Samantha.

"As you went up the mountain, the air pressure got less and less. At a certain air pressure, the device was activated. Then, when you descended from the top, the device was set off when the air pressure rose to a preset point. The device went off and cut the brake's hydraulic line."

"That must have been the strange *pop* I heard."

"Probably so. Once the line was severed, the hydraulic brake fluid escaped, and you had no brakes."

"The Ghost put the device on the car. Didn't he?"

"Yes, I suspected as much, but now I'm sure it was him, Samantha."

Samantha shook her head. Then she said, "Where did he rig the car? When did he have the chance to do such a thing?"

"He could have done it in Telluride or at Grand Lake. The device wasn't activated until the air pressure decreased to the desired point. My guess, though, is that he did it one night when you were at the Grand Lake Lodge."

"Harlan, this guy really is a ghost if he did that at night."

Harlan shook his head in dismay. He then continued, "That brings us to Ira's submarine emergency. Ira can report that better than me. Ira?"

Samantha looked up at Harlan. In her concern for herself and the twins, she had totally forgotten about Ira's problem.

Ira began, "Sorry I couldn't fly back here yesterday to be with you in the hospital, Sam. Harlan kept me informed of your condition, but it was chaos at the office, and I just couldn't leave. It turned out that there was no submarine emergency. The call to me was a fake.

"What about the military helicopter sent to get you, Ira?" she asked.

"A fake too. It was an old military helicopter restored and configured to look just like a modern one. The helicopter crew members were not military as well. Just dressed like it. The real weird part, which I should have caught, was that this fake helicopter landed at the Norfolk International Airport, and there was a limousine waiting to take me to the base. The limo driver must have had a fake ID because we were waived right through the gate at the naval base. At the time, I thought that the security guard recognized me and waived us through. I should have realized that landing at the commercial airport was not what would have been done. They'd have taken me directly to the base, especially in an emergency."

James asked, "What's all this about? Why go through all that trouble and expense just to get Ira away?"

"Here's what I think." Harlan said. "The Ghost is behind all of this. His agenda is to kill Samantha, not Ira. If he didn't call Ira away with this fake submarine emergency, Ira would have been in the car with Samantha."

"Why do this?" asked James. "By killing Ira, he would have been killing two birds with one stone. Oops! No offense, Samantha. I forgot that you still go by Dr. Stone."

"None taken, James. Forget about it."

Harlan continued. "Ira is number twelve on his hit list. Listen, I'm telling you all that Yulov is a narcissistic egomaniac. He thinks that he is smarter than we are. He put a game together, and he's playing his game. He's toying with us. He's having fun."

"What do we do next, Harlan?" asked Samantha.

"For starters, Telluride is out, I'm afraid. I don't know how the Ghost did it, but he did. He found you. He found out that Ira was coming to see you for a few days. He found out that you were staying for a few days at the Grand Lake Lodge. And above all this, he had the time to rig your car with two intricate devices and to arrange for a fake helicopter to pick up Ira. I don't know how he got Ira's phone number through his burner app. This guy is a problem. He's smart. He's clever. And most importantly, he's insane."

"I have to admit, Harlan. I am really scared of this guy. But what scares me the most is that he almost killed my two babies."

"We are all going to fly back to Langley tomorrow on the CIA jet. Tomorrow afternoon, we will have a brainstorming session and come up with a plan to protect you, Samantha. We will put you, the twins, and Ira up in a safe house tonight here in Denver. We will leave early tomorrow morning. You will be well protected. Tonight, we will discuss basic ideas of what we can do as we move forward."

"My babies, Harlan. Think about how we can protect them."

"I will, Samantha. We all will."

CHAPTER 11
GULFPORT

THAT EVENING, A MEAL WAS brought in for Harlan, Samantha, Ira, and James. They discussed what could have gone wrong in Telluride, but no solid answers were arrived at. How the Ghost had pulled off the whole assassination attempt in one month was a mystery.

After dinner, Harlan said, "The one thing that seems to make the most sense is that Telluride was too small. Too easy for someone to notice things. Things like a new single female in town with infant twins. We need to be more cunning about what we do. Our standard way of doing things is not good enough in trying to deal with this guy."

Everyone agreed. Harlan asked, "How about Gulfport, Mississippi, Samantha? Gulfport is larger than Telluride. You won't stick out there. Also, I want to double up on the security guards."

"What about Roman and Paula? How do we protect them?" Samantha asked.

"You are not going to like this, Samantha, but we have a married couple working at CIA headquarters, and they are willing to take care of the twins while you are away in Gulfport."

"I have to be away from my babies," Samantha stated as a fact and not a question.

I'm afraid so. Based on the Telluride fiasco, they are in too much danger if they are with you."

"This kills me to say this, but you are right. Can I meet with the couple? What are their names?"

"Believe this or not, but their names are Jack and Jill Hill."

"Like *went up a*?" Samantha said with a smile.

"Cute. You're not the first to say that."

Ira, who had been silent up until now said, "What are Mr. and Mrs. Hill's qualifications?"

"Well, for one thing, they are trained field agents. They can take care of themselves, if you know what I mean. Plus, they have had children of their own and are recent empty nesters."

Ira said, "Do you think the Hills and the twins could stay at my house on the base?"

"That might work out, Ira. We'll ask them."

The next morning, all four were on their way back to Langley on the CIA jet. Late that afternoon, they were in Harlan's office ready to plan and execute the next phase of trying to save Samantha's life.

Harlan called Jean Barlow, his secretary, into his office to join them. "Jean, call Jack and Jill Hill and ask them to come to my office to meet the people I talked to them about."

"Right away, Harlan."

Samantha said, "I hope all this works out, because I would feel better if the kids were with Ira. At least he would see them every day."

"One other thing," said Harlan. "We've developed a double-layered encryption capability for our cell phones. It's even better than the burner app. We'll use it to communicate with each other. It hasn't been fully tested yet, but it seems to be functioning as planned. And, Samantha, keep your eyes open for any suspicious activity and keep your gun handy. We've been underestimating this guy all along. We can't let that happen again."

"For sure, Harlan," she answered.

The meeting with the Hills went well. They were happy to set up in Ira's admiral's quarters. Samantha was pleased with them as surrogate parents to her children. When the Hills had left his office, Harlan asked Jean to call Frank Bilger and Bill Williams to begin setting up Samantha's new life in Gulfport. Meanwhile, the search for the Ghost continued.

CHAPTER 12
PLANE RIDE FROM HELL

SAMANTHA SETTLED INTO HER NEW location in Gulfport. Almost three months went by with no unusual activity taking place. The one bad thing was that the Ghost was still out there, and everyone knew that he was actively seeking Samantha. Samantha kept in touch daily with Ira with normal phone calls, and they used FaceTime to show Samantha how fast Roman and Paula were growing. Samantha missed them every minute, but knew she had to stay strong for them. Jack and Jill were doing an outstanding job in taking care of the children, and both Ira and Samantha were pleased with them.

Samantha had two new secret service bodyguards, Matthias Roberts and Nathaniel Breakstone. Matthias was one of Harlan's most senior and trusted field agents. She continued her self-defense lessons with Matthias, but he was not as skilled as Bart, and she often showed him a thing or two.

The ringtone on Samantha's phone chimed—Harlan. "Hi, Harlan. What's up?"

"Samantha. Bad news. I just heard from one of my agents that he has very reliable information that the Ghost has located you in Gulfport. I haven't checked this out thoroughly yet, but I don't want to take the chance that he could strike at any minute.

I want you, Matthias, and Nathaniel to get to the airport right away. Don't pack. Don't do anything. Just get to the airport. I will have a plane waiting for the three of you. Big John will be at the passenger drop off area, and he will tell you where the plane is waiting. You shouldn't have any trouble spotting him. Give the phone to Matthias, and I'll give him instructions. Get yourself ready to go out the door.

"Okay, Harlan. But I'm scared."

"Me too, Samantha. Let me speak to Matthias."

Samantha handed the phone to Matthias. Ten minutes later, they were on their way to the Biloxi-Gulfport International Airport.

When they approached the passenger drop off area, Samantha spotted Big John immediately. At six foot-seven and a wide body to match, he stood out amongst most of humanity. Matthias pulled up alongside him, and even before the car fully stopped, the big man crawled into the back seat with Nathaniel.

"Go straight to the next stop sign and take a right. Then follow the Air National Guard signs."

In a few minutes, they pulled up to a plane that had its twin jet engines running and ready to go. Matthias parked the car nearby, and they all ran to the waiting plane. There was a female attendant standing at the plane's doorway, and she guided them to their seats. As soon as they were strapped in, the plane began to taxi. In ten minutes, they were at altitude enroute to Langley.

Just as she was starting to try to relax a little, Samantha heard a hiss and noticed a sweet odor. When she opened her eyes, she found herself sitting in the right-hand seat in the cockpit, where a man was tying her into the seat with a rope. She was very groggy, but she had enough sense to close her eyes again, but hold her arms rigid and away from her body. She continued to feign unconsciousness. In a few minutes, she felt more alert, and she opened her eyes and looked over to the pilot seat. She saw a man wearing a pilot's uniform, and he looked very much like

Anton Yulov, except his hair was longer than in his photographs, and he sported a bushy moustache.

"Well, well, well," he said, "Dr. Samantha Stone. We finally meet face-to-face at last. Are you comfortable?"

Samantha said nothing. She only glared at him with loathing.

"I must admit, Samantha, you've been a challenge to me. Your escape down the mountain was very impressive. It's too bad you don't have enough time left to tell me how you did it."

"You almost killed my babies, you psychotic asshole."

"Now, now, Samantha, please watch your tongue. If it will make you feel any better, I was not happy at putting your babies at risk like that. I only wanted you."

"What about Bart. You killed him. He's not me. What's wrong with you? You are an animal."

Yulov smiled at Samantha and said, "Bart is merely a signature, Dr. Stone. You wouldn't understand."

Samantha glared at Yulov in disbelief at how cavalier he was about the taking of human lives.

"Dr. Stone, you've been a very formidable challenge, and I've really enjoyed getting to know you. It's been so much fun to see your likes and dislikes, listening to you, and watching you live your life."

"Watching me!"

"Yes. I've been watching you. I even have about an hour of video of you. I've seen you naked. I have pictures. I must say, you are very impressive without clothes on."

"You are a perverted douchebag," she spat. "You're no better than a squashed cockroach on the sole of my shoe. You are going to rot in hell."

"Thank you for the compliments, but as for hell, I don't believe in that sort of thing, Dr. Stone. All I know is that I am having so much fun while I'm still alive. And there is so much more fun yet to come."

Samantha stared at him in utter disbelief and hatred.

"Ahh. I think I see my ride home a few miles ahead. I must be going now, but it was very nice talking to you and getting to know you even better. But now, here's your situation. The plane is on autopilot, and you are heading right out into the Gulf of Mexico. No land in sight. I estimate that you have an hour, maybe an hour-and-a-half of fuel left. So, in the time you have left, enjoy the ride. You've been delightful."

Yulov left the cockpit. A minute later, Samantha felt the sudden change in cabin pressure as the Ghost opened the hatch and jumped from the plane. She watched as a large yacht off the starboard side of the plane came into view and Yulov's parachute descended toward it. She began a frantic struggle to free herself from her bonds. After a few minutes she got one arm free. The rest was easy. The Ghost might have been a skilled assassin, but he was poor at securing people with a rope.

When she had herself free, she jumped out of the chair. She nearly passed out before she took her first step. She was still groggy from the knockout gas and perhaps from her earlier concussion. She took some deep breaths and shook her head. Finally steady, she rushed into the cabin. To her horror, she saw that Nathaniel and the flight attendant were still strapped in their seats and both were saturated with blood. Their throats had been slit and were almost certainly dead. Big John and Matthias were still alive and were just coming to from the gas. Samantha helped them unbuckle their seat belts and asked, "Can either of you fly an airplane?"

Both men shook their heads, still trying to shake off the effects of the gas.

"That's just great! Looks like I have some work to do."

She ran back into the cockpit and strapped herself into the left-hand seat. She said aloud, "Gilbert said it was like riding a bicycle. Once you know how, you never forget. Let's hope he was right."

She studied the instrument panel for a few moments. *Come on. Come on. Remember, remember, remember. I can do this. I can do anything through Christ Jesus who strengthens me. Give me the strength, Lord. I can do this, but I really need your help.*

Her head suddenly cleared, and she noticed that she was on autopilot with a heading of 185 degrees. She knew that if she flew the reciprocal of 185 degrees, she would retrace her out bound flight line. She said, "Here we go, Lord. Please be with me." She switched off the autopilot and grabbed the steering yoke. She made a tight turn until she was on a course of 005 degrees. Fifteen minutes later, she spotted the yacht. As she approached the yacht, she descended to an altitude of 200 feet. When she was abreast of the yacht, she could clearly see the Ghost sitting on the fantail celebrating with a cocktail in his hand.

Yulov stood up as he saw the plane fly by. Samantha waved to him, and he saw what he thought was a smile on her face. When the plane had passed by, it made a left-hand turn and began to circle Yulov's yacht. As it made the circle, Samantha rocked her wings up and down as a way of saying hi to him. Yulov could again see Samantha and noticed her flip him off as she turned the plane toward Gulfport.

Yulov threw his cocktail glass to the deck, smashing it to pieces. "You bitch!" he yelled at the departing plane. "You bitch. I've underestimated you twice, but it won't happen again."

CHAPTER 13
"I HAD HELP"

ENROUTE TO GULFPORT, SAMANTHA PHONED Harlan and reported what had just happened to her. Matthias and Big John were okay, but Nathaniel and an innocent flight attendant had been murdered. "I'm fine, Harlan. Quite a bit shaken up, but I'm fine. I was face-to-face with the Ghost, and he is a very scary individual. He is insane. He can kill people without any sign of remorse or regret. But we've got him, Harlan. He's on a yacht, and I know his coordinates, and he is headed toward west Florida. Have the Coast Guard intercept the yacht and take him into custody. Be sure the Coast Guard personnel know how dangerous he is." She then gave Harlan the yacht's location coordinates.

"Thanks, Samantha. I'm glad you are okay. I'll call the Coast Guard as soon as we hang up here."

Harlan buzzed Jean. "Yes, Harlan."

"Jean, get the Biloxi/Gulfport Coast Guard on the phone and have them hold. I need to talk to them."

"Right away," she answered.

"Samantha, do you have enough fuel to get to Gulfport?"

"I believe so, Harlan. I should be good."

"Who's flying the airplane? Matthias?"

"No, Harlan. Neither Matthias nor Big John know how to pilot a plane. In fact, as we were boarding the plane, Big John told me he is scared to fly. So, I guess it's up to me."

"You are kidding me, right?

"I should be okay. I've got a little help."

"This I've got to hear about when we meet. I've got to get the Coast Guard into action to pick up Yulov. I've got a few other arrangements to make as well. When you land, I want you to taxi to the Air National Guard terminal. The guardsmen there will protect you. But stay close to Matthias and Big John. Very close. In fact, stay right behind Big John. You'll be safe there. After a pause, he said, "You do know how to land a jet aircraft don't you?"

"I've landed a plane a couple of times a long time ago. We'll see. Like I said, I have help."

As Samantha approached the Gulfport airport, she contacted the control tower and requested a landing strip to use. She was given the number, and she could clearly see the number painted on the runway. She also could see planes ahead of her regaining altitude to clear her approach and that her assigned runway was lined with all sorts of emergency vehicles with their flashing lights strobing away. This sight scared her a bit more because it clearly reminded her of the danger that she was in. Then she turned to Big John who was now sitting in the right-hand seat. "Are you sure you don't know how to fly a plane?"

"You can do it, Samantha. I have faith in you."

I don't want to lessen your faith, John, but I've only landed an airplane two times before, and both times I had a licensed pilot with me making sure I didn't kill us."

"You can do it, Samantha. I have faith in you." Big John repeated through clenched teeth.

"John, you are scared. That's the second time you said that."

"I am scared, Samantha, but I have faith in you. You can do it."

Samantha giggled nervously. "Hold onto your seat, my big

friend. It's time. Here we go." She took a deep breath and put both hands on the yoke.

She lined up the plane with the runway. "God, I hope I don't hit any of those emergency trucks." She cut back on the throttle and increased her flaps to slow down. When she felt the plane beginning to stall, she retracted the flaps a bit, and the plane picked up a little speed. She looked at the windsock on the ground, and she saw that she had a slight crosswind from port to starboard. She was descending in altitude, but she wasn't sure if her descent was too steep or not steep enough. She aimed the aircraft to the right side of the runway's center line to compensate for the slight crosswind. She passed over the start of the runway, and it felt like she was going to run out of runway before the wheels touched the ground. She increased the flaps to maximum, and miraculously, the Cessna's wheels hit the runway right on its center line. She quickly reversed the thrust of the engines and retracted the flaps fully. She slowed to taxi speed and began steering the aircraft to the National Guard terminal.

She turned to the terrified man sitting next to her and said, "We did it, Big John. We did it!"

He answered in a very shaky voice, "I knew you could do it, Samantha. But if you will forgive me, I think I shit my pants."

"Well, John. That doesn't show a great deal of faith in me. But under the circumstances, I understand—and I do forgive you," she said with a chuckle.

Samantha taxied to the spot where ten armed national guardsmen were standing. An ambulance was there with EMTs waiting with hand-held stretchers. Two security agents went onboard as soon as Samantha had opened the plane's door. The agents inspected the plane for ten minutes. They then gave permission for Samantha, Big John, and Matthias to leave the plane. Big John had to assist Matthias down the stairs because he had still not gotten over the effects of the knockout gas. The

EMTs went into the plane to recover the two bodies. Another EMT tended to Matthias. When Matthias was able to walk under his own power, the three were escorted by two agents and the ten guardsmen and were led into the national guard terminal. Once inside, a waiting doctor and nurse tended to them. Ten minutes later, one of the agents handed a phone to Samantha and said to her, "Director Bradbury needs to talk to you, Dr. Stone."

"Hi, Harlan."

"Are you guys okay?"

"We're all fine. Quite a bit shaken up. But, yes, we are fine."

"I was told you made a perfect landing."

"Really? Who told you that? I thought I used up most of the runway before the wheels hit the ground."

"Well, I was told it was perfect. Look, Samantha. Here's what I want you to do. One of the Mississippi Air National Guard planes is going to fly you, Big John, and Matthias to the Norfolk Naval Air Station. I'm taking a helicopter there in about an hour. Ira is waiting for us at his headquarters. We have a lot of talking to do." After a pause, Harlan said, "Did you really fly that airplane?"

"I had help, Harlan. Read Philippians 4:13."

CHAPTER 14
A MOLE?

HARLAN AND IRA WERE ALREADY in the small briefing room when Samantha, Matthias, and Big John entered. Ira ran to Samantha and hugged her with a sigh of relief. When Ira finally pulled away from her, he said, "What's this I hear about you flying a jet airplane?"

Samantha giggled and said, "I knew you'd be upset when you heard. But whoa! News certainly travels fast around here."

"I'm not upset. I'm just thankful that you were able to do it. But how? How do you do all these things?"

"Hey!" she said. "You two have your cups of coffee. Let the three of us get ours and get settled down in our chairs."

The latecomers got their coffee and sat down. Samantha took a few sips of coffee and looked at the others. She was silent.

Ira finally exclaimed, "Well, woman. Are you going to make us wait all day? How did you know how to fly that plane?"

Samantha smiled and said, "It's a secret."

"No, it's not," said Ira. "Start talking.

"Well, okay. I guess I owe you guys an explanation."

Ira and Harlan looked at each other in exasperation, rolled their eyes, and shook their heads.

"When I was at Oregon State University as an undergraduate

in physics, I met a guy named Gilbert Stewart. He's one of the two guys in my life that I've been engaged to, Ira. I've told you about that. Well, Gilbert was a physics major as well, and he was from Alaska . . . Fairbanks, Alaska. And he, like so many other Alaskans, had a private pilot's license. He even had his own plane. During long weekends and vacations, we would fly to Alaska , land on a lake, and camp out in the wilderness. During these flights, Gilbert would show me how to pilot an aircraft. I guess I caught on quickly because he asked me if I wanted to try and land the plane. I thought he'd never ask," she said with a smile.

Ira once again rolled his eyes then looked up at the ceiling.

Samantha continued, "Gilbert was sitting right next to me and was ready to take the controls if I got us in trouble. He talked me through it, and voila. I did it. He let me land twice. After I graduated from OSU and started working at the Naval Research Lab, I started taking flying lessons. I only took three lessons before I had to quit. I was travelling too much on my job. That's it. Any questions?"

Harlan smiled then looked at Matthias and Big John. "Did you guys know about this?"

Matthias answered, "We asked her, and she told us the story on the flight here from Gulfport."

Big John said, "I was sitting in the copilot's seat during the landing. I had faith that Samantha could do it. She kept mumbling something about Philippians 4:13. And even though I've never been scared about anything in my life, I was scared to death. Now I know what the term *scared shitless* means. I'm embarrassed to say this, but I actually shit my pants."

Everybody at the table laughed, except Big John and Samantha.

She said seriously, "I fail to see the humor in all this. I knew that Big John was telling the truth because I couldn't wait to get out of the cockpit." She burst into laughter.

Everyone, except Big John, joined her in the laughter.

After the good-natured fun at Big John's expense died down, Harlan said, "Alright. Alright. Let's get serious. We've got some decisions to make."

"Samantha. Give us a description of what happened to you today. Don't leave out any details, especially of the time on the plane with the Ghost."

Samantha retold her experience with Yulov and their conversation.

Harlan asked, "When you were talking about Bart's murder, did he use the term *signature* like you just told us?"

"Yes, he did. Exactly that term. Then he said that I wouldn't understand. He must think that I'm really dumb if I wouldn't know what he meant."

Matthias chimed in, "That's very bad news Mr. Bradbury. It means that he's going to take the life of someone else when he assassinates each hit-list victim."

"You're right, Matthias. And from what we've seen so far, it is probably one of the agents we have guarding Samantha."

"First Bart then Nathaniel."

Samantha added, "It's just another way for him to make a fool of us. He's saying, 'You can't even protect your security guards much less your client'. I told you, the man is insane."

Harlan nodded his head in agreement. "This really complicates dealing with this nut. Our best field agents are at risk."

Samantha added, "What about the flight attendant he just killed?"

"I'm not sure about that. She might have been a loose end he had to take care of. We'll do a thorough background search on her to see if she had any ties with Yulov."

Samantha asked, "Harlan, how did your agent know that the Ghost was in Gulfport?"

"After we talked when you were on the plane, I called him.

He said that an airport security guard spotted someone that he thought might be our man. He had flown in on a private jet yesterday. My agent said the airport security guard followed the man and got a good description of him. He even was able to photograph him. He called the number we provided to airport security, and he provided the photo, which was surprisingly good. We photoshopped the photo and removed the moustache and long hair off him and turned his hair back to light brown. From that, we were pretty sure it was our man, the Ghost. Not positive, but sure enough to get you out of Gulfport, Samantha."

"Harlan. How is he finding me? He finds me soon enough to set up these very complicated assassination attempts on me. I mean, look what he did this time. How did he have time to arrange the bogus—and expensive, I might add—jet aircraft ready to go? Knockout gas, possibly a fake flight attendant. How did he know that Harlan would get me out of Gulfport by an airplane? How does he know ahead of time what we will do?"

"I don't know, Samantha. This guy might really be a ghost."

Samantha thought for a moment. No one else said anything. Finally, she broke the silence and said, "I don't believe in ghosts. Harlan, is it possible that we have a mole somewhere?"

Harlan looked shocked. "It's always possible. But there are only a few people that have known what our plans were. And I trust them all a great deal. They've been with me for years."

"Who are they?" she asked.

"I have to give this some thought and do a little digging. But off the top of my head, Frank Bilger and Bill Williams knew because they arranged the relocations. There are a few people that work with Frank and Bill to set everything up. My secretary, Jean Barlow is another. Of course, the security agents we've assigned to protect Samantha, but half of them are dead. Then there's Ira and me," he added.

"Harlan, I think you should look into this very quietly. If one of them is the mole, we don't want to spook him. Pardon the pun."

"I will, Samantha. Let's see what I can find out. Meanwhile, what do we do next?"

Ira said, "He's found Samantha two times now. He will probably find her again. Is there another way to protect her?"

Harlan was thinking about this when Jean buzzed him. "Harlan, the Coast Guard is on the line for you."

"Thanks, Jean. Before he picked up the phone, he said, "They probably have Yulov in custody. Perhaps this nightmare is finally over."

"This is Director Bradbury. Do you have Yulov?"

"I'm afraid not, Mr. Bradbury."

"What the hell happened? Didn't you intercept his yacht?"

"Yes, we did, Mr. Bradbury. But he wasn't onboard."

"How can that be? Did you search the yacht thoroughly?"

"Yes, we did, sir. Apparently, he escaped on a speed boat the yacht was carrying. The yacht's master said that our man had his crew lower the boat right after the airplane circled them. He took off directly north toward the Florida panhandle. The coastguardsman then said, "We dispatched an aircraft to try to locate his boat. There's a lot of ocean out their but we may still spot him. Sorry, sir."

"Get more search planes in the air. We must find this guy and get him into custody."

"Yes, Mr. Bradbury. We will do all we can to capture him."

Harlan shook his head in dismay as he hung up the phone. Samantha then said, "I'm sorry Harlan. It's my fault. I should never have flown around the yacht like I did. He knew that I would alert the Coast Guard to intercept him. I'm sorry. I let my ego get the best of me. I just wanted to give him the finger so badly."

Ira said, "Don't worry about it. He had that speed boat on the yacht for a reason. He probably planned to abandon the yacht in any event. A yacht is easy to spot from the air. A small speedboat is not easy to see."

"Ira's right, Samantha. That's how the Ghost operates. He always has several ways to escape."

"Look," Harlan continued, "You guys need some sleep. Let's get together tomorrow morning in this room to plan what we do next." He then asked Ira, "Can I stay at your house tonight, Ira? I'll give you and Samantha some privacy. Matthias and Big John can stay in a guarded safe house."

Ira said, "My house is big. There are rooms in there that I've never seen. You, Matthias, and everyone can stay there without any problem."

"Great. We'll all stay there," said Harlan. "I doubt very much if the Ghost can do anything for a day or two after this attempt failed. I do think he is human, and he has to rethink what he should do next to get Samantha."

"Let's hope you are right, Harlan," she said.

At that very moment, Anton Yulov was being lifted from his speed boat into a hovering helicopter. He was then whisked away to a small regional airport just outside of Mobile, Alabama where a small private plane was warming up awaiting to take him to his hideout in the Blue Ridge Mountains.

En route, he thought, *That bitch has got to go. I won't fail next time.*

CHAPTER 15
A MOLE

THE NEXT MORNING, HARLAN, IRA, and Samantha met in the briefing room. Big John and Matthias were instructed to help Harlan's team in investigating how the Ghost was able to put the complicated assassination attempt together.

"It must have been nice being able to hold your children last night. The joy on your face was pretty clear."

"Yes, it was, Harlan. I hadn't touched them in three months. Thank God for FaceTime. I wasn't so shocked to see how much they had changed."

"I'm just happy that you survived your ordeal yesterday and was able to be with them again."

Harlan continued, "I convened an investigation yesterday to try to find out how Yulov did what he did. I put Matthias in charge of the team. Hopefully, we'll get a report later this morning or early afternoon. But let's talk about what we are going to do next to protect Samantha here."

Ira said, "I've been giving this quite a bit of thought since yesterday, and I talked it over with Samantha last night. We both feel that she is in danger wherever we relocate her. So, why don't we just let her stay with me and the kids right here? We can free Jack and Jill from their duties with the twins."

Harlan looked at Samantha and asked, "Are you okay with that?"

"Yes. Like Ira said, we talked it over last night, and it seems like a good plan."

Harlan cautioned, "That sounds fine on the surface, but our Mr. Yulov will have no problem getting around the security of the naval base. He's done it before. We should have you and your home surrounded by security agents. Hope you don't mind."

Samantha thought for a few moments. "Harlan. I don't want to be a prisoner in our home. I have to be busy doing something. Would it be possible to set me up in an office here at Ira's headquarters? We can set up security to get me back and forth from my office to our house. If we can do that, would it be possible to keep the Hills on to watch the twins during the day?"

"I'm sure I can arrange that, Samantha. But what is it you want to do?"

Samantha answered, "I want to get involved in catching the Ghost."

"How?"

"For starters, I would like to have access to all of our files on Yulov. I want to know everything that we know about him. Maybe . . . just maybe, I will be able to come up with something on him that will help."

"I don't know, Samantha. We've had our best psychologists and analysts poring over all this information for weeks. That's probably a dead end."

Ira said in a sarcastic voice, "Don't underestimate her, Harlan. She was probably the president of the Psychology Club in high school."

"Ira, don't be a wise guy. I'm serious here," Samantha moaned.

With a smile, Harlan said, "It wouldn't hurt, Ira. Maybe a fresh set of eyes would be just what we need. Okay, I'll set up the security details, and I'll ask the Hills to stay on guarding the twins." He then asked Ira, "Can you set her up with an office here? You know, computer, secure phone line, stuff she needs."

"Sure, Harlan. That'll be easy."

"Good. I'll have Jean send the files to Samantha electronically whenever she is set up here."

The discussion on the details of Samantha's protection continued for the rest of the morning. Just before lunch, Samantha asked Harlan, "What about the possible mole? Have you started looking into that yet?"

"No, I haven't. I want to investigate that myself. I don't want it getting around what we suspect. After we finish up here today, I'm going back to Langley. I've got some suspicions and ideas of what to do and who it might be. I'll start tomorrow."

Ira had a light lunch brought into the briefing room. About halfway through lunch, Ira's yeoman came into the room and said, "Mr. Bradbury, Mr. Matthias Roberts just called and said he has a report on his investigation."

"Good. Call him back and ask him to be back here by two o'clock to brief us."

"Yes, sir."

At two o'clock, the yeoman escorted Matthias into the room. "Hey, everybody."

"Matthias." Said Harlan. "Get yourself a cup of coffee and tell us what your team has come up with."

Matthias got his coffee, sat at the end of the conference table, and spread some papers out in front of him. "Where do I begin?" he mused aloud.

"How about the yacht? What do you have on that?"

Matthias picked up a sheet of paper and said, "We questioned the crew operating the rental yacht. They didn't know anything about who rented the yacht, just that he stressed that a high-speed motorboat had to replace one of the lifeboats normally carried by the yacht. He provided the motorboat and was the only passenger on the yacht, which normally carries twenty-five guests and a crew of eight. We also found out that a helicopter left a small regional airport near Biloxi and was found abandoned in Alabama. We feel certain that this helicopter picked up the Ghost from his speedboat. Which, by the way, was found by the Coast Guard. It was drifting with no one on board."

Ira then asked, "Matthias, how did the Ghost know that Samantha was in Gulfport?"

"That I don't know. Not yet anyway. But I do know how the Ghost pulled off his caper. For one thing, we could not locate the airport security guard who spotted the Ghost at the airport. No one like him works at the airport."

"He was a fake?" asked Harlan.

"That's right. He contacted our agent, gave him that false information, and texted him the dummy photo of Yulov."

"In other words, he wanted us to know that he was in Gulfport." Said Samantha. "Why would he do that?"

Harlan answered, "He manipulated us. He knew that our man would notify me right away. He knew how I would react. And that would be to get Samantha out of Gulfport right away. Our normal operating procedure in a quick turn-around situation like this is to use a private transportation service. One that the private companies use when they need jet service. The smaller companies that can't afford their own private company jet."

"That's right, Harlan." Mathias said. "We checked, and there are two such transportation companies that provide jet service to the Alabama, Mississippi, Louisiana area. Gulf Coast Transport and Biloxi Jet Service."

Harlan said, "We contacted Gulf Coast Transport."

"That's right, Harlan," said Matthias. "We contacted Gulf Coast Transport, but they claim that they never received a call from us scheduling a flight."

"Are they telling the truth?" asked Ira.

"Apparently. We checked their phone records, and they received no calls from us."

Harlan asked, "Did the Ghost intercept the call from us?"

"Maybe. Gulf Coast Transport never received our call."

Samantha asked, "How did the Ghost set up the aircraft so quickly? He only had an hour or so to do it."

Matthias said, "This is where it gets scary. The plane used by Yulov was not a Gulf Coast Transport unit. All their planes are accounted for."

Ira asked, "Then where did this plane come from?"

"We did a search of Cessna Citation aircraft that have been sold or purchased recently. That's the Cessna model used by the Ghost in the assassination attempt. The only one that popped up on our search was a used one for $750,000. It was bought in New Orleans nine weeks ago."

Samantha moaned, "Oh my God. I think I'm going to be sick. If the Ghost bought that aircraft nine weeks ago for this assassination attempt, that means that he knew where I was right after I relocated to Gulfport."

Everybody in the room was stunned. No one said a word for over a minute, as the reality of the situation sunk in.

Samantha broke the silence. "We have a mole."

CHAPTER 16
ADMIRAL'S ROW—NAVAL STATION, NORFOLK

IN THE NEXT WEEK, A flurry of activity took place. Samantha moved into Ira's house on Admiral's Row with the twins. This, of course, made her extremely happy. Jack and Jill Hill remained there to take care of the twins while Samantha was at work. Big John, and a new agent, Simon Prather, moved into the house and were solely responsible for the safety of Samantha. Base military security guards were used to guard the house and to escort Ira and Samantha to the headquarters building. Security personnel on the base were instructed to be on the alert at all times and to observe all security protocols that were in place—with no exceptions.

Harlan began to personally investigate the activities of all personnel that could possibly be the mole. The plan was that once the mole was identified, they would be allowed to remain in place to feed false information to the Ghost when the need arose. Harlan and Matthias compiled all the available intel on Anton Yulov and submitted it to Samantha over secure transmission lines.

Samantha began studying the Yulov files, trying desperately to get inside the head of an insane man. This was a daunting task to say the least. The CIA, working with the KGB and INTERPOL, continued the search for the elusive Ghost. But their efforts were to no avail. The Ghost remained out there and undetected.

During the third week of Samantha's new life, she called Harlan.

"Hi, Samantha. What's up?"

"Harlan, I think that I've come up with something that could pay off. I admit that it's a longshot, but hey, we're not getting anywhere with finding our man."

"What is it?"

"Can you come down to Norfolk so we can talk face-to-face?"

"I'm fully booked today, and I give my weekly intel brief to the president tomorrow morning. But I can grab the chopper in the early afternoon tomorrow. Is three o'clock okay?"

"That would be great. I'll look for you then."

"How's everything going down there?"

"Boring actually. Every day is the same."

"Samantha, in this case, boring is good. We'll catch Yulov. He'll make a mistake."

"I hope so, Harlan. I want my wonderful life back with Ira and my beautiful children."

"It'll happen, Samantha. Keep your chin up."

"Thanks for the encouraging words. I'll see you tomorrow."

"Say hi to Ira for me. Bye."

The next afternoon, Harlan walked into Samantha's office. She was swamped with papers, folders, thumb drives, and various other data storage devices. She was staring at her computer screen when Harlan said, "Hi, Samantha. What's going on?"

"Right on time, Harlan. Have a seat. I'll be with you in a minute."

Harlan sat and waited patiently as Samantha continued to look at the computer screen and take notes. Finally, she said, "Sorry, Harlan. I didn't want to break my train of thought."

"What do you want to talk about that's so important that we need to be face-to-face?"

She answered, "Because of this mole thing, I'm probably being overly cautious. I'm sorry if I'm causing you too much trouble."

"It's okay. I've learned that I shouldn't underestimate you. What do you have?"

"Let me list some things. Correct me if I'm wrong."

"Okay. Go."

Anton Yulov and Rhetta Yulov had one child. Right? A daughter."

Harlan nodded.

"They named her Anna, with a soft *a*. And she's twenty-four years of age and unmarried."

Again, Harlan nodded.

"Right after Yulov murdered Rhetta, he disappeared."

Samantha looked at Harlan for confirmation. He just stared at her waiting for something new. She continued, "Anna disappeared at the same time as our Ghost. Hasn't been seen since. No dead body either."

Harlan said, "Correct."

"It seems like Yulov and Anna had a good relationship. Apparently, he loved her very much. If this is so, then there's a good chance that Yulov took Anna with him. Right?"

"That's right. Everything you have said is correct. But don't forget. Yulov supposedly loved Rhetta, his wife, and he murdered her. No, we haven't found any bodies yet that could be Anna. We've thought of all this. But we haven't come up with any leads yet on finding her."

"Well, I did some research on Anna, Harlan, and I found one small snippet of info that may be important. She is an avid skier. Because her life has been totally turned upside down, what if Yulov wanted to try to keep his daughter happy and settled down near a ski resort. Somewhere in the Alps. Switzerland, France, Italy. I don't know."

"What are you saying here?" asked Harlan.

"I suggest that we concentrate our search at the nicest ski resorts around the world and see if we can spot her."

Harlan thought deeply for a few minutes. He finally said, "It is a longshot, Samantha. There are a lot of ski resorts in this world. But it is an approach we haven't tried."

Samantha said, "Yulov is rich. He stole over two hundred and forty million dollars from the Russian people. He wants to keep his twenty-four-year-old daughter happy. He would probably relocate near an expensive, jet-set type resort. Especially one near an international airport where he can come and go with ease. Would all this narrow down the search?"

"I don't ski, Samantha. But it should. Let me get on it. This might be another one for Matthias to get going. He can authorize the reassignments of our agents. I can also make a few calls and authorize him to work with the KGB and INTERPOL in my name. Hey, nothing else is working. Let's give this a try."

"Good," said Samantha.

Harlan then asked, "Is there anything else you want to talk about?"

"Yes, Harlan, there is. The mole. Where do you stand on that? Any progress?"

"I have some thoughts, but I'm not sure yet. I'm almost there."

"Well, what do you have?"

"I'm almost sure that it is either Frank Bilger or Bill Williams. They are the only two people who knew everything about your relocations. Everything. Where you were relocated to, your new name, your address, your job, your friends. The whole thing. I'm leaning toward Bill Williams right now because four months ago he made a sizeable deposit of eighty thousand dollars into his savings account. I'm checking right now to see if there was any reason why he could have gotten such a large amount of money. What do you think?"

Samantha looked directly at Harlan for about ten seconds.

She finally said, "Harlan, I don't think it is either Frank or Bill."

"Why not? It fits."

"You're forgetting one thing, Harlan. Besides Ira and yourself, there's only one person in the world who would know who would be at our first anniversary barbecue. Remember. Everyone there got an envelope with a unique number in it. The Ghost would have had to know who would be there to do that. Frank and Bill did not have that information. Therefore, neither one of them could be the mole."

"Well, who could it be then?"

"Think, Harlan. Who sent out the invitations? You?"

"No, it was . . ." Harlan paused. "Jean. You're saying that the mole is Jean Barlow? Samantha, she's a friend of my family. I've known her for most of my life. I hired her when I became the CIA director seven years ago. It can't possibly be her, Samantha."

"Harlan, you are letting your personal life cloud your thinking. Did you run a financial activity check on Jean?"

"I am embarrassed to say this, but I have not."

"Do it, Harlan and do it soon. If she's clear, I could be wrong, but I don't think I am."

Harlan returned to Langley that afternoon. He privately instructed Matthias to investigate Jean Barlow's financial activity. When he thought about it a bit, he realized that Jean had just bought a new car. One that seemed a little pricey for her usual taste. Also, he noticed that she was wearing different jewelry, but he didn't have a great deal of knowledge on women's jewelry, and it didn't seem important to him at the time.

Harlan went to the deputy director's office to make a secure call to his contacts at the KGB and INTERPOL informing them that Matthias Roberts would be representing him, and that they should communicate directly with him. When Harlan returned to his office, he looked at Jean in a new light, but he thought, *Please don't let it be you, Jean. You've been my life-long friend.*

The next day, Matthias called Harlan. "We need to talk, Mr. Bradbury. I have some information."

"Good. Meet me in the deputy director's office in fifteen minutes."

"Yes, sir."

Once in the deputy director's office, Matthias said, "First of all, William's eighty-thousand-dollar deposit. It's legit. He received an inheritance from his grandmother, who passed away six months ago."

"So, he's clear," said Harlan. "What about Jean?"

"Her normal bank accounts are clear. No unusual deposits. However, she established an account in a Swiss bank about eight months ago. Very suspicious. We'll really have to dig to get detailed information there."

"But it is ominous, Matthias. I think we've got our mole."

"I believe so, Mr. Bradbury. It looks like Samantha is right again, and Jean is our man."

"This really hurts. Be that as it may, and I accept it. Here's what I want you to do. Make a list of the most prestigious ski resorts in the world. Give the European ones the highest priority. Active night life is important. Where the jet-set goes to have fun. A nearby international airport is important. Assign a priority to these resorts and compile a list in priority order for me. Then I want you to look at the assignments of our field agents on this case. Reassign them to have one at as many of these resorts as we have people available. Work with the KGB and INTERPOL offices to help you on this. We are looking for Yulov's daughter, Anna. Samantha, not me, will give you all the information we have on her. Photos, age, height, color of hair, food preferences, anything we have on her. And, of course, do not let Jean know what we are doing. Everything goes to you, and you brief me privately. We will let Jean know only what we want Yulov to know. You got all this? Any questions?"

"I've got it. No questions. I'll get started right away."

CHAPTER 17
ARROW

A WEEK LATER, THE NEW direction for the search for the Ghost was finally in motion. Samantha continued her research on Yulov, especially information relating to his daughter. She hoped that her idea about Anna's love for skiing would bear fruit. They had to get this guy and get him off the streets. The life of fear, constant moving, isolation, and near-death experiences was getting very old and had her down. But, she realized she had no choice. She had to grin and bear it until the Ghost was finally caught.

On Saturday of that week, Samantha was at home with Ira, the twins, and the Hills. Big John and Simon Prather had gone to the base commissary to buy groceries for the week. Ira said, "Sam, I have to go to the office for an important meeting and to finish up some things I left hanging yesterday. Do you want to come with me and work for a while?"

"No, Ira. I've got to take a break from studying the Ghost files. I'm really down because we haven't found him yet. It's been almost a week, and we haven't heard anything on locating Anna Yulov."

"Be patient. These things take time. Look, let's take a few minutes and pray for something good to happen."

"Ira. I just love you so much. Words can't describe how much I love you. Of course, let's pray together." They kneeled, interlocked their arms, and prayed.

Thirty minutes later, Ira was ready to leave for work. I'll leave as soon as the big guy and Simon return. My meeting is in an hour. I've got time."

"That's fine. While we are waiting for them, I'll go upstairs and spend some time with Roman and Paula. That'll cheer me up."

Thirty minutes later, Big John and Simon drove up. Ira called upstairs, "Samantha. They're back. Let's give them a hand. I'm sure they bought a lot. They always do," Samantha said as she came down the stairs, "They have to. I've never seen anyone eat as much as Big John."

When they went to the mini-van, Big John and Simon were already walking to the house with several bags in their arms. Ira grabbed two more bags leaving one for Samantha. It was a plastic bag and was light because it only contained two dozen eggs. She picked it up with one hand thinking *being a woman sometimes has its advantages*. She closed the back lid of the van and started toward the house behind Ira. Big John and Simon came back out of the house to see if they were still needed. Ira turned around to see if Samantha was coming when he heard a loud *thwack*, and Samantha went flying backward in the air. She landed flat on her back at least five feet from where she had stood. When she hit the ground, she slid another few feet along the concrete driveway. The bag of eggs went flying as well and hit the driveway, broken eggs running everywhere. Horrified, Ira dropped his grocery bags and ran to Samantha, who lay motionless on her back in a spreading pool of blood. An arrow stuck straight out of her chest.

"Sam!" Ira screamed. "Big John, call 911. Simon. It's the Ghost. The arrow came from that direction. Find him and kill him!" Ira roared as he motioned toward the back of the house.

Ira got to Samantha and cradled her head in his arms. The pool of blood continued to grow. He cried, "Please, Sam. Please be alive. Please don't leave me." He buried his head in her neck with his cheek against hers. "Oh my God. Please God. Don't take her from me. Oh, please, please." Tears streamed from his eyes.

He sensed some movement from her. He pulled away to look at her. "Sam, please be alive."

He then heard Samantha say in a very weak strained voice, "Can't breathe. Can't breathe. Dying."

"Sam, stay with me. Please don't give up. Try to breathe. An ambulance is on the way. You are going to make it. Please stay with me, Sam," Ira cried.

Ira continued to hold the motionless Samantha in his arms and begged her not to die.

At that time, Anton Yulov was climbing down from a tree about forty yards away. He thought, *Well, that was fun. I have to admit, Dr. Stone, you've been the biggest challenge I've ever had. I greatly admire you. In fact, it's strange, very strange, but I think that I'm in love with you. I will certainly have wonderful memories of our exciting adventure together. Bryan Boxer, you are next.*

Yulov quickly stored his foldable bow into its carrying case. He could hear the siren from the approaching ambulance. He smiled broadly as he headed through the dense copse of trees between the houses. He reached the chain link fence separating the naval base from the Ocean View Golf Club. He slipped through the cut he had made in the fence and put his bow-carrying case into the waiting golf cart he had left there. He thought, *So much for base security. These smug Americans are so careless.* He quickly drove through the wooded rough to the golf course's parking lot. He selected one of the two cars he had left for his getaway. *Life is so much fun. I think I'll take the red car. It's the color of blood.* He got into the car and drove away.

CHAPTER 18
THE SIGNATURE CONTINUES

WHEN THE AMBULANCE ARRIVED, IRA was still cradling Samantha in his arms and was crying. The EMTs ran up to them and told Ira to move away while they tended to Samantha. Ira begged them to tell him that she was still alive. They said nothing as they continued to get Samantha on a stretcher so they could get her into the ambulance. As they were getting her in the ambulance, Ira once again asked about her condition.

"She's still alive, Admiral Coen, but she is struggling to breathe and her breathing is very shallow. We'll put her on oxygen in just a few minutes. That should help. But other than that, I just don't know. She's lost a lot of blood, and we must get her to the hospital ASAP, or we'll lose her. Do you by any chance know her blood type?"

Ira thought for a moment then said, "A Positive. What about the arrow in her chest?"

"Can't say. That will be addressed at the hospital. For right now, we can't touch it. Listen, we gotta go. Get to the hospital as soon as you can, Admiral."

The EMT jumped into the back of the ambulance. It sped off with its siren blaring.

Ira's last view of Samantha as the ambulance door was closing was the other EMT pinching Samantha's nose and blowing into her mouth.

Ira turned around slowly and saw Big John standing ten feet away. His head was down looking at the driveway and at the pool of blood left by Samantha. Ira took a deep breath and went up to Big John and said, "Where's Simon, John? Did he get that insane murdering asshole?"

Big John looked at Ira with sad eyes and said, "The Ghost got him. Put an arrow through his neck."

"My God, John. No. That can't be." But Ira saw the look of despondence on Big John's face and knew that it was true. Simon Prather was dead.

"John, call another ambulance for Simon. I've got to get this blood-soaked uniform off of me, shower, and get to the hospital as quickly as I can. Be ready to go with me. And please pray that Samantha is still alive and survives this lunatic's attack."

"Yes, sir," Big John said sadly.

When Ira and Big John ran into the hospital's emergency room, they were greeted by a nurse, who was waiting for Ira. "Admiral Coen. I am Wanda Bedford. Please come with me."

The three went into a small consultation room which contained a desk and three chairs. Ms. Bedford sat behind the desk, and Ira and Big John sat in two of the chairs. Ira looked scared and dreaded the news that Bedford was about to give him.

"Admiral Coen, I've been authorized by Dr. Gunn to give you a report on your wife."

Ira sat there expecting the worse.

"Your wife is alive and should survive."

Both Ira and Big John took deep breaths and looked up at the ceiling in relief. Ira finally said, "She'll live, but how bad is the wound in her chest from the arrow?"

"Dr. Gunn said that she will be fine. Apparently, your wife would have been mortally wounded by the arrow if she weren't wearing a body armor vest."

"She was wearing her vest? She never wears the vest she was given."

Dr. Gunn had just entered the room and heard what Ira had said. "Well, Admiral Coen, she had it on today. Thank God."

"*Thank God* is right. I can't believe she put it on."

Nurse Wanda Bedford stood up and gave Dr. Gunn the seat behind the desk.

"You must be Dr. Gunn?"

"That's me."

"How serious are her injuries, doctor. She was lying there in so much blood."

"Admiral Coen, you can call me Larry or Gunner, whichever you prefer. I go by both. To answer your question, she did lose a lot of blood. But most of the blood came from severe lacerations on the back of her head, shoulders, back, buttocks, and legs. She must have hit the concrete with a great deal of force."

"She also slid along the concrete for three or four feet after she hit."

"That explains the severity of her lacerations and abrasions," said Dr. Gunn.

"What about the arrow in her chest?"

"Well, as Wanda told you as I was coming into the room, the vest she was wearing essentially stopped the arrow, but it did penetrate enough to pierce a little into her chest. She does have a chest wound, but the arrow did not fully penetrate the sternum. She lost some blood there, and she will have a nasty bruise on her chest for quite some time."

How is she now?" asked Big John.

"She was having a great deal of trouble breathing. But the quick action of the EMTs to give her CPR followed by oxygen got her breathing normally by the time she reached the ER. We cleaned and dressed her abrasions and chest wound. We gave her a sedative, and she is resting comfortably. She is now being moved to a private room. She will be fine."

"When can I see her, doctor?"

"She will probably sleep for about eight hours, just to let you know. But she should be settled in her room in about ten to fifteen minutes. After that, you can go to her room at any time. I suggest, however, that you get some rest and get something to eat. Both of you."

"I'd like to see her now and hold her hand for a few minutes. If that's okay?"

"That's fine. I completely understand."

"Big John. Are you coming?"

"Of course. If you'll let me hold her other hand."

Ira and Big John thanked Dr. Gunn and left to find Samantha's room.

When they located Samantha's room, they quietly entered, not wanting to disturb her. She was sleeping peacefully and breathing normally. Ira was shocked at first because the top of her head was totally bandaged up, and she had the ever-present oxygen tube nestled on her nose. She had a bag of blood and the normal saline drip bag in operation as well. Ira wanted to pull back her sheet to see how her wound from the arrow was bandaged. He resisted the temptation and sat in a chair next to the bed. He took her hand in his, squeezed it gently, and began to cry. Big John pulled up a chair next to the bed and took her other hand in his. With tears running down his cheeks, Ira looked at Big John and said, "God, John, I love this woman. I thought I'd lost her."

Big John looked at Ira and said, "Don't take this the wrong way, Admiral, but I love her too. I've loved her since the first time I opened the door for her that November evening at Carter House."

"Don't worry about it, big man. You're not the only one that's happened to."

CHAPTER 19
ANOTHER BULLET DODGED

AT SIX O'CLOCK THE NEXT morning, Ira's cell phone woke him up. It was nurse Bedford calling. She told him that Samantha had awoken about four o'clock. They had been busy cleaning and dressing her abrasions and chest wound and trying to get her to eat. Bedford reported that she was still affected by the sedative, but she kept asking for Ira and the babies.

Just before eight o'clock, Ira and Big John approached the nurse's station. "How is Samantha Coen? Room 313. Is she okay?" he asked in rapid fire.

"Calm down, Admiral. She is fine. One of you can go in to see her now, but I must warn you, she suffered very painful injuries, and we have her under strong pain medication. She may still be a little uncomfortable and incoherent at times."

"I understand. Can I go in now?"

"Yes. But your friend will have to wait his turn."

"John?" Ira turned to Big John.

"I'll be in the waiting room, Admiral. Take your time."

Ira thanked him and hurried into Samantha's room.

Ira saw her lying down but awake. "Hi, Sam," he said as he entered.

"God, Ira. I thought you'd never get here. Where are the twins?"

"Big John and I brought them, but the hospital staff said that we should take the kids to the nursery for now. They will bring them to your room in a half hour or so. How are you doing?"

"Okay, I guess. I'm hurting all over. It really hurts to lie on my back, but that's what I have to do most of the time. They keep coming here to rotate me and take my vitals. When they are rotating me, it hurts like hell."

"The nurse told me that they were pumping pain meds into you."

"Ira. What happened? Everything is a fog to me. I only remember that I couldn't breathe, and I thought that I had died. It was horrible."

Ira told her what he had seen. The sound of the arrow striking her in the chest. Her flight backward. The blood. The horror of thinking that she had died. His discussion with Dr. Gunn.

"Apparently, I dodged another bullet. Or in this case, an arrow," she laughed at her joke, but then grimaced in pain caused by her laughter.

When Ira stopped laughing, he got serious and said, "Sam, I do have some bad news. Simon Prather was killed by the Ghost. He left his signature."

"Oh, no, Ira. How many more are going to die because of me?"

"No, no, Sam. You're not to blame for all this. It's that idiotic madman that's to blame. Certainly not you."

"I suppose you are right. But it hurts so much to see men I've grown very close to lose their lives. What really hurts is that they have been assigned to protect me from the Ghost, and they are the ones dying. Not me."

She began to cry, and Ira handed her a tissue to wipe the tears from her cheeks.

When Samantha had regained her composure, Ira said, "Sam, there is something that I've got to ask you."

"What's that?"

"After all these weeks of you refusing to wear your protective vest, what made you put it on yesterday?"

"It's strange, Ira. Right after we prayed together yesterday, I went up to be with the twins. Jill had just fed them. I had Paula up on my shoulder trying to get her to burp. Well, she did burp, but a lot of stuff came up with it. I had burp curd all over my blouse. I put her down and went to our room to get a fresh blouse from the closet. I pulled the blouse I wanted out, but it was caught on the hanger that I had the vest hanging on. The vest was just there staring at me. Then, for some reason, something told me to put it on. I obeyed that feeling and put it on."

"Sam, that vest saved your life. Without it, you would have certainly been killed by the Ghost's arrow.

"Well, we prayed for something good to happen. That's not exactly what we were looking for, but . . ."

"God does work in mysterious ways," Ira interjected.

"That He does, Ira. That He does."

They smiled knowingly at each other, then Ira bent over to kiss her. They kissed passionately for several seconds, pulled away, and continued to smile at each other. Suddenly, Samantha's eyes widened. She said with urgency, "Does the Ghost know that I survived his attack?"

"Probably not. Why?"

"Bryan Boxer. He's in danger. We've got to announce that I'm alive. If we don't, Bryan is in immediate danger. The Ghost might already have a plan in place to kill him."

"Lord, Sam. You are right. I'll contact the media right away. I'll alert Big John to take extra careful care of you. I'll call Harlan and bring him up to speed and to cover Bryan sooner rather than later. We've got to help Big John while you are in the hospital. He's good, but we need more."

As Ira was leaving the room to talk to Big John, Dr. Larry Gunn was entering the room followed by an entourage of medical students and interns.

"How's my favorite patient doing?" Doctor Gunn asked Samantha with a smile.

"I'm doing great, doctor, and I have to get out of here ASAP."

An hour later, Big John came into Samantha's room followed by six armed guards. Samantha was already dressed and waiting in a wheelchair. Despite Dr. Gunn's objections, Samantha was wheeled out to a waiting limo. She was carefully helped into the car, and it sped off to Ira's house on Admiral's Row. At the house, a hospital bed had been set up in one of the rooms, and a registered nurse was putting away needed medications and supplies to take care of Samantha. Dr. Gunn volunteered to have Samantha Stone Coen as his sole patient and to move into Ira and Sam's home until he was no longer needed. Also under heavy guard, Roman and Paula were taken home from the hospital nursery.

CHAPTER 20
SAMANTHA'S PLAN

ANTON YULOV WAS SITTING AT the dining room table of the modest condo he had purchased near Boone, North Carolina. He was going over his final plans to eliminate number six on his hit list, Master Chief Bryan Boxer. He thought, *This should be easy. Straight forward.* The biggest challenge to Yulov was how to eliminate the CIA secret agent guarding Boxer. He thought, *The bow would be fun. But no. I just used that on Dr. Stone.*

He then said aloud, "I really admired that woman. She had spunk. Never begged once for her life on the plane. Getting her was the most fun, and most challenging, I might add, of all my prey. I'll miss her."

Then, something he heard on the TV caught his attention. He heard the news reporter say, "And next, we will bring you a bizarre story of a near death incident from a stray arrow. That story next from Norfolk, Virginia."

Yulov thought, *That can't be. I saw the arrow hit her dead center in the chest and knock her flying. She has to be dead.*

When Yulov got in front of the TV, he waited impatiently until an obnoxious commercial ended. A field reporter appeared on the screen and began talking about a Navy Admiral's wife who was struck by an arrow that seemed to come out of nowhere. The scene then switched to a bed in which a woman was lying and who had a big smile on her face.

Yulov looked closely at the woman and said, "Yes, it is that bitch, Stone. She can't be alive. I saw the arrow hit her in the heart."

He focused on the interview with the woman and heard her say "I'm sure it was a stray arrow. I just happened to be in the wrong place at the wrong time," she said with a smile. "But we are going to investigate this, and if we find out it was on purpose and we know who fired the arrow, I'm going to hunt him down myself and kill him."

Yulov stared at the TV as she said her final words, and he noticed two things. Her angelic smile had been replaced with a serious look of conviction. And he noticed that the right hand lying on the sheet had its middle finger extended.

Yulov knew that she knew who fired the arrow. He said, "She's talking directly to me. That bitch is taunting me. Challenging me. She's only a woman. How dare she challenge me. Okay, Dr. Stone. Take your best shot. We'll see who wins this game. This is going to be fun. Hombre e mujer. Man against woman. Bryan Boxer you'll just have to wait. I've still got an arrogant bitch to kill."

The next two weeks went by slowly. Samantha steadily recovered from her abrasions and chest wound. She cut her hair short because she had scraped most of her hair off the back of her head when she slid on the concrete driveway. As the abrasions there healed, her hair was beginning to grow back. However, the process was extremely itchy. At the start of the third week following the arrow assassination attempt, Samantha was beginning to get stir crazy. She wanted out of the house, but her requests were rejected by Ira, Harlan, and Dr. Gunn.

"How much longer, Gunner? How much longer are you going to keep me locked up?"

"I think you are close to not needing me by your side. You are healing well. You have a lot of energy. And I see that you want to be more active than you have been. That is all good. Two or three more days, and I'll be out of your hair." Dr. Gunn laughed at his little joke.

Samantha glared at him for a few seconds before she said, "Thank God for that. Don't get me wrong, Gunner. I love your company, and I will miss you. But I've got to move on. I have things I need to do."

"I will miss you too, Samantha. More than you know."

One hour later, Samantha was lying in bed reading a file on Anna Yulov for, perhaps, the tenth time. Her phone chimed, and she saw that it was Harlan.

"Hey, Harlan. What's up?"

"Hi, Samantha, are you going to be home tomorrow?"

"Nice one, wise ass. You know I'm a prisoner in my own home."

"I guess you're right, Samantha. I was just having some fun with you. Seriously though, I've got some news that I'd like to share with you. I've got some business with Ira, and we can get together right after our meeting. Maybe three o'clock?"

"Great. See you then. Is it good news, Harlan?"

"Yes, it is."

The next afternoon, Harlan and Ira walked into Samantha's small office.

"Hey, guys. Have a seat and give me your news, Harlan."

Harlan sat down and smiled. "Samantha, I think your ski resort idea has paid off. One of our agents placed in Grindelwald, Switzerland, Rodrigo Ortiz, is pretty sure he has spotted her. He was able to take a photo of her. She's in the background, but we were able to blow it up and enhance it a bit."

Harlan slid a photo onto the coffee table they were sitting around. Samantha picked it up and studied it for about thirty seconds.

"It's her, Harlan. I'm sure of it. I've been looking at photos of her for weeks, and I know her face and her body. Look at the highlighted cheek bones. Look at the shape of her nose and compare them to this."

Samantha opened a folder, shuffled through some photos, and pulled one out. She handed it to Harlan, who in turn, gave it to Ira. They compared the two photos for a few minutes. Finally, Harlan said, "The hair is very different. Color, length, style. But definitely a resemblance."

"I'm sure of it. Look, I need all the information you can get me on Grindelwald. Bars, clubs, spas, jet-set hangouts, ski slope maps, roads, transportation services. Everything. I need to know all about Grindelwald and the surrounding area. I know all about Anna. Now I need to know about where she lives."

"What are you talking about, Samantha? You don't think that you are going to Switzerland, do you?"

"Of course, I am going. That asshole Yulov is mine."

"No, no, no, no, Samantha. Don't even think about it. You are not doing this."

Ira chimed in, "Come on, Samantha. Be reasonable."

"Look you two. That maniac has almost killed me three times. He's put me in the hospital twice. He's put an arrow in my chest. Abandoned me on an airplane to die. He's been spying on me. He has videos of me, and he has pictures of me naked. And most important of all, he almost killed my two babies. Harlan, Ira, if you guys don't work with me on this, I'll fly to Switzerland myself and go after him."

"Ira, please talk some sense into your wife."

"Harlan, one thing that I've learned from my time with her is that when she has her mind made up, there is no way that I can make her change it."

"This is insane."

"I agree. It is insane. But another thing I've learned about her is to not underestimate her."

"Ira, are you siding with her on this? Are you crazy, too?" She's your *wife* for God's sake. She'll be going after one of the most dangerous men in the world. She won't have a chance against him."

Samantha interjected, "Look, Harlan. Hear me out. Yulov's daughter is his Achilles' heel, perhaps the only weakness he has. I want to go to Grindelwald, meet Anna, make friends with her, and try to get her help in trapping this psychotic, egomaniac father of hers."

Ira said, "Work with her, Harlan. I don't like it any more than you do. But she has a better chance of surviving with you helping her than if she goes it alone."

"Good Lord, Ira. I can't believe that I am going along with this. It's insanity."

"Harlan, thank you," Samantha said. "We've got a lot of work to do in the next few weeks."

"This is absolutely crazy." Harlan sighed deeply, then said with resignation, "What is your plan, Samantha?"

"I have to admit, I don't have it all worked out yet. But for starters, we need to use our mole, Jean, to get the Ghost away from his daughter. I will be in Grindelwald, I will find Anna, and I will try to strike up a relationship with her. I will have to play all this by ear. If I can convince her who her father really is, she might be able to help me set him up. If she knows who her father is and still supports him, I will have to come up with a scheme to use her to get him without her realizing what she is doing. Harlan, Ira, I'm going to have to make this up as I go. The thing that I have going for me here is that I know more about Anna than anybody else in the world. I know that I will be able to read her body language and read between the lines of what she says."

Harlan said, "We will have to be very careful on how we use Jean. If Yulov figures out— or even suspects—that Jean's identity has been compromised, then her life and yours will be in great danger. Also, we've got some intense training to give you. You are not a trained field agent. There are things you need to know and things you need to be able to do. Normally, we do this training in Virginia. But I'm afraid that if we use normal training protocols, Jean will find out. I would like to set up special training here at Naval Station Norfolk."

"Harlan, this may seem strange to you, but I would like to have Jared Townsend and Josh Freeman with me in Switzerland. They are extremely capable Navy SEALs. We won't be traveling together, but maybe we could 'accidently' bump into one another in Grindelwald. I will feel more comfortable knowing they are there if I need them to talk to or to protect me."

"I don't like that either, Samantha, but I understand why you want to have them there. I'll arrange to have them take the training with you here in Norfolk."

"Thanks, Harlan." She then asked, "What's our timetable?"

"Samantha, you are still recovering from your last assassination attempt. You need more time."

"I'm fine, Harlan. Let's change the way I look as much as possible. I can't dye my hair because of the abrasions and possible infection. But I have cut it much shorter. Even though it is short, maybe we can curl it a bit. That would give me a different look. What about getting me some push-up bras to make my boobs look bigger? I'd like that."

Ira shook his head and said, "Come on, Samantha. Get serious. Your boobs are fine."

"I am serious. Men look at things like that. Don't forget, the Ghost said he has pictures of me naked. The pervert."

Harlan said, "We need at least four weeks of training."

"I'm a fast learner. Let's do it in three."

Harlan shook his head and said, "It's four weeks, or I change my mind about this crazy plan."

"Okay, four weeks. Once we have all these details ironed out, we can pick a date that I go to Grindelwald. We'll have to come up with a scheme to get the Ghost away from there so I can meet Anna without running into him. Also, Harlan, have Rodrigo, your agent in Grindelwald, continue to observe Anna. I need to know if she has a boyfriend, where she likes to eat, where she skis, her favorite slopes, everything. Her normal schedule. When she shows up at the resort to ski. The more information I have, the better."

"I'll have Matthias get the word to him, and I will contact Townsend and Freeman right after we are through here. I'll see if they are good about this insane plan. If the president finds out about what we are doing, my job is history."

"Hey, Milsap is a lame duck. His two terms are just about over. He's only got a little over a year left in office. You'll most likely be replaced by the new president."

"Yea, but that's better than being fired. Oh God. What have I been talked into?"

The next four weeks were a flurry of activity for Samantha. Most of the time was spent at a training center set up at the Naval Station Norfolk. It was intense training, but she enjoyed being with Jared Townsend and Josh Freeman again. When they had a chance to talk, they usually reminisced about the exciting times they shared on the SOOF mission in the Sea of Okhotsk. They also asked her several times to relate what happened during the three assassination attempts on her life. Samantha was surprised at the depth of her field agent training. It included such things as communications, use of various types of firearms, hand-to-hand self-defense, the importance of patience, observation/spying techniques, cyber technology, and many other aspects of the trade. It was like drinking out of a fire hose, and she hoped some of it was sinking in.

But there was one thing she noticed about herself. It seemed like the three assassination attempts on her life had somehow heightened her awareness of her surroundings. She observed things that before would have gone unnoticed. She could look at a license plate on a car and instantly memorize it. She could hear sounds that before would have been lost in the background noise. She now remembers the smallest of details. She had heard that this sort of thing had often happened to soldiers who had escaped life-threatening, intense combat situations. She wondered if this new capability she seemed to have was similar.

With the training almost completed and with Samantha seemingly completely healed from her wounds, a date of October 27, ten days away, was selected for her departure to Grindelwald.

Harlan, Ira, Jared, Josh, and Samantha met at Ira's headquarters in Norfolk to go over the plan for the mission. Harlan said, "Samantha, this has been pretty much your scheme, so why don't you go over it with us one more time."

"Okay. Here it is again. And as always, if any of you see a flaw in the plan or if you see some way, *any* way, we can make it better, please chime in. First, being sure that Yulov is not in Switzerland. We are going to arrange three relocation cities for me. Yuma, Arizona, Bar Harbor, Maine, and Ann Arbor, Michigan. Since the Ghost has found me at the other locations, we are going to make it look like that we are trying to confuse him with three possible sites. I am going to make the choice as to which one at the very last minute. Even Harlan does not know. I will have flight reservations to all three cities. I will choose which one at the airport just before I'm supposed to leave. Several days before I leave for Grindelwald, I will talk to Jean and hint to her that I'm leaning toward Bar Harbor because I'm from Maine. But I'll tell her that I'm not sure. Hopefully, the Ghost will bite on that and go to Maine and spend some time looking for me there. When he realizes that I'm not in Bar Harbor, we will have Harlan mention Yuma several times in front of Jean. She might report this to the Ghost. We will have a female agent in Yuma pretending to be the relocated me. After two weeks, we will get her safely back here. Hopefully, all this will buy me about two weeks to get a relationship going with Anna."

Samantha took a deep breath and said, "Harlan, can you give me an update on what we know about Anna's activities in Grindelwald?"

"Sure. As you know, I am getting daily reports from Matthias as to what Rodrigo in Grindelwald is finding out. Jean does not know about this. Anna's name is now Anna Kennedy, and she hails from Toronto, Canada. She now pronounces her first name with a nasal *a* and not a soft one. Her credit card bills are being paid by her father, Anthony Kennedy. Rodrigo has not found out where she lives yet, but she stays at the Grand Hotel Regina about four or five days a week. The other days in the week, she presumably stays at her house. She skis just about every day and doesn't seem to have a favorite slope. She parties heavily and has been seen in the company of several different men. The men she has been seen with have all been put together very well, if you know what I mean. Muscular, he-man type guys."

"Like Josh here," interjected Samantha.

"Yea, like Josh."

Josh smiled and flexed one of his bicep muscles.

Samantha smiled at Josh and said, "What do you think, Josh? If the need arises, would you be willing to make a move on her?"

"I guess I could. Sure, if the need arises, I could give it a go."

"Hopefully, it won't come to that, Josh."

"How will you handle Anna?" asked Harlan.

"She parties hard. I will try to meet her at a club. I will turn on my charismatic charm to get her to talk with me. I will probably try to get a skiing date with her. But I want to get a significant amount of time with her alone so we can talk. I'm hoping to get a solid, trusting relationship with her in about a week. Hopefully, the Ghost will be preoccupied trying to find and kill me during my time with Anna Kennedy from Toronto.

"Jared, Josh, what will you two be doing?" asked Harlan.

Jared spoke, "Basically, we will be on a skiing vacation and trying to keep an eye on Samantha and to protect her, if necessary. I mean . . . I *could* make a move on Samantha if it helps our cover . . ."

"Just don't get *too* close, Jared," Ira interjected.

"Don't worry, Ira. She'll be in good hands."

"That's what I'm afraid of."

"Come on you two. You're acting like little boys," said Samantha with a big smile on her face. She continued, "Let's face it. We are going to have to make this up on the fly. We don't know where she will be coming from with respect to her father. Jared and Josh will be going to Grindelwald two days before me to scope the scene out and get familiar with the village."

"Right," said Harlan. "And Rodrigo will be a taxi driver to take you to the hotel from the airport. He will also have a suitcase for you which will have firearms, communications devices, and surveillance equipment. He will have a number for you to call when you need transportation or help for any reason."

Samantha said, "Okay, guys. Any questions, changes, suggestions for improvements?"

There was a chorus of agreement.

Eight days later, Jared and Josh were on a flight to Bern, Switzerland, and Samantha met with Harlan in his office.

"Jean, can you come into my office? I want to make sure we have Samantha all set up for her relocation."

"Be right in, sir."

When Jean was comfortably seated, Harlan said, "Are Samantha's plane tickets all set up for Bar Harbor, Yuma, and Ann Arbor?"

"Yes, sir. She has electronic tickets for all three. The three flights all leave within twenty minutes of each other. All she has to do is check in, then board."

"Good. Are the other two female agents briefed on how to interact with Samantha at the airport?"

"Yes. They are ready. As soon as Samantha makes her choice, the other two will board the flights to the other cities."

"Great," said Harlan. "Do you have her credit cards ready?"

"Yes, Harlan. They are in my desk. I have five different cards which she can use randomly. I also have two encrypted phones and one thousand dollars in cash. You should be ready to go, Samantha."

"Okay, Samantha. Get your stuff from Jean when you leave. Do you have your revolver?"

"Yes, Harlan. Same procedure as before in getting through security and on the plane with a firearm?"

"Yes, Samantha. Your revolver won't be a problem." Harlan did not say in front of Jean that Samantha would be taking a military flight to Switzerland.

"Okay then. Looks like we're set. Let's get rolling."

As Jean and Samantha left Harlan's office, Jean said, "I'm sure glad I'm not you, Samantha. You've been through so much. All this must be very hard on you."

"It is, Jean. What hurts the most is that I have to be away from Ira and my two children. It's tough."

Jean then added, "I know that you are going to make your decision at the last minute, but are you leaning toward any one of the three?"

"It will be a very last-minute choice, Jean. I'm kind of hoping that I choose Bar Harbor. You know, being from Maine and all. But we'll see."

"Well, good luck, Samantha. I wish you the best."

As Samantha left Jean's office, she said under her breath, "Traitor, bitch."

CHAPTER 21
NOT A CARE IN THE WORLD

LATER THAT DAY, JARED AND Josh took a commercial red-eye to Bern, Switzerland as scheduled.

The day before Samantha's decision day and her flight to Switzerland on a military aircraft, Harlan was with Ira in a secure area. Ira said, "Harlan, this may be the last day I ever have with Samantha."

"I don't like to think like that, Ira, but you may be right. What do you have in mind?"

"I would like to have dinner with her in a nice restaurant and spend the night alone with her where we are safe."

"I'll support that, Ira. What do you have in mind?"

"I've got two restaurants picked out. I can choose which one on the way. We can stay one more night in the safe house with no agents inside."

"Okay, how can I help?"

"Provide us an armed car with agents to drive us to the restaurant. Have agents as patrons at both restaurants. Inside and out. Then give us a ride back to the safe house. We'll be fine."

"You got it, my man. What time?"

"I will make reservations at both restaurants for eight o'clock."

"Okay, is seven thirty a good time to leave the safe house?"

"Perfect."

After a pause, Harlan asked, "Ira, how are you handling this whole thing with Samantha?"

"Harlan, I've got to be honest with you. I am sick about it. I may never see her alive again. Plus, she's letting her hatred for this man control her. You know Samantha. She doesn't hate anyone. In fact, she loves everybody. And I'm afraid this hatred might cause her to do something rash and cause a mistake—a fatal mistake."

"Ira, I know this crazy man has tried to kill her, but why is she all of a sudden hating someone if that is so unlike her?"

"I'm positive it's because the Ghost almost killed Roman and Paula."

"Yea, I'm sure you're right. The love bond between a mother and her children is something we men will never understand."

"Tell me this, Harlan, how is Samantha doing overall? This CIA training?"

"I've got to tell you, Ira. I've never seen anyone pick up all the nuances and technical skills needed by field agents as quickly as she has. She was actually teaching the instructors, for God's sake. She handles firearms better than any woman I've ever seen. Her self-defense and taekwondo skills are remarkable. She can break-and-enter almost anywhere. She's got it all. My biggest fear is that the Ghost will recognize her."

"I'm worried about that too. But overall, you're making me feel better, Harlan. I found out on the SOOF mission that she is unflappable under pressure. She prays for help constantly, but when decisions have to be made quickly, she is decisive and calm. And she is, just as you said, a quick learner."

"Yea, and she can fly a plane," Harlan said with a smile.

"She can fly a plane," Ira agreed. They both shook their heads and laughed.

"Okay. Let's get you back to the safe house. We'll pick you up at seven thirty."

At 7:30, the armored car was waiting for them at the safe house. On the way, Ira handed the driver the address of the restaurant he had chosen. By 8:10, he and Samantha sat at a small intimate table sipping their wine.

"This is really nice, Ira. Good choice. I hope the food is as good as the ambiance."

"Let's hope so because it does have a great reputation for its food."

Samantha looked down at the table then looked up into his eyes and said, "Ira, I have to say that I am so sorry for doing this to you. I know how much this pains you. It's just something that I must do. I hope you understand."

"Sam, I really don't understand why you feel like you have to do this. But I do know that you feel it is something you *must* do. I also know that I would never have been able to talk you out of it."

"You know me too well."

They placed their entrée order and continued to drink their wine. They held hands, gently at first, then squeezed them tighter.

"Sam, promise me that you won't take any unnecessary chances. Keep a cool head, and please remember that you have two Navy SEALs there to protect you."

"I'll do my best to do that, Ira."

After a long pause where they both looked at each other intently, Ira said, "Sam, I love you more than life itself. You've got to come back to me." Tears began to run down his cheeks.

"I can't promise you that, Ira, but I can promise that I'll do my best."

Ira just looked at her and continued to weep.

Samantha then said, "Ira, I want you to promise me one thing—if I don't make it back, take care of our babies and tell them good things about me."

"I promise." Ira choked up as he said these words. Tears streamed down his face.

An elderly couple was sitting at a table on the other side of the room. The woman said to her husband, "Look at that table over there, Myron. A handsome naval officer holding hands with a beautiful woman. I'll bet they don't have a care in the world."

The next day, the airport plan went perfectly. A Samantha look-alike boarded the flight to Bar Harbor, and two other agents occupied her reserved seats on the flights to Yuma and Ann Arbor. Samantha, meanwhile, was at Joint Air Base Andrews securely fastened into her seat for her flight to Meiringen Air Base, Switzerland, then the helicopter trip to Alpnach Air Station where she would meet Rodrigo for her taxi ride to Grindelwald.

PART THREE

THE CAT AND MOUSE GAME

Anton Yulov's Chalet Helicopter

CHAPTER 22
RODRIGO ORTIZ

THE NEXT MORNING, SAMANTHA WAS shuffled from her military transport at Meiringen Air Base in Switzerland into a waiting helicopter for a short flight to Alpnach Air Station near Grindelwald. When she got off the helicopter, she was escorted to a waiting taxi. The taxi driver introduced himself. "Hi, Samantha, I'm Rodrigo Ortiz, your friendly taxi driver in Grindelwald."

"Rodrigo. It is so good to meet you, at last."

"Good to meet you as well. Commander Townsend and Lieutenant Freeman arrived two days ago and are comfortably settled in at the Grand Hotel Regina. You have been booked in a room right next to theirs. Let's get going. It's about a twenty-five-minute ride from here. Sit back and enjoy the beautiful scenery here in Switzerland. Oh, and by the way, you can call me Rod."

"Great, Rod. I'll take your advice and enjoy the views. But first, do you have any updates on Anna Kennedy?"

"Not much, other than she was in the village last night, and I believe that she will be skiing today."

"Good. I'll be plagued with jet lag, and I'd like to take it easy for a few hours. Hopefully, I will be able to get a little sleep. Maybe I can bump into her tonight. Do you have any idea of where she may go for dinner or for partying later?"

"Her favorite night club is the Eiger Zone. Just to get in costs fifty Euros, and it's kind of pricey for drinks, but a lot of the rich young adults go there. A lot of pairing up takes place."

"Good to know, Rod. Where does she eat dinner? What are her favorite restaurants?"

"Hard to say, Samantha. She bounces around. Often, she's with a male friend, and he probably determines where they go."

"Okay. Try to keep an eye on her and call me whenever you have her location."

"Will do, Samantha. You can speed dial me on one. Jared and Josh are on two and three. We all have you on four. In case of an emergency, Harlan is on five."

Samantha thanked Ortiz and sat back in her seat to enjoy the vistas on the way to the Grand Hotel Regina in the center of Grindelwald village.

Check-in was smooth, and when she was in her room, she noticed that a small suitcase had been included with the two large suitcases she had packed. In the suitcase was another handgun and several boxes of ammunition. Also included were some surveillance and eavesdropping equipment, lock-picking devices, and two additional cell phones.

Samantha thought, *Well, I guess this makes me an official CIA spy.*

Samantha unpacked and called Jared. "Hey, Jared. I'm here."

"Room 212?"

"Yeah. You?"

"Room 214, right next to you. Leave your door unlocked, and we will be right over. You decent?"

"Yes. Come right in."

Josh and Jared came into Samantha's room. Josh held his index finger to his lips signifying Samantha to be quiet. Jared immediately scanned the room for listening devices. When he had found none, he said, "We can talk now. We can't be too careful."

"You are right. Any updates on Anna?"

"No. We have spent the two days we've been here just trying to familiarize ourselves with the village."

Josh added, "Anna usually goes dancing every night. She has a lot of energy. She skis all day then parties at night. I don't know how she does it."

"She turns twenty-five in two weeks. That's how."

"I guess you're right. She left an hour ago to go to the slopes. She'll probably get back around sixteen hundred—oops! Sorry, Samantha. About four o'clock."

"Don't worry about it. They use the twenty-four-hour clock here, we might as well too."

"Most of the time, Rodrigo said she goes to the Eiger Zone dance club. That might be a good place to start."

"I agree. How about if I get there at . . . twenty hundred? Is there a problem getting in?"

"I think so. I'll see if Rodrigo can get you on the A-list with the doorman."

"Have Rodrigo get you guys on the A-list as well. I may need you in there some time."

"Will do."

"Good. Does Rodrigo know my name is Carrie Sheffield?

"He does. We'll be calling you that as well."

"I have to get a few hours of sleep before tonight. I'll see you guys about six thirty. I mean eighteen thirty."

Samantha was exhausted and fell right into a deep sleep. She woke with a start. When she checked the time, she saw that it was only five o'clock. She had plenty of time to shower, get dressed, and get something to eat in the café restaurant of the hotel.

When she was relaxing in the café with a cup of coffee, she saw Anna come in wearing her skiing clothes. A young woman about Anna's age was with her. They both ordered a coffee to go. It was definitely Anna. A shiver ran through Samantha's body when she realized that this was the Ghost's daughter, Samantha's prey. Or maybe vice versa. Samantha studied Anna as she was handed her coffee and walked out of the café. She noticed that her English was good with a North American accent and that she walked erect and with confidence. She was definitely an athlete and confident in herself. Samantha looked down at the table and said softly, "I can do this. With Your help, I can do this."

CHAPTER 23
ANNA KENNEDY

"NAME PLEASE," DEMANDED THE LARGE man guarding the door of the Eiger Zone.

"Carrie Sheffield," Samantha stated firmly.

After looking at his printed list for her name, he said, "Go right in, Ms. Sheffield. Enjoy yourself."

"Thank you. What's your name?"

"Klaus, Ms. Sheffield."

"Glad to meet you, Klaus. You can call me Carrie," she said with a flirtatious smile.

"Thank you, Carrie. Have a great time."

As she entered the dance club, she thought, *Never hurts to make friends with the bouncer.*

Samantha went into the main room and saw that the action was already in full swing. The DJ had lively dance music playing, and the dance floor was packed with gyrating bodies. She found an open spot at one of the two bars in operation and ordered a cocktail. She knew that she had to nurse the drink so she could keep a clear head if she encountered Anna. Not a minute went by, even before she had been handed her drink, a man asked her to dance. She politely refused and told him that perhaps later she would like to dance with him. When she received her drink, she walked around the club observing the location of the restrooms and emergency exits. She surveyed the locations of the tables and sitting areas and, of course, was ever watchful for a sight of Anna Kennedy.

At about 8:30, she spotted Josh. He was sitting in an easy chair in one of the lounge-type sitting areas sprinkled throughout the club. They looked at each other impassively giving no sign of recognition. A few minutes later, she saw Jared. When they had made eye contact, he moved his head slightly to the right several times. When Samantha looked in that direction, she saw Anna on the dance floor with the very same guy that had just asked Samantha to dance with him when she was ordering her drink at the bar. Anna didn't seem to be paying too much attention to him because she was looking past him and smiling at other people.

Samantha quickly went up to Jared and said, "Would you like to dance?"

He announced, "I'd like that very much."

Samantha led Jared to a spot on the dance floor close to where Anna was dancing. Near the end of the song, Samantha bumped into the man that Anna was dancing with. "I'm so sorry. I got carried away. Oh—hi," she continued. "Do you remember me from the bar?"

"Yes, I do," he said with a hopeful smile.

"Well, if your lady friend doesn't mind, I may say yes the next time you ask."

"That would be great," he responded with an even bigger smile on his face.

She then turned to Jared and said, "Thanks for the dance. I enjoyed it."

"Great. See you around."

She then turned to Anna and said, "I'm so sorry I bumped into you guys."

"Don't worry about it. It happens all the time around here. You're the first person that's ever apologized."

Samantha found a seat where she could observe Anna, who was at a table that was more or less surrounded by a u-shaped couch. Anna laughed frequently and seemed to be having a good time with the group she was with.

Finally, she saw Anna excuse herself, and she started walking toward a restroom. Samantha followed her into the restroom about thirty seconds behind. When Samantha walked in, Anna was not in sight. Samantha busied herself at one of the sinks. When Anna came out of a stall and went to a sink to wash her hands, Samantha caught her eye in the mirror and said, "Hi." After they exchanged smiles, Samantha said, "I want to apologize to you."

"Why is that?"

"It was so rude of me to tell the man you were dancing with that I would dance with him later. I mean, he could be your boyfriend. I can't imagine what you think of me."

"Hey, don't worry about it. You did me a favor. He's been asking me to go to dinner with him for several nights now, and I'm starting to run out of excuses to say no."

Samantha then decided to take a chance. She said, "I kind of sensed that you weren't that interested in him by the way you were looking around to others."

"You sure picked up on that. So, thank you." After a pause, Anna continued. "I haven't seen you around here before. Are you a tourist on a ski vacation? Are you alone?"

"Yes, to both questions. Got here just this morning. Ski vacation. I'm alone." Samantha paused for a couple of seconds, then said, "Tragically, my fiancée was killed in a car accident about a month ago. I was with him when it happened, and I was badly injured. I can show you the wounds if you want. I'm trying my hardest to get over the loss. The heartbreak is tearing me up inside."

"Oh, I am so sorry for you. But believe it or not, I share your pain."

Samantha shook her head and, somehow, created a tear in

her eye. Anna quickly handed her a tissue from the dispenser and said, "Look, why don't you come to my table, and I'll introduce you to my friends."

"I would love that. You are so kind."

"My name's Anna. Anna Kennedy. What's yours?"

"Carrie. Carrie Sheffield."

"Come on, Carrie. Let's help you get over the sorrow you are trying to deal with—or at least put it aside for a while."

"Thank you, Anna. I needed this. I was beginning to feel so lonely."

When they got to the table, Anna introduced her to the three people sitting there, two men and a woman. The men were German, Gunther Kemp and Heinrich Schlosser, and the woman was Russian, Irina Rossova. Samantha noticed that they all spoke English to one another. However, when Anna spoke to Irina, they conversed in Russian. Samantha did not let on that she could speak Russian, and she carefully listened when they were speaking to one another. Anna related to the others Samantha's tragic story, and they all expressed genuine sorrow for her. They all made her feel comfortable and part of the group. One of the German men, Heinrich, asked her twice to dance, and he seemed to have an interest in her.

At about 11:30, it was apparent that the others were beginning to fade and were starting to excuse themselves to retire for the night. Soon, it was just Samantha and Anna at the table. Samantha was also beginning to feel the effects of jet lag, but she didn't want to let an opportunity to talk to Anna slip by. Fortunately, Anna bailed her out of the situation. "Listen, Carrie, I know that you must be exhausted tonight from your flight over and jet lag. I know you want to get some sleep, and I don't want to keep you up. But me and the others are going skiing tomorrow. Want to join us?"

"Why, Anna. Thank you for asking. I'd love to. What time?"

"I'm staying at the Grand Hotel Regina. I can pick you up at eight o'clock. Is that too early?"

"No. I'm at the Regina as well. I can meet you in the lobby. What about breakfast?"

"Let's meet in the hotel's café at seven. Irina's at the Regina as well. We'll meet you in the café. We will leave for the slopes right after breakfast. Do you need equipment?"

"I have clothes, but I'll have to rent everything else. Skis, boots, poles, helmet."

"No problem. I'm friends with the rental guy at the ski area. I'll have him fix you up with the perfect stuff. I'll call him from the café in the morning. He'll probably have everything ready for you when we get there."

"Sounds great. See you at seven."

When they stood up to leave, Anna came up to Samantha and gave her one brief kiss on each cheek, and said, "It's been great meeting you, Carrie."

Samantha thought, *This couldn't have gone any better.*

Anna gave Samantha a ride back to the hotel. When Samantha got back to her room, she called Jared and Josh and asked them to come to her room. She briefed them on how well it went with Anna at the Eiger Zone and her skiing date with Anna.

"I don't know where we are going to ski. She didn't tell me. But when I find out, I will text you and let you know where. I'd like to have you there just in case. Can you guys ski?"

"Hey, we're SEALs. Skiing is a piece of cake. Right, Jared?" After a pause, Josh asked, "You can ski, can't you?"

Jared gave Josh a penetrating stare and said, "Better than you, Josh."

Josh said, "I guess the answer is yes, Samantha. We know how to ski."

Samantha shook her head and said, "Anna has her own car, and we are going right after we have breakfast. I'll try to tell you where as soon as I can when I know. Her friend Irina is going with us as well. I'm not sure, but I think the two German guys will be there too. Irina is staying here at the Regina, but I don't know her room number. We'll work all this out. I'd like to have a dinner date with Anna tomorrow night for some alone time. I'm not sure how Irina fits into all this. I haven't figured that out yet, but I think she isn't just some friend of Anna's. I got this from some of the discussion they had tonight."

"You're right. She may not be just a friend."

"Look, guys. It's late. We need some sleep if we're going skiing tomorrow."

CHAPTER 23
IRINA, GUNTHER, AND HEINRICH

THE NEXT MORNING, SAMANTHA WALKED into the café, and Anna and Irina were already there drinking coffee. "Morning, Carrie. Get yourself some coffee at the counter. Our server will take our order when you have your coffee."

"Okay. Be right there."

During breakfast, the three talked small talk trying to get to know one another better. Samantha noticed once again that Irina's English was not very good, and like in the dance club, she and Anna spoke in Russian. Their conversation seemed innocent enough because it was mostly to explain what Samantha had just said. One time, Irina did say something that caught Samantha's attention. She said to Anna, "Keep your eye on her," but Samantha wasn't sure if the statement was sinister or telling Anna to watch out for Samantha on the slopes.

Samantha then asked Anna, "Where are we going to ski today?"

"We're going to Black Rock. It's one of my favorites. It's very challenging, Carrie. Are you up to it?"

"Let's hope so. But that does sound good. How far away is Black Rock?"

"If we leave now, we should be there by eight forty-five. It's a bit of a ride but well worth it."

"Good. Before we go, I need to let some of this coffee out. I'll be right back."

When Samantha got into the restroom stall, she texted Jared with the information he needed. When she was washing her hands, Anna and Irina walked into the restroom. "We decided we needed to let out some coffee as well. I also want to call my dad to let him know what we are doing today."

A shiver went through Samantha knowing that this young woman would be talking to a man who had tried three times to kill her.

At Black Rock, Anna introduced Samantha to Guy Friedman in the rental area. He looked her over intently and said, "Nice."

Anna responded, "Come on, Guy. Can't you wait until the second time you see her before you hit on her?"

"Give me a break, Anna. I was just assessing her size so I could get her the right equipment." He turned back to Samantha and said, "You going to the Eiger Zone tonight? If so, I'll be there."

"Guy!" Anna yelled.

"Okay. Okay. I'll get Carrie's stuff."

When Guy went into the back to get Samantha's gear, Anna said, "That guy has hit on every woman in the world, I'm sure of it."

"Don't worry about it. It's kind of flattering. Besides, it helps me forget what I'm trying to deal with . . . a little."

When Samantha was fully outfitted, the three women got in the cable car for the ride to the top. The area had just had its first snowfall of the season, and the view was spectacular. And for a few minutes, she totally forgot about her mission here in Switzerland. In fact, she was really looking forward to the exciting ski adventure before her. When they arrived at the top, Gunther and Heinrich were there waiting for them.

Anna spoke directly to Samantha, "Carrie, I assume that you are a skilled skier, but just follow me down to the Stage Two area where we can all join up. The run from Stage One to Stage Two is all piste—compacted snow. It should take about fifteen to twenty minutes. If you want to go faster, we can."

"No. Let's see how I do. This is a first for me."

"Well, I won't go too fast. We'll have a good time together. This is going to be fun."

As they were ready to start their run, Anna said, "Carrie, isn't that the guy you were dancing with last night when you bumped into me?"

Samantha looked to where Anna was pointing, and she saw Jared and Josh. "Yes, it is."

"Before we start, why don't you go over and ask him and his friend to join us. He's kinda cute. So's his friend."

Samantha was taken by surprise and said, "I don't know, Anna. That seems kind of forward to me. Suppose he says no? Suppose they're gay?"

"Come on, Carrie. You're in Switzerland. Besides, you'll never see them again. Here, I'll go ask."

"Anna. No, no."

Anna walked up to Jared and said, "My friend over there was wondering if you'd like to ski down to Stage Two with us, but she was too shy to ask. Do you and your friend want to join us?"

Jared was a little shocked at this invitation. He looked at Josh for a reaction. Josh nodded. Jared said, "Sure. Why not. We'd love to join you."

Anna led the process of the introductions, and they began their run to Stage Two. Anna, an accomplished skier, quickly set the pace down. Within five minutes, Anna and Samantha were almost out of sight of the others. When they reached Stage Two, Samantha was only about five seconds behind Anna.

"You are one heck of a skier, Carrie. I usually have to wait five minutes for the others to get here. Where did you learn to ski like that?"

"Maine. But I have skied all over the US. This is my first time in Europe."

"You'll have to take me to Maine sometime. I'd love to go there."

"I'd love to. Maybe we can go there someday."

"Tell you what, Carrie. This piste is a little boring. Let's go off-piste. We just had our first snow of the year, and there is fresh virgin powder off the main slope, and I know a few exciting ways down. Jumps, moguls, tight areas between trees, and even some sharp cliffs to avoid. Are you up to it?"

"I don't know about the cliffs part, but sure. Let's give it a go."

"Here come the others. We'll tell them what we're going to do."

"Do you think Irina will be comfortable with four men?"

"Trust me. Irina can take care of herself when it comes to men."

Anna explained to the others that she and Samantha were going to go off-piste, and that they could all meet at the base and take the cable car up again. None of the others wanted to go off the trail, so Anna said, "Okay, Carrie. I know where to go, so I'll lead the way down. Try to keep up. If I see you falling behind or in trouble, I'll wait for you. Ready? Can you handle fresh soft powder?"

"Let's do it."

The run down was exhilarating for Samantha. Anna was truly an expert skier, and she had all she could do to keep up with her. But she was able to. When they reached the Black Rock Base Stage, both girls were giddy with excitement. Anna came over to Samantha and gave her the hardest hug she had ever received. Anna said, "I haven't had this much fun in my whole life. I've never had anyone keep up with me like you just did. What a blast."

"I've never done anything like that before. I've got to admit that it was downright scary at times. We've got to do that again."

"Let's get some lunch, and we can do it again today. What do you say?"

"Sounds like a good plan to me. I'm famished."

In the restaurant, they met up with the others, and Anna couldn't stop talking about how Samantha had handled the off-piste run. Samantha blushed numerous times and said how scared she was on the way down.

By late afternoon, as they were loading their skis onto Anna's car, Irina had to visit the restroom. Samantha took this opportunity and asked, "What are your plans for tonight?"

"Usually, I go back to the Regina, shower, change, and get something to eat. Then I go dancing. Two, sometimes three times a week, I go to my dad's house to check it out. I sleep over there when I do. Tonight, I'm at the Regina. What do you have in mind, Carrie?"

"I was thinking that you and I could go to a nice restaurant somewhere and get to know each other better. Just you and I."

"That's a great idea. I'd love that."

"Do you know a nice place we could go? My treat."

"Of course. I know a great place. Kind of pricey. Still want to treat?"

"Absolutely. Since I'm buying, you make the reservation. Deal?"

"Deal. How about twenty hundred?"

"Perfect. What about Irina? She seems to stick very close to you. Will she mind if we leave her out?"

"Probably. But I'll deal with her. Leave that to me."

"How should I dress?"

"It's casual but wear something nice. Show off that amazing body of yours, if you know what I mean. A lot of good-looking, rich guys go where we are going. You never know."

"Gotcha."

★★★

Back at the hotel, Samantha immediately called for a meeting with Jared and Josh. She told them of the extraordinary success she had with Anna, including her dinner date with her later tonight. Alone. No Irina.

"What's bothering me is that I really like Anna. She seems so genuine, and I believe that she really likes me."

"Samantha," said Josh. "It could be a like-father like-daughter situation. She could be as evil and sly as he is."

"Josh is right," said Jared. "Why else would he take her with him when he escaped from Russia? He's so careful in what he does and bringing his daughter with him could be a real liability to him."

"I suppose you two are right. I need to keep that in mind. But I can't help having the feeling that she is just a fun-loving young woman and that the feelings she is expressing for me are genuine."

"Maybe they are. Let's hope so. But please, be ever mindful of who she is and how dangerous she could be. For all of us."

"Of course. I'll keep that in mind. But there's going to come a time when I'll need to make the critical decision to open up to her or not. I have no choice, and I'll have to let my intuition guide me on this."

"Just be careful, Samantha."

Samantha nodded in agreement then said, "What about Irina? What's your read on her?"

Jared said, "She seems to stick very close to Anna. She doesn't say very much to any of us, probably because her English isn't very good. She speaks in Russian to Anna. I don't know what they are saying."

"Well, I do," said Samantha.

"You speak Russian?" Josh blurted.

"Harlan never told you?"

Jared said, "No. This is news to us. Where is Irina coming from?"

"There doesn't seem to be any collusion between her and Anna. Mostly innocent stuff."

"What do you mean *mostly*?"

"At breakfast yesterday morning, she told Anna to watch me closely. Could have been innocent."

"Or more of a warning to Anna," said Josh.

"Perhaps. I'll keep an ear out for her," Samantha said with a smile.

Samantha continued. "What about the Germans? How do they fit into this?"

Jared said, "They're very blah. They don't say much. Typical Germans. You danced with Heinrich a couple of times. He might be interested in you. It's hard to say if they are good guys or bad guys."

Josh said, "There's something about Heinrich Schlosser."

"What is it?" asked Samantha.

"I can't really say. It just seems like I've seen or met him before. I don't know what it is. The way he walks. His German accent. There's just something familiar about him."

"How is that possible, Josh? When could you have met him before?"

"I don't know, Samantha. But if I have, it'll come to me."

"Do you two think you should try to make friends with them?"

Jared responded, "No. I think that could complicate things. I think that we should just continue to observe them and look for anything that could be sinister."

"I agree," said Samantha. "Besides, I'd like for you two to be at the ready if I need you."

"What's the plan, Samantha?"

"At dinner tonight, I'm going to try and feel out Anna. We should have reservations for eight o'clock at the restaurant. I'll try to get the name to you as soon as I know. Maybe one of you can be close by and the other trying to observe the Germans and Irina.

Josh said, "Anna seems very observant and may spot me or Jared again at the restaurant. That wouldn't be good. What if we have Rodrigo near you, and Jared and I can handle the other three?"

"Good idea. Anna has unfathomable energy and will probably want to go dancing after dinner. I'll try to excuse myself because of tiredness and jet lag and skiing all day. I'd like to meet back here after my dinner with Anna and compare notes. Anna mentioned something about skiing tomorrow at Wengen's Lauberhorn. It might be even more of a challenge than Black Rock. If that's so, I need to get some sleep tonight. I'll really need to be rested and alert for tomorrow."

"Okay. Call us when you get back from dinner," said Josh.

Jared added, "Good luck tonight, Samantha."

"Pray for me, Jared. I'll feel better than hoping for good luck."

CHAPTER 24
DINNER WITH ANNA

"BOY, ANNA. YOU SURE KNOW how to pick out nice places. This restaurant is unbelievable."

"It is nice. But, like I said, it's going to cost you. The appetizers and salads start at about thirty Euros."

"Uh oh. I might have to cut my vacation here a little short," Samantha said, wide-eyed.

"Don't worry about it, Carrie. I can pay the bill."

"No, Anna. I'm good for it." Samantha then changed the subject and asked, "How did Irina take not being invited tonight?"

"Not very well, I'm afraid."

"She's Russian. How do you know her? And where did you learn to speak Russian like you do?"

"First question first. I met Irina about a week after we moved here a year and a half ago. We've been good friends ever since."

"She doesn't live in Grindelwald, does she? I mean, she has a room at the Regina. That's not the cheapest place to live. How can she afford it?"

"She's like me, I guess. She has a rich family paying her way. That's what she told me anyway," Anna continued, "That brings me to your question number two. I'm really not Canadian. I'm Ukrainian. Born and raised there. Kiev, Ukraine. Lived in Moscow for twelve years. That's why I can speak Russian."

"Why did you leave Russia, become a Canadian citizen, and spend most of your time in Switzerland?"

Anna hesitated for a moment. Before she could respond, Samantha added, "Am I being too personal here, Anna? You don't have to answer."

"No. It's okay. It's just that it's a little complicated. And quite frankly, I'm not quite sure how to answer your question."

"If you don't mind, just give it a try."

"Okay, here goes. In April a year ago, my mother died suddenly of a heart attack. My father was devastated by her death. He said that he couldn't stay in Moscow and even Russia anymore because it created too many painful memories of my mother. Within two weeks after her death, we left everything behind and moved here to Switzerland. He bought a beautiful chalet just outside of Grindelwald. I wondered why we moved so quickly, but I was overwhelmed by the sudden death of my mother and moving to this skiing mecca. I didn't openly question it. Soon after we moved here, my dad told me that we were going to become Canadian citizens. I asked him why, and he said that he had a lot of very important business in the US and Canada and being a Canadian citizen would benefit him. I spend most of my time here because of my passion for skiing. It's no problem for him because he prefers it that way. He spends most of his time in Toronto and the US."

"I assume he pays all your bills."

"Yes, he does. He covers my credit card bills every month."

"What does your dad do?" Samantha asked in a matter-of-fact way.

"To tell you the truth, Carrie, I'm not sure."

Samantha asked, "He must be doing pretty well to have a chalet here, supporting all your needs, and a home in Toronto."

"I've asked him what his business is, but he always gives me some vague answer, like 'imports and exports.'"

"What did he do in Russia? Maybe that'll give you a clue."

"It's interesting. My dad had a successful career in the Russian air force. He was a general when he retired. Then, on a whim, he decided to jump into the political arena, and he ran for the office of the minister of finance of Russia. My mom and I tried to talk him out of it, but he ran anyway."

"What happened? Did he win?" Samantha asked knowingly.

"Yes, he did. But it was through some tragic event. He was behind in the polls, and for some reason, his opponent committed murder and had to drop out of the race. My dad won without opposition."

"Wow. I can see why you might be confused. From what you are telling me, your dad should be able to live a comfortable life, but not as extravagant as this."

Samantha continued to pursue this topic. "Do you know anything about your dad's life before he became a general?" Samantha asked with a little trepidation.

"No. He would never talk to me or my mom about his early life. I do know that he was on the Soviet Olympic archery team. He's proud of that, and he practices his archery skills all the time. In fact, he has an archery range set up here at the chalet and at the house in Toronto." Anna paused. "Carrie, why are you so interested in my dad?"

"I don't know, Anna. He seems to be an interesting enigma. He really intrigues me, I guess. Do you want to change the subject? I don't want to pry."

"No. It's okay. It's just that I don't really enjoy talking about him that much."

Samantha found this comment very intriguing. It could mean that she was forcing Anna into revealing too much about her dad. Or it could mean that Anna just didn't like her dad that much. Samantha thought that she should think and pray about how she should pursue this deeper.

Their main course was placed before them. Their wine glasses were refilled, and they both enjoyed a marvelous meal.

After dinner, they sat looking at each other as they sipped their coffee. Finally, Anna asked, "You are a very beautiful woman, Carrie. Have you ever been married?"

Samantha looked down at the table for a few moments and then said, "No. I've been engaged three times. The first two I broke off because I couldn't honestly say I wanted to spend the rest of my life with them. Well, you know what happened to my third. He was killed about a month ago." Samantha took a deep breath and wiped away a tear with her napkin. "What about you? Been married?"

"No. Wanted to once, but like you, it ended in tragedy before we got married."

"That's what you meant when you said you could relate to my pain of losing my fiancée in an accident."

"Exactly."

"If it's not too painful, can you tell me what happened?"

Anna was silent for five or ten seconds before she said, "Almost four years ago, I was twenty-one, and I fell in love with a boy. We decided that our love was deep and true, and we decided to get married. When I told my dad, he was furious. He did not like the boy, and he forbid me to marry him. He said I was too young, and he gave all kinds of other reasons why I shouldn't marry him. I never disobeyed my dad, but I did this time. I told him we were going to elope. I never saw my father so mad. But I was determined. Well, two weeks before we planned to run off with one another, my fiancée was killed in a boating accident."

"Anna, that is so like what happened to me. Were you in the boat when it happened?"

"No. Unlike you, I was given the news of his death."

"How did your dad take the news? Was he happy?"

"Unbelievably, he took the death hard. He seemed genuinely grieved and expressed his sorrow for me."

Samantha thought how much of a monster this man was. He was evil right to the core. She expressed her sorrow for Anna, then she returned to Anna's friend Irina.

"Irina intrigues me as well."

"I like Irina, but she can be a little overbearing at times."

"What do you mean?"

"I'm going to be blunt here. Irina is in love with me. She knows that I will never let that happen between us, but she still keeps trying to get a relationship going between us."

"Irina is a lesbian?"

"Yes."

"Wow! I didn't see that coming."

"Yeah. That's why she took being excluded tonight so hard. She's jealous of you. I'm sure she's noticed the way you and I are attracted to each another."

"I don't want to cause any trouble for you. I'll only be here for a week or so. Two at the most."

"Don't worry about it, Carrie. Irina needs to grow up and accept rejection once in a while. Besides, you are a breath of fresh air for me. It's true, I am greatly attracted to you, but not sexually. I like men. But I really do enjoy being with you."

"I enjoy being with you too, Anna." Samantha was shocked that when she said this, she wasn't lying.

"Are you up for Wengen Lauberhorn tomorrow?" It's quite a challenge."

"Sounds like fun."

"Same drill as today? Breakfast at seven?"

"Breakfast at seven," Samantha repeated.

"Okay. Great. Ready to go to the Eiger Zone for cocktails and dancing?"

"Anna, I'm going to have to pass on that tonight. I'm totally exhausted from trying to keep up with you on the slopes, and the jet lag hasn't quite left me yet."

"I understand. I'm still going to the club for a little while, but I'll stop by the Regina to let you off."

"I appreciate that, Anna. Look. Can we do this again tomorrow? Your dad's treat?"

"You've got a date. I can't wait. But tomorrow, I'll be asking the questions. I want to know about your life."

At the Regina, before Samantha got out of the car, Anna reached over and took one of Samantha's hands and squeezed it gently and said, "This has been the best day I've had since leaving Russia. I'm so glad we met."

Samantha went up to her room in a daze, wondering what exactly just happened. She texted Jared, and they were in her room almost immediately.

"Well, what happened?"

Samantha relayed the details of her dinner with Anna. When she was finished, she said, "I know that this is probably stupid of me, but I really believe that she doesn't know what her father is. I was trying to catch her lying to me, but she answered all my questions truthfully and was open about everything. No excuses. No embellishments. Just direct honest answers."

"Do you think we can be open to her about her dad?"

"I think so, but the key word is *think*. I'm not sure. When she said that she didn't like talking about her dad, I sensed a fear of him in her.

"You think she's afraid of her father?"

"I do. But I'm not sure. I need to come up with some way to probe her for more information. Another thing that has me in a daze is this. She expresses strong feelings for me. She hugs me, kisses me on the cheeks, but when she took my hand in the car, I felt a very strong feeling of attraction for me."

"Do you think she's a lesbian like Irina?" asked Jared.

"No. I don't think so. Anna was blunt when she said she likes men. Irina doesn't have a chance with her. She made that very clear."

"Overall, how do you feel about her?"

"I like her. I like her a lot, and I so hope that she is being honest with me."

"So do I."

"What about Gunther and Heinrich. Anything happen with them?"

"Not really. They were all at the Eiger Zone and hung out together. The Germans talked to each other quite a bit. Irina looked depressed. Didn't smile very much. Probably thinking about what you and Anna were doing."

"Poor girl. I feel sorry for her." Samantha then looked at Josh and asked, "Any thoughts on where you've seen Heinrich?"

"Yes. One thing I've come up with is this. Five years ago, I was a wet-behind-the-ears Navy SEAL, and my first mission was on a multi-national exercise with German and French special warfare guys. Heinrich reminds me of one of the Germans. I'm not sure though."

Samantha said, "Call Harlan and see if Heinrich Schlosser and Gunther Kemp were ever in the German special warfare service, the KSK. If they were, that's very important to know. If we have to deal with two of those guys, we could be in trouble. They are killers"

"That they are. The German KSKs are vicious killers," added Jared.

"You know, there's one thing that has been bothering me. Have any of these four people tried to take a picture of us? If they have a photo of any of us, and they are on the Ghost's payroll, he will know what's going on. I'm sure he knows what all of us look like."

"Not openly, anyway. But any of them could have sneaked a shot."

"Let's keep this in mind. No pictures."

"Got it," said Jared. "What's the plan for tomorrow?"

"Pretty much a repeat of today. Skiing at Wengen Lauberhorn and some alone time with Anna. You guys can keep an eye on Gunther, Heinrich, and Irina. Hopefully, Harlan will get some info on the Germans. Let's get some sleep."

CHAPTER 25
YODELER'S PARADISE

IN THE MORNING, SAMANTHA WALKED into the café, and like the day before, Anna and Irina were already at a table with their coffee. Samantha went to the counter and ordered her coffee. At the table, the small talk seemed normal, but Samantha noticed that Irina was looking at her with a hard stare. No talk was made about Anna and Samantha's "date." Samantha appreciated the fact that Anna did not mention it because she would have had a hard time talking about the topics discussed in front of Irina.

The skiing part of the day went almost exactly as the day before. Jared, Josh, and the Germans joined the three girls. However, Samantha did notice that Anna went out of her way to talk to Josh before anyone began their initial run down the slopes. Also, during lunch, Anna sat beside Josh and talked to him often.

During the afternoon run, Anna told Samantha to follow her. Midway down the first run, Anna went oft-piste and raced downhill through the soft virgin powder at high speed. Samantha matched every move that Anna made. It was a downhill race, and Samantha was determined to keep up. When they reached the bottom, it was a dead heat. Both girls released their ski-boot bindings, removed their helmets, embraced, and rolled in the snow laughing hysterically.

"No one's been able to do that, Carrie," Anna said as she hugged Carrie. They broke the embrace, got up, and fell into some undisturbed snow powder. They began making snow angels like a couple of young kids. They walked into the lodge holding hands and laughing audibly. The other five came into the lodge fifteen minutes later. Irina saw Samantha and Anna sitting on a couch talking intimately. She turned away and walked into a restroom.

"Uh oh. Irina's pissed," said Anna.

Samantha responded, "Let's not aggravate her any more than she is."

"You're right," Anna agreed.

"Your dad pays for dinner tonight, but can you also make the reservations since you know the restaurants here and I don't?"

"Done. I've got a nice out-of-the-way place picked out. We can leave the Regina at nineteen forty-five—quarter of eight."

"What's the name?" asked Samantha.

"It's called Yodeler's Paradise. You'll love it. Much more intimate than last night."

"Sounds great. What's the dress code? Sexy like last night?"

"Casual. Not nearly as formal. Meet me in the lobby at nineteen forty-five. I'll handle Irina."

"Better you than me. If looks could kill, I'd be dead by now."

At eight o'clock, Samantha and Anna were seated in a one-table, very intimate room. "When you said more intimate, you weren't kidding. The table's only two feet above the floor, and we are sitting on cushions at the only table in the room. Were you telling me the truth when you said you like men?" Samantha said jokingly.

"I was. And speaking of men, what do you think of Jared's friend, Josh?"

"I saw you flirting with him today. Are you interested?"

"He's really cute. Have you checked out the body on that guy? He's a real hunk."

"He is cute. But I think Josh and Jared are gay. You don't have a chance."

"Oh yeah? Watch me. What about Jared, Carrie? He's a hunk too. Could he take your mind off things?"

"I'll have to think about it, Anna. But I have been thinking about what we talked about last night."

Right then, the sommelier came into the room to take their wine order. Anna said, "Dad's paying the bill tonight, so let's splurge a little bit." She looked at the wine list and said to the sommelier, "A bottle of the Chateauneuf-du-pape. The best year, please."

The sommelier's eyes opened wide and said dutifully, "Excellent choice, madam."

After they clinked their wine glasses, Anna said, "Okay, Carrie, what did you want to talk about? Then it's my turn to ask the questions."

"Anna, I'm going to be bold and direct here, and I hope I don't offend you. Last night we talked at length about your life and your father. When I went to bed last night, I couldn't stop thinking about what you said. I'm worried about you."

"What do you mean? Why are you worried about me? You hardly know me."

That's true, but for some reason, I am greatly attracted to you personally. Maybe it's because your relationship with your father resembles the one I had with mine."

"In what way?"

"My father seemed to love me, but in some ways he was aloof. He didn't always tell me things I felt he should. It turned out that his business dealings were not always legal. I don't want to get into that right now. Maybe later. You and I seem to have many things in common. Strange fathers. Tragic loss of a loved one.

Passion for skiing. So, I need to ask you this, and you don't have to answer if you are uncomfortable. After all, I am still really a stranger to you, and I will understand."

"Carrie, I feel the same strong attraction for you. So, go ahead and ask. What do you want to know?"

Samantha paused, knowing that this was a pivotal point in getting Anna to open up to her. It could go either way. But this was the time. She stared at Anna for maybe five seconds, then she said, "Truthfully, what do you think of your father?"

Anna's eyes widened, and she stared at Samantha for a long time. She finally said, "Despite what you have just told me, I have to admit, I didn't see this coming."

"Anna, your father is a puzzle to me, and last night you said that you didn't like to talk about him much. Why is that?"

Anna stared at Samantha and shook her head. She continued to stare at her and said nothing.

"Anna, I know this is hard for you, but open up to me and be honest."

"Carrie, I've only known you for a little over two days, but somehow, I am attracted to you in a way I've never experienced before. And because of that, I'm going to tell you something I've never ever told anyone."

"What is it, Anna? Tell me."

Anna began to say something, then stopped. She began again, and again she stopped.

"Go ahead, Anna. Say it."

After another long pause, Anna said, "Carrie, I hate my father."

"Why?" Samantha asked. "He's your father. Why do you hate him?"

After another long pause, Anna said, "Carrie, let me count the ways."

"Start from the beginning, and I'll keep track."

Anna began hesitantly. "He is so mean to me and was to my mother. He totally controlled the household. We had to get permission from him for everything. My mother couldn't even buy a bra without his consent. He has a furious temper, and if we ever disobeyed him . . . Carrie, it was horrible."

"What did he do?"

"He was abusive to us. Mentally and physically."

"He was physically abusive to your mother? He hit her?"

"Yes, he did. And me."

"He hit his own daughter?"

"Not just hit us, Carrie. He beat us terribly. One time, I watched him beat my mother." Anna paused then said, "I never saw so much blood in my life."

Samantha gasped.

"Do you remember that I told you that he was furious when I told him that I was going to run away with my boyfriend?"

"Yes, I do."

"Well, he beat me so bad, I was in the hospital for four days. That's why we put the elopement off for a few days. I was in the hospital recovering from the beating he gave me."

"My God, Anna. I am so sorry for you."

"He mentally tortured me as well. When I was very young, he threatened to drop me off at an orphanage if I misbehaved. To me at the time, that was a fate worse than death. He threatened my mother that he would divorce her and tell everyone that she was cheating on him. That's only a fraction of what I've had to deal with in my life."

"Anna, I just don't know what to say right now."

The entrees were placed before them, and the sommelier refilled their wine glasses.

When he had left the room, Anna reached across the table and took Samantha's hands in hers.

"Carrie," Anna said, "Let's forget about this and enjoy our

dinner and each other's company. Just being with you like this fills me with joy."

Samantha nodded her head, looked at Anna, squeezed her hands, and said with a genuine caring smile. "I agree. Let's enjoy the rest of the evening."

As they ate, they shared small and funny experiences of their lives. Eventually, the smiles turned to laughter. But despite the happier atmosphere, Samantha was planning her next move toward fulfilling her objective of enlisting Anna into trapping her father.

As they finished their after-dinner cup of coffee, Anna said, "I'm so sorry for burdening you with the dark side of my life. I should never have opened up to you the way that I did."

"Anna, Anna, Anna, don't worry about that. I'm so glad that you did. My heart truly grieves for you, but I do want to ask you one last question. And again, it's very personal, and you don't have to answer it if it makes you uncomfortable."

"What is it, Carrie?"

"Anna. You are going to be twenty-five in about two weeks. You are an adult. Why haven't you left home? Why don't you just leave him right now? Run away."

"Believe me, Carrie. I've often thought about doing that, but there are several reasons why I haven't. For one thing, my father has not provided me with any financial security I could use if I were on my own. Second, I don't know where I would go. And third, and this is tied to the second reason I just gave, I am so afraid of him, that I know he would find me and come get me. Then I don't know what would happen to me."

"My God, Anna. You really are in a bind."

"I am, and I don't know what to do."

Samantha thought for a few moments and said, "Let me think about your situation tonight. I have a few ideas, but I want to think about them a little bit before I present them to you."

"Carrie, I don't know what you have in mind, but I just felt my heart jump with a little hope for the first time. What do you have in mind?"

Samantha looked down at the table deep in thought. After about thirty seconds she said, "Let's you and I spend tomorrow together. Just you and me. No skiing. No friends. We can talk your situation over and discuss our options. What do you say?"

"You said, *our* options." She then said, "I would love to do that, Carrie. Tomorrow is a day I go to the chalet to check it over. My dad requires that I do that about twice a week. Why don't you come with me? We'll have all day to talk and discuss *our* options," she said with a smile.

"Perfect. Do Irina and the Germans know that you are going to the chalet tomorrow?"

"Yes, they do. We can leave at seven before they leave for the slopes. Is that good?"

"Yes, it is. Here's what I suggest. If you are up to it tonight, go to the Eiger Zone and be with your friends for an hour or two. Don't let them know about any of this. Act your normal jovial self. I will go back to my room and think about your situation and some of the ideas that might be workable. Is all this agreeable to you?"

"Oh, yes. I can't wait for tomorrow."

Twenty minutes later, they were parked in front of the Grand Hotel Regina. Once again, Anna reached over and took Samantha's hands in hers and squeezed. She said, "Carrie, I wish that you were a man."

A few hours later, Jared and Josh met with Samantha in her room. "How did it go?" asked Josh.

"I think it went very well. With one reservation," she added.

Samantha relayed the discussion she'd had with Anna at Yodeler's Paradise.

Jared asked, "Why didn't you just come out and tell her what her father really is?"

"My intuition told me to wait, talk it over with you guys, pray, and think over my next move before I act. Remember, we were taught to be patient and not to rush into things. Plus, things are going so well with Anna. I'm actually a day or two ahead of where I thought I'd be with her. I was trying to come up with a suggestion to her of where we could be totally alone together, but once again, she solved my problem for me when she asked me to go to her chalet with her tomorrow. It's perfect because I can look over the place for information on the Ghost. Information that we might be able to use."

Josh said, "Good point." Then he asked, "You mentioned that you had a reservation about how it went with Anna. What is it?"

"As sincere as Anna seems to be about the story she's told me about her father, I have to keep in mind that she may be as clever and devious as he is—and just as evil. Impossible as it may seem. And . . . I might have committed a major blunder, but she didn't seem to pick up on it."

"What kind of blunder?" asked Josh.

"I said to her that she was going to turn twenty-five in two weeks. She has never told me how old she is or her birth date. How would I know that?"

"Uh oh. She didn't question you on that?"

"No. And as soon as I said it, I knew I had made a mistake. I looked for a reaction, but I got none. I really didn't have an answer ready if she called me on that."

Josh said, "Maybe, under the euphoria of hope, she didn't catch it. Then again, it may hit her when she's reliving her time with you tonight."

Jared added, "Make sure you have your handgun close by tomorrow. Watch her closely. Don't turn your back on her at any time. Be very careful. Remember, you will be alone with her. There will be no one around to help."

"I will." After a pause, she asked, "How did it go at the Eiger?"

"Pretty routine. We were all together at a table when Anna arrived. Irina and Anna talked in Russian quite a bit. It seemed like Irina was asking a lot of questions, and Anna was trying to answer them."

"True," added Jared. I didn't sense that Anna was giving Irina any secret information." Jared looked at Josh and Samantha and said with a smile, "What I did notice was that Anna asked Josh to dance several times and that their bodies were rubbing together during the slow dances."

"Hey," Josh responded. "She's a gorgeous woman. I'm a man. What do you want me to do?"

Samantha giggled and said, "She's after you, Josh. Be careful."

Before Jared and Samantha could tease Josh anymore, Jared's phone chimed. Jared looked at the phone's screen and said, "It's Harlan. Maybe he has some info on the Germans."

He pushed a button and said, "Harlan, what do you got?"

Jared listened intently. "Yes, sir . . . I understand . . . I'll tell them." When he ended the connection, he said, "We've got a problem. Josh was right. Heinrich and Gunther were in the German special forces, but under different names. April, a year ago, two special forces guys went AWOL and haven't been found. They disappeared from the planet. One of them, probably Heinrich Schlosser, was on the multi-national exercise that you were on five years ago, Josh."

Samantha said, "It looks like the Ghost recruited them to keep an eye on Anna."

"What does this mean for us? How much do they know? Have they figured everything out, and have we been compromised?" asked Josh.

"We need to be very careful around them," said Samantha. "Let's assume they know who we are. But watch them closely for signs. We can't let you guys be alone with them, especially when no one else is around. Be on the alert that they can try to take you out at any time."

Jared said, "We'll be ready at any time to defend ourselves."

"Good. I'll try my best to recruit Anna tomorrow. Also, tomorrow, I think it's important to brief Rodrigo on what's going on. We need him close by and ready for action if we need him. This German thing has changed our timetable. I thought I was ahead of the game but not anymore. Any other issues?"

Josh asked, "What about Irina?"

Samantha answered, "I haven't figured her out yet. She could just be a love-sick girl hoping that Anna will change her mind. But on the other hand, she could be working with the Germans." Then she added, "And with Anna, for that matter."

"Okay, let's get ready. Tomorrow is a big day for us."

CHAPTER 26
SAMANTHA TELLS ALL

SAMANTHA MET ANNA IN THE hotel lobby just before seven o'clock. She asked Anna, "Should we get some breakfast before we go?"

"No. Let's go right away. I don't want to bump into Irina and have her see us together again. I'll make us something to eat at the chalet."

Once in Anna's car, she told Samantha that the trip to the chalet was about thirty minutes. After twenty minutes of normal driving, Anna turned off the road onto a gravel road for the next ten minutes that went straight to the chalet up a slight gradient. "This is a private road that goes to the chalet. You can see it up ahead."

Samantha could see a beautiful structure off in the distance. She said, "It looks beautiful."

"Wait until you see it up close. It's something else."

When they drove up to the chalet, Samantha exclaimed, "This is magnificent. Your dad must have paid a fortune for it."

"I'm sure he did."

Anna parked her car in front of the garage located on the side of the house, which was out of sight from the front door. They walked around the side of the house to the front, and once inside the chalet, Anna said, "I'll make us something to eat, and then

I'll give you a tour. After that, we can talk."

"Sounds good. I'm pretty hungry."

During the tour, Anna pointed out the master and two other bedrooms downstairs and the two bedrooms upstairs. Also downstairs, were a large gathering room with a large fireplace and a large playroom/lounge in the center of which was a professional sized billiards table. But what really interested Samantha during the tour was a locked room on the second floor that Anna referred to as her father's study. "It's locked, and I'm not allowed to go into that room," she said with a great deal of annoyance in her voice.

They eventually went into the pool room to sit and talk. Before they sat down, Samantha looked out a window and asked, "Anna, what's that building about a hundred meters from the back of the house?"

"That's the one thing my dad had built during the year and a half that he's owned it. It's actually a hangar for his helicopter."

"There's a helicopter in there?"

"Yes, and you can't see it from here, but the doors open in the back to a concrete landing pad. That's also where my dad practices his archery skills. He has an archery range set up there."

"Does he fly the helicopter much?"

"Not often. He told me that he wanted it there in case he ever needed it. He uses the helicopter just to exercise it and keep it flight worthy."

Samantha shook her head in wonder at her opponent, the Ghost.

Before they sat down to talk, Anna said, "If you don't mind, Carrie, I'd like to go pee."

"Go. I'll be right here."

As soon as Anna left the room, Samantha took a bug detection device from her purse and scanned the room. Just as she was putting the device back into her purse, Anna walked into the room.

When they sat down, Anna spoke first. "Before we get into

my situation, Carrie, I'd like to ask you something. I want you to give me an honest, no bullshit answer."

Samantha was taken by surprise by this action from Anna. She had scripted in her mind how she wanted this meeting to go, but this question by Anna changed things.

"What do you want to ask me?"

Anna looked directly into Samantha's eyes and said, "Who exactly are you, Carrie? How did you know when my birthday was and how old I was? Why the interest in my father? Why do you want to help me? You don't even know me. Tell me. I want to know."

Samantha was a little shocked at the directness of Anna. She looked at Anna for a long time as she considered her answer. She finally took a very large deep breath and exhaled slowly through her mouth. Her intuition told her to be upfront and honest with Anna. No beating around the bush. She had her purse by her side with her gun on top just inside the open zipper. She was ready to grab for it in an instant, if necessary.

She began, "You are right, Anna. I'm not Carrie Sheffield. My real name is Samantha Stone Coen."

Samantha studied Anna's face intently looking for some reaction to the mention of her name. She saw none other than a wrinkling of her eyebrows.

"Anna, I will answer all your questions. Trust me. Here we go. First of all, your father has been trying to kill me for over a year."

"What!" Anna exclaimed. "That's crazy! Why? He doesn't even know you!"

"I'll give you all the details. But first, let me tell you who your father really is. The bottom line is that he is a professional, international assassin."

Anna gasped in audible disbelief and shock. Samantha nodded her head.

"We are quite certain that he killed at least twenty-eight

people when he was in the Soviet Union's special warfare force, the *spetsnaz*. We believe that he killed two of the Soviet Union's Olympic archery team members so he would be added to the Olympic archery team. He murdered your mother's fiancée so she would marry your father instead of her fiancée. He framed his political opponent for murder so he would be elected Russia's minister of finance. We also believe that he killed his disgraced political opponent and made it look like a suicide. We know that he assassinated two CIA agents who had obtained information about a top-secret facility built in the Sea of Okhotsk. I'll tell you more about this in a few minutes."

Anna said, "This can't be true. No one can be that evil"

"Anna, I hate to tell you this, but it gets worse. Much worse. Let me go on. I just mentioned the two CIA agents a minute ago. He also killed a CIA department head in her home. When he killed her, her husband also died with her. He was what your father calls *collateral damage*. Along the same line, when he killed the two Soviet Olympic team members, four innocent people lost their lives with them. Also, collateral damage. Anna, your father has no regard for human life."

"Carrie, or Samantha, whatever your name is, I believe what you are telling me, but I still can't grasp the fact that my father has done all this."

"I know that this is hard to believe, but here is the worse part for you. Please prepare yourself for something that might make you sick."

"What is it, Samantha? What are you going to tell me?" Anna asked in a trembling voice.

"Anna, it hurts me to say this, but your mother did not die of a heart attack."

Anna responded in a very shaky voice, "But the doctor's report said that it was a massive heart attack."

"Anna, she died of suffocation. She was smothered to death

with a pillow by her husband, your dad."

"My God, no, Samantha. You are making this up. Tell me what you just told me is not true."

Samantha just looked at Anna and said nothing.

"Why would he do such a thing? The death certificate said she died of a heart attack."

"Your father paid the doctor to fake the cause of your mother's death. Incidentally, that doctor has disappeared. We feel that your dad might have killed him because he was what we call *a loose end*."

"My God, Samantha. My God."

"There is one other thing that will probably hurt you deeply. Your boyfriend, Georgi."

"No, Samantha. Please don't tell me that my father killed Georgi too."

Samantha looked at Anna with sad eyes. Anna began crying. She buried her face in her hands, and she began to shudder in grief.

"Anna, I'm so sorry that I have had to tell you all this. It hurts me to see you in such pain. But just cry it out of your system. I'll wait. I have more to tell you. Just take your time."

Anna stood up and walked around the room with her hands to her mouth and choking back tears. It took about ten minutes for her to regain her composure. When she had calmed down, she managed to say, "Go on, Samantha. What more evil has my dad done?"

"I'm sure you are aware of what happened in Russia a year and a half ago."

"Yes, just before my dad and I left Russia after my mother died." Anna paused as she choked up again at the thought of her mother. Finally, she continued, "Just before we left Russia, there was a military conflict, and a great deal of Russian lives were lost. It sounded to me from the news that Russia initiated the conflict, but my dad insisted that it was the West."

Samantha shook her head several times and said, "Here's what really happened. Your father was one of the leaders of one hundred and twenty-eight high-ranking, rogue military leaders that were planning a political and military coup designed to establish world domination for a new Russia. The coup failed, and as you said, unfortunately many Russian lives were lost. Following the failed coup, we started rounding up the military leaders to put them on trial for their crimes. Well, we captured a hundred and twenty-seven of them, and one escaped—your father. As the minister of finance for Russia, he stole more than two hundred and forty million dollars from the Russian people. Now you know why he ran for the office of minister of finance and why his political opponent was disgraced and murdered. Today, you and I are sitting in some of the money he stole—this chalet. Now you know why you and your father left Russia so quickly, established a residence in a remote part of Europe, and established Canadian citizenship. With new names, I might add. Does all this make sense to you so far?"

"Unfortunately, it is all starting to sink in and make sense. It's making me sick."

"Let me continue, and you will see how I fit in to all this. Your father has escaped capture numerous times. And he decided to get revenge on the people that were responsible for the failure of the coup. He has a list of eighteen people, one through eighteen. So far, he has assassinated the first four on his list. Anna, I am number five. Last May, he warned me that I was next. Number five. So far, he has tried to kill me three times. And only by the grace of God, has he failed. But in those three attempts on my life, he has put me in the hospital two times, caused me all kinds of injuries, which I can show you by the way, and most important of all, he has almost killed my infant babies. They would only have been collateral damage to him."

Anna said, "Samantha, you are married?"

"Yes, I am. Heading for a year and a half."

"If my father is trying to kill you, why are you here?"

"I just got tired of running and hiding. Looking over my shoulder all the time. Jumping at every sudden, strange sound. Being separated from my husband. Worried about my twin babies. I decided to become more proactive and go after him."

"How did you find him here? Can I ask you that?"

"You, Anna. I found him through you."

"Me? How?"

Samantha paused before she answered. She finally said, "Anna, I am so sorry about being dishonest with you about so many things in my life. But I had to win over your trust before I could open up to you. That's why I bumped into you on the dance floor. I had to meet you and tell you a string of lies about myself. My father was not a criminal. My fiancée didn't die in a car accident. And yes, as I said, I am married. I'm so sorry."

Anna looked at Samantha with critical eyes. She finally nodded her head and said, "I understand why you've done what you done. I would have done the same. I forgive you. Please, tell me what I need to know."

Samantha then proceeded to tell Anna how she located her through her passion for skiing, and how she hoped to enlist her in capturing her father.

Samantha concluded her argument with, "Anna, I feel that I have made a strong case against your father. To save my life, and perhaps the lives of others, I really need your help. What do you say? Will you help me?"

"I can't believe that this has happened to me. But, of course, I will try to help you. But remember, I am in a bind myself. How can I get out of the situation that I am in?"

"This will not be easy, Anna. I'm going to be very frank here. If you help me and your father finds out, I believe that, even though you are his only daughter, he will try to kill you, as he did your mother and countless others. If you help me, your life is in danger."

"Samantha, I believe that my life is in danger whether I help you or not. Of course, I will help."

Samantha said, "The first thing that must be done is to get your father off the streets and in prison where he belongs. Once that is done, I will take you with me to the United States and get you a new productive life there. I promise that I will be with you all the way. I have friends in very high places that will help me take care of you—the president of the United States, just to name one. Are you with me?"

"Of course, I am. What do you need for me to do?" Anna paused, then said, "Do you really know the president of the United States?"

CHAPTER 27
"HELLO, MR. DIRECTOR"

"FIRST OF ALL, I NEED to know all I can about your father. Likes, dislikes. Hobbies. Fears. Idiosyncrasies. Anything you can think of that would be of use to me and maybe save our lives. Second, is there anything in this house that would help. For example, we need to get into his study upstairs and search that room extensively. What does he have in the garage, attic, and closets? Anywhere. We need to go out to the hangar and see what he has out there. Third, do you communicate with him regularly? If so, what do you talk about? What information does he give you? Does he tell you when he is coming home, or does he just appear here? Anna, I need to know anything you can think of that will help us."

"What about my friends, Irina, Gunther, and Heinrich? What should I do about them?"

"Anna, two things. First, the two Germans are working with your father. He has hired them to watch you and to, perhaps, protect you. As far as Irina is concerned, we are not sure where her loyalties lie. We are assuming that her loyalties are with your father. Second, Jared and Josh are with me. They are Navy SEALs and are here to protect and to help me. And now, to protect you."

"Josh is here with you? Is he married?"

"Jared is married, but Josh is not." When she said this, she detected a faint smile of relief on Anna's face.

"Samantha, I just can't believe that all of this has been going on, and I have never picked up on any of it. I must be so naïve."

"No, you are not, Anna. You are an innocent woman surrounded by very clever and evil manipulators. Your father, Irina, and your German friends are not nice people."

"Thank you, Samantha, that makes me feel a little better. Where do we start?"

"It's lunch time. Let's eat something. We can then talk about the Ghost, as we call your father. We can search the chalet for things he might have here that could help. Then we can talk some more. We have a lot of talking to do. But please keep this in mind. Outside of this room, do not talk about anything that could alert your father. I have scanned this room for bugs. Until I scan the other rooms, please consider them bugged. This is very important."

Anna nodded her head in understanding, then she said, "Should we go back to the Regina tonight?"

"Don't you sleep over when you come here?"

"I do. But I usually show up the next morning at a ski slope we have picked out."

"Let's do that. Let's keep everything as normal as possible. Pick out a ski area and text your friends. I'll let Josh and Jared know the plan. Do you have a plan B ready if we need to spend tomorrow here instead of skiing?"

"I can get sick and beg off."

"That takes care of you. I'll have to come up with a plan B for me. Perhaps a shopping spree in Bern."

"Let's make some sandwiches."

After lunch, they started their search of the chalet. Samantha's main interest was in the locked study on the second floor. The Ghost had installed a new lock on the door, and they could not open it. Samantha had brought a lock picking set with her, but her initial attempts at unlocking the door didn't work. Samantha decided to try again later.

"I don't want to spend all day trying to unlock this door. I want to call Harlan for some advice. He may be able to help."

"Who's Harlan?"

"I'll explain everything when we talk again. But for now, he's the director of the CIA."

"Samantha, who are you? You have friends like the president of the United States and the director of the CIA?"

"It's a long story, Anna. I'll tell you everything tonight. Let's check out the garage." But before they went to the garage, Samantha sent a picture of the lock to Harlan and called him for advice on how to defeat it.

Once in the garage, Samantha checked for bugs then asked, "What's under these tarps, Anna?"

The big one covers my dad's Range Rover. The smaller two are snowmobiles. One's my dad's, and the other one is mine."

"Hmmm. Interesting."

They spent the rest of the afternoon looking through boxes in the garage and in the small attic of the chalet. While they were eating their evening meal, Harlan called with instructions on how to use her tools to open the lock guarding the Ghost's study.

Samantha said, "Thanks, Harlan. I'm pretty sure that I'll be able to pick the lock now. I was doing it wrong before. Any news on the Ghost?"

"As usual, we don't know where he is. As far as we know, he is still in Bar Harbor looking for you. We have Jean bugged, and he has called her several times for any additional information she might have. Of course, she has none. Hopefully, he will stay in Maine for a few more days. However, you never know with him. I'll keep you informed."

"Thanks, Harlan. It's going well with Anna. Do you want to say hi to her?"

"Sure. Put her on."

Samantha handed the phone to Anna.

"What do I say?" Anna whispered.

As Samantha handed the phone to Anna, she whispered, "Say hello. He's a nice guy."

Anna took the phone, pursed her lips, and finally said in a very shaky voice, "Hello. Mr. Director?"

"Hi, Anna. We are so sorry that we have put you in the middle of all this. I know that it must be a shock for you, and you must feel like you are in a whirlwind."

"Thank you, Mr. Director. I am in shock. But I thank you and Samantha for opening my eyes to all this."

"Take care of my Samantha there. She's precious to me."

"She's precious to me as well, Mr. Director. I will try."

"Bye, Anna. Please give the phone back to Samantha. I have a few more things to tell her."

"Bye. Thank you." Anna was in a daze as she gave the phone back to Samantha.

Ten minutes later, Samantha ended her call with Harlan. Anna said, "I can't believe I just talked on the phone with the director of the CIA."

"Like I said, he's a nice guy. You'll like him."

Anna shook her head in wonderment.

They spent the rest of the evening going through boxes and discussing Anton Yulov, Anna's father, the Ghost.

CHAPTER 28
THE HANGAR AND
THE STUDY

SAMANTHA SPENT A GOOD PART of the morning trying to unlock the study lock with no luck. She finally said, "I'll get this sucker open, but I need to take a break. Let's go out to the hangar and see what that can give us."

They walked the 100 meters to the hangar and went around to the back. When they reached the doors, Samantha said, "Oh crap. He's got a digital lock on the doors."

"My dad has always used his birthday for digital locks. Maybe he did here." Anna punched in the six digits, but nothing happened.

"What did you do? Month, day, year?"

"Yes."

"Try day, month, year."

Again, nothing happened.

"Okay. Try year, month, day."

When Anna punched in the numbers in that order, the hangar doors began to open.

"Yes!" Exclaimed Samantha.

When the doors were fully retracted, they saw a beautiful,

all-white helicopter standing regally in the center of the hangar. They went inside and began exploring. Near one of the doors was a charcoal barbecue grill. "Like I told you last night, my dad likes to grill when he's here. He buys expensive steaks in the village, and he cooks them for us."

"What's in the closed case over there?"

"I don't know. Let's go see."

Inside were three beautiful, Olympic-style archery bows hanging neatly on hooks. Also in the case were numerous arrows with different type arrow heads neatly stored in quivers.

Samantha shivered when she thought of her encounter with one of Yulov's arrows.

"My dad loves launching arrows into targets. You may have seen his range that he has a few meters from here. He prides himself at his accuracy at long range. He is able to hit the center from fifty meters."

"Yes, I saw the stands. Look, over there are the targets he puts on the stands."

"When he's here, he practices his archery skills for hours."

Samantha started to inspect the helicopter. She got in and stared at the instrument panel for a long time. She found manuals in a compartment near the pilot's seat. She took numerous pictures of the manuals and of the helicopter, in general. They spent about an hour searching the helicopter for anything that could be of use. They found nothing of value.

"Let's go back to the chalet. I want to try the door lock some more. We've got to get into that study. That's where we will hit paydirt."

Once in the house, Samantha began working on the door lock in earnest. After about fifteen minutes of frustration, Anna came up with a tray of sandwiches and some soup. They sat on the floor outside the locked study door and began eating. Anna asked, "What are we going to do if we can't open the door, Samantha?"

"I'm not going to let this thing beat me. I'll get it open. Right then, Samantha's phone vibrated. It was a text from Harlan with an attached video. Samantha opened the video, and it was a technician demonstrating how to pick the lock. The directions that Harlan had provided earlier were for a similar but different lock. The video clearly showed Samantha what tools to use, how far to insert them, and how to twist them to retract the bolt. Within two minutes, the locked snapped open, she turned the doorknob, and the door opened smoothly.

Samantha scanned the room for bugs and found none. "There's got to be something in here, Anna. Otherwise, your father wouldn't have forbidden you to go in, and he wouldn't have installed such a difficult lock. Let's get to work."

The room was fairly spartan as far as furniture was concerned. Besides the large double-pedestal desk and desk chair, there was one couch facing a TV on the wall. There were two matching four-drawer file cabinets against another wall. Each wall had at its center a generic Swiss-scenery picture. All in all, it was a very blah room.

Samantha said, "You start looking through the desk drawers, and I'll tackle the file cabinets. But before you touch anything in any of the drawers use your phone and take a picture of the way everything is situated. Got that?"

"Yes, I'm on it."

Samantha began opening the folders in the file cabinet drawers. She found surprisingly little that she felt would be useful. The only interesting documents she found were receipts for various purchases the Ghost had made, including the Cessna Citation purchased in New Orleans for $750,000. The yacht and helicopter rentals used in the Gulfport assassination attempt were also there. She went through both file cabinets in fifteen minutes. Anna went through the desk with the same results. Nothing useful.

Anna sat on the edge of the desk, and Samantha sat in the couch.

"There's got to be something here, Anna. Why would he forbid you to come in here if there wasn't something he didn't want you to see? Why would he put such a sophisticated lock on the door?"

Anna nodded in agreement.

"Let's look at the desk again. None of the drawers were locked, right?"

"Right. The center drawer and the five pedestal drawers all opened. No locks."

Samantha looked in all the drawers. Nothing of value. She thought for a while then said, "The deeper drawer on the right-side pedestal seems to operate with a little more difficulty than the others. It seems heavier even though there is little in it."

"You're right, it does."

Samantha opened and closed it several times. "Something is a little strange here." She emptied the drawer of a few near-empty folders. To her, it looked normal. She felt the tops of the inside sides of the drawer, then she felt something that could be a button. She pushed it, and the front of the drawer bottom popped up. She lifted the drawer bottom up, and it came out of the drawer revealing a shallow hidden compartment.

"This could be what we're looking for." On top of some papers was a fully loaded pistol. Samantha put the pistol on the desk and pulled out the two sheets of papers that had been under the gun. On the papers were several lines of random numbers and alphabet letters. Eight lines on one sheet and four lines on the second.

"What's all this mean, Samantha?"

"I'm not sure. But I have an idea. This must be important for him to hide them in this secret compartment. Look at this line of alphanumeric characters." Samantha pointed to a particular line. It read, LU33 595KSU 661 BL 881—22.5. I could be wrong, but I think the LU is a country code, maybe Luxemburg. The two numbers following the country code could be the International Bank Account Number, the IBAN. The next series of numbers up to the dash could be the bank account number."

"What's the twenty-two point five after the dash?"

"Again, I'm not sure, but it could be the amount of money in the account. Probably in millions of dollars or euros."

What you are saying is that each of these lines represents an offshore bank account in which my dad has put the money he stole from Russia. In this particular line, it is twenty-two and a half million dollars."

"That's exactly what I'm saying. But, again, It's a guess on my part."

"This does make sense, Samantha. You told me yesterday that he stole more than two hundred and forty million dollars from Russia. Let's add up the totals and see what we get."

They added up the total of what Samantha had guessed was the money in each account.

"Anna said, "Two hundred eighteen point six million dollars. Take away what he has already spent or kept out of the accounts, and we are in the ballpark. It looks like you are right."

"Looks that way. Or it could be an incredible coincidence."

Anna then asked, "What's this last line of numbers? It is different than the rest."

"I was wondering that too. It is six pairs of double digits."

"Could it be a safe combination?" suggested Anna.

"It very well could be. Does your father have a safe in the house?"

"Not that I know of."

"Hmmm." Samantha scanned the floor looking for a possible floor safe. She then looked at the pictures on the walls.

Anna saw this and said, "A wall safe behind a picture."

They both ran to the walls and began removing the pictures.

Sure enough, a safe was hidden behind one of them. Samantha took the sheet with the numbers on it to the safe. She read the numbers aloud to Anna and she turned the dial accordingly. The safe did not open.

"What do we do, Samantha?"

"Nobody said any of this was going to be easy. Let me think a minute."

After a minute of thought, Samantha said, "With the hangar doors, he set the combination backward of what is normally used. Maybe he did the same here."

Samantha read aloud the six double digit numbers in reverse order. Anna entered the numbers and pulled down the handle. The safe opened. The two girls said, "Yes!" simultaneously.

Samantha took a photo of the contents in the safe. In the front of the safe was another fully loaded handgun with several ammunition clips. Behind the gun were two stacks of passports for different countries, six for the Ghost and six for Anna.

"Looks like he had more travel plans for us. Our pictures, but different names for us on each passport.'

Sitting on top of a folder were two stacks of hard currency. Samantha estimated that there was about a hundred thousand in each stack. One in dollars, and the other in euros.

"He wanted to be prepared if you two had to leave in a hurry. There's about two hundred thousand in euros and dollars there, Anna. This also tells me that he probably has millions stashed away in safety deposit boxes, airport lockers, and God knows where else all over the world, just in case he needs it. This is what he does."

Samantha opened the folder and took out the manilla envelope that was inside. She removed a stack of photos from the envelope. The topmost photo was of Samantha. Below hers were photos of Anna's mother, Mr. and Mrs. Smith, and Mary Graham. Each of these photos had a diagonal line drawn through them.

Anna said, "If I had any doubt that my dad had killed my mother, it is gone now. I know for sure that everything you've told me is true. My dad is a monster."

"Look, Anna. I have to take pictures of these two sheets of account numbers and send them to Harlan. If they are offshore account numbers, perhaps the CIA can freeze or empty the accounts. We need to put everything back into the safe exactly as we found it. Same for the desk and file cabinets. I mean exactly. Use the photos we took. When you are through with the desk, I want you to memorize the safe combination and practice opening it several times from memory. Let's get busy and restore this room in a way that he won't know that someone's been in it. Memorize the combination exactly. We may need to get into it in a hurry.

Samantha took photos of the two sheets and sent them to Harlan along with her thoughts as to what the numbers meant.

When they were finished, they once again checked the room to be sure they hadn't made a mistake.

That night and the next day, they continued to talk about Samantha's time on the *Hawkbill* in the Sea of Okhotsk, the destruction of the SOOF, and her idyllic life with Ira during the first year of their marriage. She also recounted every detail of the three assassination attempts on her life. In addition, Samantha kept prodding Anna's memory about her father.

CHAPTER 29
"GET OUT AS FAST AS YOU CAN"

THE NEXT MORNING AFTER BREAKFAST, Samantha and Anna checked over the house to be sure there were no signs of any unwanted poking around. Samantha practiced picking the study door lock until she could do it in under two minutes. They then sat down with a cup of coffee and talked.

"Anna, your father is a clever and observant man. Do not underestimate him. As I said before, if he feels that you have deceived him, he will not hesitate to kill you. It is critical that you act normal and as you always do when you are around him. When he returns from the US, we will have a plan in place to get you out of here, probably skiing, and our men will move in to capture him. Now, this is important, I am going to give you an encrypted phone which you must have with you at all times. Be sure, be absolutely sure, that he doesn't find it. If he does, you are dead. I'm sorry, but I need to be blunt here. We've set up speed dial numbers. Speed dial one is for our CIA man, Rodrigo Ortiz. Number two is for Jared. Number three is for Josh. I am number four, and Harlan is number five. Heaven forbid if you have to call Harlan. If you do, we will probably all be dead. When you get back, tell Irina, Gunther, and Heinrich that you are finally feeling better, and you'd like to go skiing. I will call you to tell you that I am all shopped out in Bern and will be returning to Grindelwald tonight for a few days before I head back to the States. We have not seen each other since last Sunday when we skied at Wengen Lauberhorn. Are you comfortable with this story?"

"Yes, I am."

"I'll be in my room at the Regina. I have things to do, and I will lay low until it's time for me to get back from Bern late this afternoon. We can all go to the Eiger Zone for some dancing and drinking. All normal stuff. But we will be planning our actions to capture the Ghost when he gets back here."

"Okay, Samantha. Sounds good."

"Anna, pray that everything goes as planned. If it doesn't, we could be in lots of trouble. Your father is a very dangerous man."

"I really don't know how to pray, Samantha."

"When I have a chance, I'll teach you. It's easy, and it's important to know how."

"I'd like that."

"Good. Let's get back to the village."

When they were about halfway down the snow-covered private road from the chalet, they saw a car turn onto the private chalet road.

"Oh my God, Samantha. That looks like my dad's red Range Rover. He's come back early! What do we do?"

"Don't panic, Anna. I'm going to crunch down out of sight where my feet are. Tell him that you have to go to the village, and you will be back to the chalet very soon."

"God, Samantha. I'm scared. Why did he come back early? Maybe he knows. I'm so scared."

"Take a few deep breaths. Relax. Try to keep a clear head."

Samantha ducked down under the dashboard and tried to make herself comfortable. In about two minutes, the cars approached each other.

Anna said, "I wish you had taught me how to pray before we left the chalet."

"Just ask the Lord to help you get through this."

The cars slowed, and Anna lowered her window when the cars were side by side.

"Hi, sweetie. Where are you going?"

"Hi, daddy. I'm going to the village for a few minutes."

"Good. I'll pull over and go with you."

Yulov turned off the car motor and opened his door.

"No, daddy. I have to go alone."

"Why, sweetie? I'll keep you company."

"No, daddy. I have to go alone." Anna furiously thought about what to say. She thought to herself, *Please, God. I need help. Tell me what to say.*

Yulov was out of his car and began walking toward Anna's car. Anna blurted out, "Daddy, I'm going to the village to buy you something. I wanted to surprise you when you got home. It won't be a surprise if you come with me. Please, don't take my fun away. I'll be back very soon."

"Well, okay, but I want a kiss first."

Anna quickly opened her door and rushed to the Ghost and met him before he reached her car. She threw her arms around him and hugged him hard.

"I'm so glad you are home. I didn't expect you back this soon."

Yulov hugged her in return and said, "Things didn't go as I expected, so I decided to come back and see you. I heard that you weren't feeling well."

Anna hesitated. "I was a little sick. Probably something I ate. I'm feeling better now. I'm especially feeling better now that you are here. Let me go now so that I can get back with your surprise."

"I can't wait, sweetie. Get back soon."

"I will. I promise."

Breathing very hard, Anna got back into her car and headed

down the road. In the rearview mirror, she saw the Ghost waving to her as she picked up speed.

"Samantha, I almost died back there."

"Is he still looking?"

"No. He's back in his car and headed toward the chalet."

When Samantha crawled back into her seat, she put her gun back into her purse. Anna watched as she did this. Samantha said, "I'm glad I didn't have to use it. I was so crunched up down there, I probably would have shot myself or you rather than him. But let me say this, Anna: you were magnificent."

"Thank you, Samantha. I took your advice and asked God for help. It must have worked because I didn't know what to say or do. Then I did."

"So, *sweetie*, what are you going to buy your father to surprise him?"

"I told you last night that he loves expensive vodka. He especially likes Absolut Crystal. It costs about twelve hundred euros a bottle. But he can afford it," Anna said with a laugh. "I just hope the liquor store has some."

"He may not be able to afford it soon if Harlan can freeze his accounts."

"When will you know?"

"I asked him to set up the procedure but to not activate it until we are through here. I didn't want your father to know until we are ready for him to know. If he found out his accounts were frozen now, he'd know that you were responsible."

"I am in danger, Samantha, aren't I?"

"Try not to think like that. We are almost finished here. Just act normal, *sweetie*."

"Come on, Samantha. Give me a break. My dad's been calling me that as long as I can remember."

Samantha giggled loudly.

Then Anna asked, "how did my dad know that I had been sick?"

"I was wondering the same thing. One of your friends had to tell him."

"Which one?"

"If I had to guess, I'd say Irina. But I'm not sure."

They drove into Grindelwald village fifteen minutes later and pulled up to Grindel Liquors. Anna returned to the car with a bottle inside a decorative gift bag. "They had it. When I told the clerk that I was surprised he had Absolut Crystal in stock, he told me that he sells quite a few bottles of this expensive vodka every week."

"There are quite a few rich people around here, sweetie."

"Can it, Samantha!"

"Okay. Okay. Drop me off at the Eiger Zone. I'll call Rodrigo and tell him to meet me there. He can drop me off at the Regina. I don't want anybody seeing you and me together. I'll stay in my room as planned. I have some important things to do. You can get together with your friends at the slopes or anywhere. Just act normal and glad to see them again. And remember, we haven't seen each other since we had dinner the other night."

"Okay. What about Josh and Jared?"

"I'll contact them and ask them to meet me in my room. I want to brief them on what we found at the chalet, and I hope they have more info on the Germans."

Samantha called Rodrigo and asked him to meet her at the Eiger Zone as soon as he could. She also alerted Jared and Josh to meet her in her room when they could get there.

At the Eiger Zone, Samantha had to wait five minutes for Rodrigo to drive up. As Samantha was getting into Rodrigo's taxi, she repeated to Anna, "Act normal. Call me if you need me. Speed dial four."

"Okay, Samantha. Will do. Pray for me."

"I promise I will, Anna. I promise I will."

On the way to the Regina, Samantha briefed Rodrigo on

her past two days with Anna as well as the close encounter with the Ghost on the chalet road. At the Regina, Samantha quickly got out of the taxi and checked out the lobby looking for Irina, Gunther, or Heinrich. Seeing that they weren't there, she hurried to the stairs and up to her room. When she was in her room, she immediately called Harlan.

"Do you have the videos I asked for?"

"I do. You should get them in about ten minutes. And we still don't know where the Ghost is. We lost him two days ago."

"I know exactly where he is. He's here at his chalet just outside of Grindelwald."

"What! Samantha, you've got to get out of there. Jared and Josh too. He must know you're there."

"I agree. Make flight arrangements at Meiringen Air Base and Alpnach Air Station to get us home. Anna is coming with us too. We've got the Ghost at his chalet. We can capture him. Do you have enough men in place and ready to go?"

"I hope so. He's as slippery as an eel. I thought I'd had him before."

"I told you about his helicopter. He also has two Range Rovers. A white one and a red one. He's got two snowmobiles in his garage. As far as I know, these are his only means of escape. When can your guys move in?"

"We'll have everything in place by midday tomorrow. Good job, Samantha. I think we've got him now. Will you be ready to leave tonight?"

"I think so. Jared and Josh should be here any minute. We'll talk it over and have Rodrigo drive us to Alpnach Air Station for the helicopter ride to Meiringen for evacuation."

"Again, good job. This nightmare is almost over. See you in a couple of days."

"Bye, Harlan. Thank you for all your support."

An hour later, Jared and Josh came into Samantha's room.

She was watching a video on her phone and taking notes.

"What took you so long?"

"We were skiing at Black Rock with Irina and the boys when we got your call. We told them that we had to go because Josh was not feeling well. I'm sure they left right after we did. What's going on?"

Samantha briefed them on her activities with Anna and on the evacuation plan.

"What about, Anna? asked Josh. How are we going to get her out safely?"

"Here's what I think should work. Anna can go with her friends to the Eiger Zone. Everything normal. Right at ten o'clock she can excuse herself to go pee. She can sneak out the back door, and we'll be waiting for her in Rodrigo's taxi. He can take us directly to Alpnach Air Station. A helicopter will be waiting for us."

"Suppose her father forbids her to go out tonight?" asked Josh.

"I hadn't thought of that. I've seen her at work, and she's very resourceful. She'll come up with something."

Josh said, "We are not leaving here without her, Samantha. No man left behind."

"Okay, Josh. You are right. Let me think for a while and come up with a plan B."

At five o'clock, Samantha said, "I'm sorry, Josh. But everything I come up with that might work involves her getting away from her father at the chalet."

"Come on, Samantha. There must be something we can do.

Before Samantha could answer, her phone vibrated.

"It's Anna. I don't like this." Samantha accepted the call. "Anna, what's up?"

Anna screamed, "You've got to get out of there. He knows. He tied me up in a chair and is coming to the village to get you. He phoned the Germans and told them to kill Josh and Jared.

They could be there at any minute. Get out of there! All of you!"

Jared and Josh immediately sprang into action and raced to their room.

Samantha calmly asked Anna, "How long ago did he leave the chalet?"

"About ten minutes ago. He could be at the Regina in less than twenty minutes. You don't have much time."

"What's your situation?"

"I did what you did on the plane when he tied you up. I kept my arms rigid and slightly away from my body. My bonds were loose, and I was able to get free and call you."

"Okay. Listen to me. Rodrigo's going to take me to the chalet to pick you up. Dress warm in case we need to travel on foot. Be ready. I'll be there as quick as I can."

"I'll be ready, Samantha. Hurry, but please be careful."

Samantha rushed to the street, jumped into Rodrigo's waiting taxi, and they sped off to the chalet."

CHAPTER 30
"BIG OAKS FROM LITTLE ACORNS GROW"

JARED AND JOSH RAN TO their room to get their guns and warm coats.

Jared said, "Josh, they may be coming for us, but we need to be the aggressors. That's the SEAL's way."

"I agree. What's the action word?"

"Let's use *acorn*."

"Acorn it is."

"You have Heinrich. I'll take Gunther."

"Gotcha."

"They'll be here shortly—that is if they're not here already. We have an advantage because they don't know that we have been warned."

They took the stairs and raced down to the lobby.

Jared said, "I don't think they'll try to take us out with people around. But be ready if they do."

Josh nodded in agreement. When they were in the lobby, they saw Gunther and Heinrich coming into the lobby from the side door that goes to the outdoor parking lot. Their eyes caught sight of one another, and Josh waved to the Germans with a smile on his face. They smiled back and said hi.

"Hey, guys," Jared said. "I really enjoyed skiing today. You?"

The Germans said that they did. Then Gunther asked, "Are you feeling better, Josh?"

"Yes, I am. I got nauseated up there at the slopes, but I feel better. In fact, I'm feeling pretty good right now."

Jared said, "Let's have a beer in the pub and plan our skiing for tomorrow." He added, "I'll buy."

They went into the Regina's pub, and Jared ordered four beers. Before they were halfway through their beers, Gunther said, "Let's go to the Eiger Zone early. We can get some snacks and drinks there and get an early start. Thursdays are always great there because the ladies get their drinks at half price. A lot of fresh meat. If you know what I mean," he said with a wolfish grin.

"Great idea," said Josh.

"You bought the beers, Jared. I'll drive us to the Eiger," said Gunther.

"You got it, man. Let's go hustle up some fresh meat."

As they went through the parking lot toward Gunther's car, they were crossing an empty parking spot. Jared said, "You know, in the States, we have a saying: *Big oaks from little acorns grow.*"

Immediately, Josh and Jared formed a 'C' with their right hands and used a tiger claw punch to the side of the German's necks. Both the surprised Germans gasped for breath and crumpled unconscious to the snow-covered asphalt of the parking lot.

"Call Rodrigo, Josh. Get him here ASAP. He took Samantha to the chalet to help Anna almost an hour ago. He should be back here by now."

"I'll disarm these killer clowns."

Two minutes later, Rodrigo drove up.

"You got ropes in the cab, Rodrigo?"

"Better. I've got large nylon ties. We can secure these guys with those."

★★★

Yulov parked his car in the underground parking lot at the Regina. He used the stairs to get up to the second floor. He carefully went up to Samantha's room, Room 212, and knocked on the door.

"Maintenance," he said. There was no response. "Maintenance. There may be a serious problem with your room." Still no response. He looked down the hall, and he saw a maid entering a room. The Ghost followed her into the room. She was talking to an elderly couple. The Ghost pulled out his silenced revolver and shot three times. He said, "Sorry folks. Wrong place, wrong time." He laughed as he took the master key card from the dead maid. He entered Samantha's room and thoroughly searched it. She was gone.

Where could that bitch be? he thought.

He went down to the café to see if she was getting something to eat. He hid and surveyed every table. She was not there. He went to the lobby desk and asked the gentleman manning the desk, "I'm looking for the American girl in Room 212. Have you seen her?"

"Yes, sir. I believe that she got into a taxi about an hour ago. I believe it was her."

"Thank you."

Yulov thought, *She could have gone to the Eiger Zone or back to the chalet. I'd better warn Irina.* As he was leaving the café, he saw the Germans with the two Americans going toward the side entrance to the outdoor parking lot. Gunther caught Yulov's attention and nodded to him. *Good*, Yulov thought. *That's the end of the Americans. But where's the bitch? She's the one I really want.*

Yulov called Irina's number, but he got no answer. A few minutes later, he tried again, and again she did not answer.

"Something's wrong," he said under his breath. "I'd better get back to the chalet." He quickly took the stairs to the underground parking lot.

CHAPTER 31
HELICOPTER

A HALF HOUR EARLIER AT the chalet, Samantha said to Rodrigo, "Thanks, Rod. I'll take care of Anna. You head back to the Regina and help Jared and Josh. They need to deal with some tough dudes and are in great danger. But keep your phone handy. I may need you."

"Good luck, Samantha."

"Thanks. But pray for me. I will need it."

Samantha ran up to the front door and found it locked. She quickly punched in the four-digit combination that Anna had given her. She ran toward the pool room, and Anna was coming out of the room as Samantha approached. They embraced tightly for a moment then went into the pool room.

"Are you okay?"

"Yes, but I'm quite a bit shaken. I am so glad to see that you are all right. What about Josh? Are he and Jared okay?"

"I'm not sure. But they can take care of themselves. We've got to get out of here before your father gets back. We've got some things to do, and we need to do them in a hurry."

"What can I do, Samantha?'

"First of all, we need to get into the study right away."

When they turned to leave the pool room, they saw Irina

standing in the doorway pointing a gun at them.

"Well, well, well. What do we have here? Back up. Both of you," she ordered.

Samantha and Anna backed up with their hands in the air.

"Mr. Yulov will be pleased that I have you both. That'll get me a nice bonus, I am sure."

Samantha said, "Your English has really improved overnight, Irina."

"I was getting tired of talking Russian all the time. It's nice to be able to talk in my native tongue."

"Look, Irina. Yulov won't give you a bonus. In fact, you're going to be a loose end. He'll kill you like he does everyone else."

"I don't think so, Carrie. But nice try."

Anna said, "Irina, if you let me go, I know that we can be close friends. Even closer than we've been."

"Are you propositioning me, Anna? That won't work because I'm not really into girls. But I could be. I really am attracted to you. My sexual needs have been taken care of by Gunther and Heinrich. But I've often fantasized how great it would be if you joined us. A menage a trois is great, but a menage a quatre would be even better."

"God, Irina. You are sick," blurted out Anna.

Samantha said, "I am serious, Irina. Yulov is going to kill you."

"I don't think so. He and I have had a thing going for almost five years. He's in love with me."

Anna screamed, "You were screwing my dad when my mother was alive?"

"Yes, my dear. And it disgusts me as much as it does you. But he pays really well."

"You're nothing but a filthy whore."

"Don't knock it if you haven't tried it, you naïve little girl." Irina smiled at Anna.

Samantha asked, "How did Yulov find out that I was here?"

With a smile of satisfaction, Irina answered, "I was suspicious of you and how you both got so cozy with each other so quickly. When Anna got sick, which she never does, and you disappear on some crazy shopping trip to Bern, I really thought something was up. I called him yesterday morning and told him what was going on. He sent me a picture of you. You were naked, by the way. Nice. When I saw the picture, I wasn't sure. But eventually, I knew you were Samantha Stone and not Carrie Sheffield. I called him a couple of hours ago to tell him. To my surprise, he had already flown back last night, and I reached him right here at his chalet. He told me to get here ASAP, and I did. I was hiding in the garage when you drove up." Irina smiled broadly in satisfaction.

Then her smile faded, and she continued, "Enough of this chitchat. Yulov wants you alive, Stone. He wants you to watch as he kills his traitorous daughter. But even though he wants you alive, I won't hesitate to put a bullet in both your heads. I want you both to get into that closet. And if either of you shows your face outside the closet. I'll kill you. Trust me on that."

Irina backed them toward the closet. She told Samantha to open the closet door and get in. When she motioned with the gun for Samantha to get in the closet, Anna hit Irina's wrist with her fist, and the gun went flying, skidding away on the floor. Irina reacted quickly, spun around, and kicked Anna in her chest with the bottom of her foot—a classic taekwondo spinning back kick. Anna grunted then hit a wall with her back and fell to the floor gasping for breath.

Samantha thought, *Uh oh. That was a perfect taekwondo kick. I may be in trouble.*

Irina grabbed a pool cue from a rack on the wall and stalked toward Samantha, who slowly backed up. When Irina yelled and charged toward Samantha with the pool cue in the air, Samantha did a body roll across the pool table, grabbing the yellow-striped nine-ball in her hand as she rolled to the other side. During the roll on the table, Irina tried to hit Samantha with the pool cue. She missed Samantha's head by an inch. The cue broke into two jagged pieces when it hit the edge of the table. In an unbelievably quick flash, Irina grabbed the loose piece of the cue, circled the table, and was once again facing Samantha.

Samantha backed up as Irina approached her, one half of the pool cue in each hand. Samantha assumed a fighting stance with her right foot slightly forward of her left and knees bent. Samantha thought, *Relax. Let the tension leave your body. A tense body is bad. Keep a clear head. Remember what you have learned. Wait for the right moment, then act.*

Suddenly, Irina yelled and charged toward Samantha. Samantha instantly fired the nine-ball into Irina's chest. Irina grunted and fell to her knees in pain. Samantha quickly took two steps forward and, keeping her wrist and fist firm, she hit Irina under her jaw with an uppercut punch using the fleshy, underside of her open hand. Bolts of pain shot up both sides of Irina's head, and she was knocked backward by Samantha's blow. Irina lay on her back, writhing in pain.

Samantha quickly turned toward Anna to see if she was all right. Anna had gotten up and was breathing with difficulty.

"I'm okay, Samantha. That kick came out of nowhere and it hurt. I had the wind knocked out of me. But I'm okay now."

"Good. But we must act fast. The Ghost could be here any minute. Get the rope that the Ghost used to tie you up with and tie up Irina's hands and feet. Get that filthy whore into the closet. When that's done, get Irina's phone, her gun off the floor, go upstairs, and get a pillowcase from one of the bedrooms. I've got to go pick the lock on the study door. Meet me there when you are through here."

Anna tied Irina up, took her phone from her, retrieved the gun, then rolled the struggling Irina into the closet. Then with great effort, she pushed the couch against the closet door. As she was starting up the stairs, Irina's phone vibrated. She looked at the phone's screen and saw that it was from Yulov. When she reached the second floor, she saw Samantha working on the lock. She ran into a bedroom and got a pillowcase. Irina's phone vibrated again. Again, it was from Yulov. When she returned to the study room door, she heard the deadbolt retreat, and Samantha opened the door.

"My dad just tried to call Irina. Two times."

"He'll know that something's wrong, Anna. We've got to move fast. Open the safe as quickly as you can and put everything into the pillowcase. I have a few things to do at the desk."

When Anna had the safe open, she slid its contents into the pillowcase. She saw Samantha writing something on a sheet of paper.

"What's next, Samantha?"

"I'll be finished here in a minute. Bring the pillowcase, run out to the hangar, and open the doors. Remember, year, month, day. I'll be there shortly."

Anna hurried to the hangar and punched in the combination. The doors began to retract. A minute later, Samantha was there and climbed into the helicopter. She got into the pilot's seat and began flipping switches. The engine powered up and the rotors began turning slowly.

"Samantha, what are you doing? You can fly a helicopter?"

"Never have, Anna. Never have."

"Do you know how?"

"We'll see. How long ago did the Ghost try to call Irina?"

"Fifteen or twenty minutes ago."

"He'll be here in about ten minutes."

"We've got to hurry."

"I know. Fortunately, this thing has wheels on the runners. I should be able to taxi us out of the hangar."

Samantha did some more switch flipping, and the helicopter

slowly began to move forward. When they had taxied out of the hangar and were on the landing pad, Samantha said, "It has to warm up for a few more minutes. I have to go back into the hangar. Stay here. Get the gun that was in the safe out of the pillowcase, and get the ammo clips out as well. Be sure it has a loaded clip in it, remove it off safety like I showed you and keep it handy."

Samantha ran into the hangar. Two minutes later, she was back in the pilot's seat.

"Okay, Anna. Here we go. Say a prayer."

The rotors picked up speed, and a high-pitched sound filled the air. Samantha adjusted the cyclic rotor pitch control, and the helicopter vibrated.

"What's happening?" Anna yelled over the noise.

"Be patient! Let me figure this out. I haven't done it before, and it's not easy. The controls are very sensitive."

Right then, a bullet penetrated a plexiglass window of the cockpit.

"It's him, Samantha! He's here!" Anna screamed.

"Anna. Open the door, lie flat on your stomach, and fire back at him. Keep him from taking aim."

Anna did as she was told. She fired a shot at her father. Freshly dropped snow filled the air, making it more difficult for Yulov to shoot accurately, but two more of the Ghost's shots penetrated the windshield into the cockpit. Anna fired shots back to keep him off balance. He continued to run toward the helicopter in a zig-zag line, ducking as Anna shot at him.

The helicopter lifted off the ground and began to spin around slowly. Then the spin increased in speed. Samantha frantically pushed on one of the anti-torque pedals, and the helicopter began to spin in the opposite direction. But too fast. The tailspin increased in speed and the tail rotor missed the hangar by inches.

"I've got to get the feel of this," she muttered out loud. She gently pushed the second pedal, and the spin gradually decreased.

With a few more adjustments, Samantha finally stopped the unwanted spin, got some control of the helicopter, and gained a few meters of altitude. The helicopter flew erratically toward the chalet garage, but it bounced on the ground several times. On one of the bounces, the helicopter hit the ground with great force sending Anna rolling to the other side. Samantha finally got the feel of the very sensitive cyclic pitch-control stick and was able to reach the chalet garage and rest the helicopter on the ground about twenty meters from the three cars parked there.

Samantha yelled, "Put a new clip in the gun just like I showed you. Run over to the cars and shoot out at least two tires of all three cars. More if you can. Do this fast. We've got to leave before the Ghost gets here."

Anna jumped from the helicopter and ran to the cars shielding her eyes from the blowing snow. When she reached the cars, she shot out all the tires on the three vehicles and quickly returned to the waiting helicopter.

"Good job, Anna. Strap yourself in. I'm not sure what I am doing here. No telling what's going to happen. Pray for us. And here we go."

Meanwhile, Yulov was cursing Samantha as the helicopter headed erratically for the chalet. He was about to run back to the chalet when he saw smoke coming out of the open hangar doors. He ran inside to see what was burning. Once inside, he saw his archery case fully ablaze. He quickly grabbed a fire extinguisher and ran to the burning case. Just as he reached it, the half-empty can of charcoal lighter that Samantha had used to start the fire, burst into flames, sending Yulov backward as he shielded his eyes. When he recovered, he found his three prized archery bows and the arrows fully ablaze.

He screamed in agony, "You bitch! I'm going to kill you!"

In the helicopter, after several near crashes, Samantha was able to regain altitude and was beginning to get some sort of a feel for the controls. By gently adjusting the anti-torque pedals and the cyclic pitch-control stick, she was able to keep the helicopter in the desired direction with a level flight. When she felt more comfortable, she headed for Grindelwald. She said through gritted teeth, "Anna, call the SEALs. See if they're okay. If they are, tell them to meet us at the Medical Elective medical facility just outside the village. Rodriguez knows where it is. They have a helicopter pad there. Tell Josh and Jared that we will fly to Alpnach Air Station for evacuation. Also, tell them to have a doctor there that can treat a gunshot wound."

Anna looked at Samantha and yelled, "My God, Samantha. You've been shot. You're covered with blood."

"I'm okay Anna, but, as you can see, I'm bleeding quite a bit. Find something to make a tourniquet with. Use your bra if you have to. I've got to concentrate on keeping this beast in the air. This is not an easy thing to do, and I'm struggling."

When the Ghost's hatred for Samantha calmed down, he ran to the chalet and to his study. On his way past the pool room, he heard Irina screaming. He went in and pushed the couch out of the way and freed Irina from the closet. He left her laying there and did not untie her. He ran upstairs to the study and immediately saw that the safe was open and empty. He swore under his breath. When he looked at the desk, he noticed a pen lying on a sheet of paper. He picked up the paper and read aloud, "Hi, Yulov. I've got your money. I've got your daughter, sweetie. I put sugar into the gas tanks of your Range Rover and your two snowmobiles. And for good measure, I let the air out of the car tires with an axe you conveniently left in the garage for me. Now, keep looking over your shoulder because we will be tracking you down. See you soon. Oh, by the way, who's the bitch now, ASSHOLE?"

Yulov ripped the paper into shreds and threw the pieces onto the desk. He yelled loudly, "Whoever you are, I'm going to kill you, and I'm going to love doing it!"

CHAPTER 33
MEDICAL ELECTIVE
MEDICAL FACILITY

IT TOOK ALL THE CONCENTRATION that Samantha had to get the helicopter to the Medical Elective medical facility and land it safely. When she shut the helicopter down, she passed out in her seat. A waiting doctor rushed onto the helicopter. He yelled for some oxygen and began tending to her blood-soaked arm. Anna asked, "How is she?"

"It's a flesh wound in her upper arm. The bullet passed through cleanly. She's lost a lot of blood, but she'll be fine."

Oxygen was administered to her, and she began to come to. When she shook her head to clear the cobwebs, Anna asked her, "Are you okay?"

"Okay, I guess, but my arm hurts like hell, and I feel faint and a little nauseous. In the movies, when a guy gets shot, he keeps on going like nothing has happened to him. My arm really hurts, and I can't imagine doing anything."

Anna said, "Well, you kept flying the helicopter like nothing had happened."

"I don't remember any of that, but I guess I did. We are at the medical facility, aren't we?"

As the doctor and Anna helped Samantha leave the helicopter, Jared, Josh, and Rodrigo came running up to them.

"Anna told us that you've been shot, Samantha. Are you hurt bad?"

"Just a flesh wound, Jared. I'll live. But it really, really hurts."

All three took turns carefully hugging Samantha. Josh then turned to Anna, and they embraced firmly.

Josh said, "I thought I would never see you again, Anna. I'm so happy I was wrong."

"I thought the same thing about you when I heard my father tell the Germans to kill you. Josh, keep holding me. I was so scared. I don't know what I would have done without Samantha. She never panicked. She is amazing."

Josh said, "Trust me. I've seen her in action on a nuclear submarine with torpedoes coming at us and just a few seconds away from killing us. She never flinched. I know what you mean."

Jared said, "The hospital said that they would fly everybody directly to Meiringen Air Base in their medical helicopter. There are seven of us. Us five and the two Germans. They have room for all seven. We will turn the German killer clowns over to the CIA guys at Meiringen."

Samantha asked, "What about capturing the Ghost?"

Jared responded, "Harlan got the team ready to go early, and it is descending on the chalet as we speak. He should be in custody in an hour or two."

"I can't believe that this nightmare is just about over. I want to see Ira and the twins so badly."

"But we've got to get your arm taken care of. We'll have a wound specialist fly back with us to the States."

"Where did Josh and Anna go?" asked Samantha.

"I think they went back to Rodrigo's taxi to be alone."

"Interesting," mused Samantha, as she once again grimaced in pain.

PART FOUR

RETRIBUTION

The Defense of Freedom medal

CHAPTER 34
REUNION

ENROUTE TO MEIRINGEN AIR BASE on the medical helicopter, Samantha fell asleep, helped by the strong pain medication injection she was given. At Meiringen, Gunther Kemp and Heinrich Schlosser were turned over to German military police and would face charges of desertion, a serious crime in the German military.

On the flight to the US, Samantha continued to rest comfortably. Jared and Rodrigo also got some needed rest, but Anna and Josh talked intimately during the whole flight to Joint Base Andrews near Washington, DC.

At four thirty that afternoon, they landed at Andrews, and the five, Samantha, Jared, Josh, Rodrigo, and Anna were ushered into a waiting helicopter and flown to Langley, Virginia—home of the CIA.

They were then escorted into a briefing room near the assistant director's office. A light evening meal was provided to them, and they all wolfed the food down. When they finished, Harlan, Matthias Roberts, and Admiral Roger Flaxon walked into the room. Samantha quickly stood up to greet Flaxon, but she fell back into her chair and grimaced in pain. Harlan, Matthias, and Roger rushed over to comfort her.

Through gritted teeth, she said, "I'm sorry guys. I was so glad to see you, I got carried away. I shouldn't have stood up so suddenly. I'll be fine."

Flaxon said, "We have plenty of time for hugs, Samantha. Just take it easy."

Harlan asked, "Do you need another pain shot, Samantha?"

"No. I'd rather not. Not now, anyway. I need to be awake for the debrief."

"If you're sure about this, we can get started," said Harlan.

When everyone was seated, a couple of carafes of coffee were brought in. Harlan began the discussion. "I'm going to be blunt here. No beating around the bush. I hate to say this, but the Ghost got away."

"What!" Samantha yelled. What happened? How did he escape? I thought we had him trapped."

"Calm down, Samantha. Please. Matthias coordinated the raid on the chalet. I'll let him explain what happened."

Matthias stood up and said, "Sorry, Samantha. You did all that we had hoped for and so much more." Matthias paused, then he said, "Much more."

Harlan added, "You've blown us away, Samantha. So have you three," he said, looking at Jared, Josh, and Rodrigo. He continued, "You too, Anna. What you did to help us here, well, I can't begin to show you how much we appreciate it."

Samantha interjected, "This is all well and good, Harlan. But tell us how that insane pervert got away."

Harlan said, "Matthias?"

Matthias stood there with a solemn face. "I coordinated the raid from here. I authorized the raid to begin when you were still at the medical facility near Grindelwald. We had two helicopters in the air and ten agents surrounding the chalet. When we stormed the chalet, Yulov was not in it. We found Irina Rossova in the pool room, both her hands and feet were bound, and she had been shot in the head. Dead, of course. The team thoroughly searched the chalet, but he was nowhere to be found. Our helicopters began searching the area. What we found were cross country ski tracks away from the chalet. We followed the tracks to a lean-to that the Ghost used to shelter and hide a car for a possible escape if he needed it. He had a very short drive to a busy road and escape. And that's it, guys. He escaped."

Flaxon asked, "What do we do now? Samantha's life is still in jeopardy."

"So are the others on his hit list," Samantha added.

Harlan said, "Anna's life is in jeopardy as well. She's not on the hit list, so he could go for her at any time. But let's look at the positive side. Thanks to Samantha and Anna, we have leveled the playing field considerably. We've recovered from his accounts most of the money he stole, and we are now returning that money to Russia."

Samantha said, "But he's probably far from broke, Harlan. Knowing how he thinks, with his multiple ways of escape, he probably has a ton of money stashed away. In his escape car, for example.

Matthias added, "But he doesn't have an unlimited budget available to him now. It'll be a lot tougher for him to stage an elaborate assassination attempt like he has done in the past."

Samantha said, "Look everyone. I'm tired, I'm hurting, and I'm depressed. But even more than that, I want to hold my husband and my two babies in my arms. Sooner rather than later."

Harlan agreed. "We'll helicopter you down to Norfolk, Samantha."

"Can Anna come with me? I want her to meet Ira. And I want to be sure she is safe."

"Of course. Do you agree to go with Samantha, Anna?"

"Absolutely. I wouldn't have it any other way."

Samantha asked, "Harlan, is Jean Barlow still on the payroll?"

"Yes, she is. I think we are still good there."

"Let's keep the knowledge of Anna being with us away from Jean. I have a kernel of an idea of how we can address our next move against the Ghost. But I want to think and pray about it for a while."

"I understand. I'll get the helicopter ready to fly you to Norfolk. Everybody, let's plan on getting together tomorrow afternoon in Norfolk. Admiral, can you make it down there tomorrow?"

"I have a few things on my agenda tomorrow. But I'll see if I can rearrange my schedule. I'd like to be there. Samantha, I hope your idea will be ready for us to consider and discuss. I'll see if I can come up with some ideas of my own."

"I agree." Said Harlan. "Samantha's ideas intrigue me. Let me know, Admiral. Jared, Josh, can you guys make the meeting?"

"Yes, Mr. Bradbury, we can be there."

"Great. Rodrigo, you, and Matthias can fly down there with me. We'll leave here at eleven."

"Yes, Mr. Director," they both said at the same time.

After the short meeting had broken up, Matthias escorted Samantha and Anna to the waiting helicopter, and they were soon enroute to Norfolk Naval Air Station.

"Samantha, I can't believe how much my life has changed in less than a week. A week ago, I was living a carefree life and skiing with people who I thought were my friends. Now, one of them is dead, and the other two will be going to prison. And here I am, flying to Norfolk, Virginia in a CIA helicopter. I can't believe it. It is bizarre."

"Well, it's all true. In less than an hour, you will be hugged by the commander of all the US submarines operating in the Atlantic Ocean and the Mediterranean Sea. My husband."

"Samantha, I am so sorry you were shot and now are in so much pain because you were trying to save me."

"Anna, I love you. How could I have abandoned you and left you behind with that monster of a man?"

"But you could have. You risked your life for me."

"I don't think like that, Anna. The thought of fleeing and leaving you behind never, ever, crossed my mind. We've got a lot of skiing to do together. But first, we must get the Ghost behind bars."

"Samantha, I'm sorry. I never thought about the fact that he might have cross country skis hidden somewhere or that he had another car hidden for him to escape with. I'm sorry."

"Don't be, Anna. This man has been one step ahead of us for a long time. As Harlan once said, 'he's as slippery as an eel.'"

Thirty minutes later, the helicopter landed at the Norfolk Naval Air Station. When the doors were opened, Samantha saw Ira holding one of the twins and Big John holding the other.

Samantha yelled, "Ira! I love you!" She gingerly climbed down the short step ladder that had been placed outside the helicopter door, and she ran to Ira. He handed Roman to Big John and softly embraced Samantha, being careful to not put pressure on her slinged arm.

"To hell with the arm, Ira. Squeeze me. I ache to feel you against me."

"Sam, I worried I'd never see you again alive. I'm so happy right now, I can't describe it. Sam, are you crying? Outside of the time I told you that Simon Prather had been murdered, I've never seen you cry before."

"I guess I am, Ira. But these are tears of joy." She turned to the big man standing next to Ira and said, "Hi, Big John. Good to see you. I'll hug you later. I have to hold my babies first."

Despite having her arm in a sling, Samantha was able to take both the twins from Big John and cradle them lovingly. She then kissed Big John on the cheek, and he grinned from ear to ear.

When Samantha had kissed her two babies, she turned to

Anna who was patiently waiting a few feet away. "Anna, this very large teddy bear here is a dear friend of mine. You can call him Big John."

They smiled at each other, and Big John bowed his head slightly to Anna and said, "Glad to meet you, Anna. It's an honor."

"Likewise, Big John."

"Anna, this is the love of my life, Ira Coen. Ira, this is Anna.

They approached one another and hugged tightly for a long time.

Ira said, "I'm so sorry how your life has changed. You must be in shock."

"I am, sir. But I've had Samantha come into my life, and because of that, it all has been worthwhile. But you are right, I am in shock, but I am happy."

Samantha gave Roman and Paula back to Ira, and said to Big John, "Come here, big guy. But please, watch my arm."

She hugged Big John and said, "Thank you for taking care of Ira for me while I was gone."

"Thank you, Samantha. It's only been a week, but I've died every minute of that week worrying about you. So has the admiral."

"Well, I'm back, and we've got a Ghost to catch."

CHAPTER 35
DINNER AT IRA'S

THAT NIGHT, IRA HAD A great meal catered by the base Officer's Club at his quarters. Enjoying the festivities were Ira, Samantha, Anna, Jack and Jill Hill, Big John, and a new security agent, Joe Pinto. Joe was an expert martial artist, and he had been instructed to further Samantha's considerable skills of self-defense. Samantha laughed at this name of self-defense because most of her training involved how to kill her adversary. Also sitting at the table was Dr. Larry "Gunner" Gunn, who had nursed Samantha back to health from her arrow chest wound and her backside abrasions. Dr. Gunn had requested to be assigned to treat Samantha's gunshot wound.

During the joyous evening, no one mentioned the fact that the Ghost was still at large and was almost certainly planning another assassination attempt on Samantha's life.

Anna, who didn't stop laughing all night, announced at one point, "My life has really changed in just a few days, but I've got to say this, I've never felt more welcomed in my whole life. I couldn't be happier than I am right now. I want to thank you all from the bottom of my heart." After she said this, each one there took a turn giving Anna a hug and a kiss on the cheek.

At about ten o'clock, Ira's phone buzzed, and he answered it.

"Oh, hi. Yes. She's here. I'll get her. It's for you, Samantha. It's for you," he repeated as he handed her the phone.

"Who is it?" she silently mouthed as she took the phone. Ira smiled and shrugged his shoulders.

"Hello?" she asked.

Her eyes widened considerably.

"James!" she exclaimed. "Why are you calling me and at this hour?"

James Milsap, president of the United States said, "Welcome home, Samantha. I want to thank you for a job well done."

"But James, we failed to get the job done."

"True. But not through any fault of yours. You performed your part with perfection."

"Well, thank you. But I feel that I should have figured out he had cross country skis hidden somewhere. That doesn't sound like perfection to me."

"Samantha, trust me. I don't know of anybody else who could have done the job as well as you."

"Thank you, James."

"Harlan tells me that you were wounded in the line of duty?"

"Yes, I caught a stray shot when I was in the cockpit. It's only a flesh wound in my upper arm. It will heal. No big deal."

"From what Harlan tells me, you were shot in battle trying to save the life of a civilian you were trying to protect. I can't award you the Purple Heart medal, which is for uniformed military personnel, but I can present your case to congress to award you the Defense of Freedom medal. That's the civilian equivalent to the Purple Heart."

"Oh, James. Don't be silly. I don't deserve that."

"Case closed, Samantha. The request goes to congress tomorrow. I expect a quick approval."

"James, don't embarrass me like that. Please."

Milsap ignored Samantha's plea. He asked, "Is that person

whose life you saved available? I'd like to talk to her."

Everyone there had been listening to Samantha during the call wondering who she was talking to. Ira sat there with a huge, knowing smile on his face. Samantha pointed to Anna and held the phone out to her. Anna crunched up her shoulders and her eyebrows, pointed to herself, and softly asked, "Me?"

Samantha nodded and handed the phone to Anna.

As Anna took the phone, she gave Samantha a questioning look. Samantha just smiled.

"Hello? Hello? Is this James?"

"Hi, Anna. This is James Milsap. How are you doing tonight?"

"James Milsap? President of the United States?"

"One and the same, Anna. How are you?"

"Mr. President. I don't know what to say?"

"I'll take that as you are doing fine. I just wanted to thank you for helping Samantha the way you did. What you did was brave, and I know it took great courage on your part. If the world had more people like you, it would be a far better place to live."

"My God, Mr. President. I'm at a loss for words."

"Look, Anna, I want to assure you that all your needs will be taken care of by the people of the United States. I will make sure that you will have a productive and rewarding life in your new country."

"Mr. President, I don't know what to say but thank you."

"Bye, Anna. Nice talking to you. Hopefully, we can meet soon so I can thank you in person and give you a hug. Bye now."

Anna stood there with her mouth agape, just holding the phone in her hand. She finally said, "I just talked to the president of the United States."

Samantha took the phone from her hands and said, "What did he say?"

"I don't know. I don't know what he said. Oh my God. I just made a fool of myself to the president."

CHAPTER 36
"YOU FLEW A HELICOPTER?"

THE NEXT AFTERNOON, THE GROUP began to convene in a secure meeting room at COMSUBLANT, Ira's headquarters. The last ones to arrive were Harlan, Matthias, and Rodrigo. Admiral Roger Flaxon had notified Ira earlier that morning that he couldn't arrive in Norfolk until later that afternoon. When all were settled in, Harlan asked Ira, "Well, how was your night last night? Did you sleep well?"

Samantha and Ira smiled at each other lasciviously. Ira said, "We had a great night. We didn't get much sleep, however."

Samantha added, "Yeah, it was great. But it was pretty hard on my arm," they both looked at each other again and smiled.

"That's not what I meant, you two. Too much information."

Anna chimed in, "I heard them. They were trying to make another set of twins."

Harlan said, "I'm serious here. We've got some important decisions to make, and you guys are clowning around."

Anna said, "From what I heard, I wouldn't call it clowning around."

Everyone in the room laughed except Harlan.

"Enough of this! Let's get started," Harlan said in exasperation. He continued, "Let's start at the chalet. What can we learn from that? Samantha? Anna?"

Samantha began with a recount of what happened with Irina in the pool room. She then described the events in the hangar, the shootout with the Ghost, and the difficulty she had trying to keep the helicopter in the air.

Ira interrupted her at this point. "Wait a minute. Wait a minute here. Are you trying to tell me that you were flying the helicopter? Nobody told me this. Harlan?"

Harlan looked at Ira with a grin on his face. "Surprise, surprise, Ira. Yes, she flew the helicopter to safety."

"How . . . how in God's name did you know how to fly a helicopter? And don't tell me you were the president of the helicopter flying club in high school."

"As a matter of fact, I was, Ira."

"Get serious. There is no such thing as a helicopter flying club in a high school. How did you do such a thing?"

"Okay, Ira. Don't burst a blood vessel. Harlan sent me several videos on how to fly the make and model of the helicopter the Ghost had in his hangar."

"You learned to fly a helicopter by watching a few videos?" Ira asked with disbelief in his voice. "That is not possible! No one can do that!"

"I guess I did. But believe me. It wasn't easy. I almost killed Anna and me a few times."

Ira shook his head with his mouth agape as he stared at Samantha. He took a deep breath and asked, "How did you get shot? Can you tell me that? You're probably going to tell me that you were the president of the how-to-get-shot club in high school."

"Oh, Ira. Here's how it went. The Ghost put several shots through the chopper windows. One of them, or maybe a ricochet, got me in the arm."

"And with a bleeding and painful wound, you flew the helicopter from the chalet to Grindelwald? Without crashing?"

"I don't remember much of that part. But apparently, I did.

The whole thing is very foggy in my mind."

Anna interjected, "Let me add this. She landed the helicopter at the chalet so I could shoot out the tires of the cars the Ghost could have used to escape."

"Samantha, you continually amaze me," said Ira.

Harlan said, "Amazing isn't the word for it. Anything else? Anna?"

"No. Nothing, Mr. Bradbury. We are just lucky to be alive."

"Jared, Josh, Rodrigo? Any lessons learned? Anything at all with you dealing with the Germans?"

Josh said, "I agree with Anna. We escaped by the skin of our teeth. If Anna hadn't been able to free herself from her binds and call us to warn us, we'd probably all be dead right now."

"Thank God for that. Okay, we are here now and alive. How do we keep Samantha and Anna that way? Any ideas of which direction we should go?"

No one said anything for several seconds. Finally, Samantha broke the silence. "I said yesterday that I had a kernel of an idea of something we could try. I wanted to pray and sleep on it and give it some more thought. We've already established that Ira and I didn't get much sleep last night. But despite that, I have thought about my idea a little more." She looked at Ira and grinned. Harlan rolled his eyes and shook his head several times.

"What's your idea, Samantha?" he asked with exasperation.

Okay, seriously. Here is a basic idea of what I am thinking. There are a lot of problems and holes that will have to be identified, considered, and taken care of if it will work. If Jean Barlow's role as a conduit of information to the Ghost is still workable, we can feed him information through her and perhaps lure him into a trap. In my mind, a big *if* is this: the Ghost is smart and very perceptive. He may not have faith in Jean anymore."

"True," said Matthias. "He didn't get true information from her on the Bar Harbor relocation."

Harlan said, "Okay, let's assume that Yulov can still trust Jean. What do we do?"

"First of all, we have to convince Jean that Anna is still loyal to her father. If we can do this convincingly, Jean could pass this on to Yulov, and he may try to use Anna to get more information to him through Jean on how we are going to trap him."

"Hold on. I have a question," said Ira. "How can we convince Jean that Anna is still loyal to her father? Didn't you tell us that Anna shot at him during the escape? Why would she have done that if she still believes in him?"

"Good point, Ira," said Anna. "I did try to hit him. I'm pretty sure he knows that it was me shooting at him."

Samantha responded, "We've got to come up with some convincing stories to make this work. I know that."

Rodrigo chimed in, "Even if we convince the Ghost that Anna is loyal to him, wouldn't he be taking a huge chance by reaching out to Anna through Jean? After all, Jean is his mole in place already. He'd be putting his source, Jean, in jeopardy."

Samantha replied, "That's a very good point, Rod. But that's a chance we need to take. But here's where I'm coming from. I'm starting to think like he thinks. Strange as that may seem. But I believe that he still loves his daughter, even though he wants to kill her because he feels she betrayed him. If we can convince him that she never really wanted to betray him, he will want to get her back. Remember, his ego is as big as Mt. Everest. I believe that he will try to use Anna to know what our plan is to capture him. He will think that by knowing our plan, he can defeat it, kill me, and get his daughter back all at the same time. If he can do this, he can laugh at us till the cows come home. I think that this would be a challenge that is impossible for him to resist."

"I don't know," said Harlan. "This seems like a longshot to me. Too many *ifs*."

"I agree with you, Harlan. But that's the idea I came up with.

If anyone has a better idea, now is the time to put it on the table."

Josh said, "What about you, Anna? Are you comfortable with Samantha's plan? Do you think that you could fool your father into believing that you are still on his side?"

"I don't know. I guess it depends on the plan we come up with."

"Samantha?" Matthias asked.

"I have some ideas. Let me think about it a little more. The plan we come up with to capture him is critical if this is going to work."

Jared stated, "Okay. We fool Jean into believing that Anna wants her father back. Jean then convinces the Ghost that Anna will work for him. He buys this, and he tells Jean to contact Anna and solicit her help. How do we cause this to happen? Jean contacting Anna."

Anna said, "I'm sure that we can improvise something where Jean and I can be alone. I can tear up a bit, and maybe she'll confide in me that she might be able to help. Once we do that, our communication channel is opened. We're in."

"We'll have to set up something where it looks like we think Anna is working with us, and we don't suspect that she isn't. If we can do this, it should be fairly simple then to create some alone time between Anna and Jean."

Harlan said, "I don't know how all this is going to come together. Like I said a few minutes ago, too many *ifs*. But again, I've seen several times before where Samantha's hare-brained schemes have, somehow, paid off. If we go along with this idea, I want you all to be on your toes to notice if anything is going wrong. Remember who we are dealing with here. This guy has been outsmarting us since the very beginning. He's smart, perceptive, clever, and insane. We don't know what he will do. I want everybody here to think about Samantha's plan. Let's reconvene here tomorrow afternoon so we can start putting meat on the bones of the plan that Samantha has outlined. Anything else before we end this meeting? No? Okay, tomorrow here at two o'clock. Samantha, your idea. You lead the meeting. And no *clowning around*," Harlan said with a little grin on his face as he tried to interject some uncharacteristic humor. Everyone just looked at him with serious expressions on their faces.

That evening, Samantha and Ira were in bed. When they had finished "clowning around" and trying to make another set of twins, Ira said, "Sam, I have to agree with Harlan. Your idea must have a lot of things go right if it has any chance of working."

"I agree with that, Ira. But like I said, I think that I have a fairly good idea of what makes this butthole think. The big *if* to me is whether the Ghost really loves his daughter. I mean, he wanted to kill Anna when he felt she had betrayed him. How could he do that to his only daughter? Especially one that he cares for or loves? But I keep thinking that he took her with him when he fled Russia. My God, he had just killed his wife. He could simply have left Anna behind. By taking her, he made his escape and new life so much more difficult. Then he sets her up in a skiing mecca because he knows she has a passion for skiing. And there is one other small thing that tells me that he has a lot of affection for her. He calls her *sweetie*. As a father, would you call your daughter something like that if you didn't love her in some way?"

"Probably not."

"On top of all this, he hires three people to protect her. Why would he do all those things if he didn't love her?"

Ira nodded his head in agreement. He thought a bit and said, "All you are saying is true, Sam. But the part of hiring three people to protect her could have an entirely different reason. He could have been trying to protect himself in case she was found out. Found out by somebody like us."

"That's true, Ira. But I just feel that all the other reasons I gave outweigh the point you just made. Also, the size of that man's ego cannot be overstated. He is a narcissistic egomaniac. We are just small pieces in an elaborate game to him, game pieces that he can manipulate as he so chooses. That's how he thinks."

"One thing you're forgetting, Sam. You have gotten the best of him four times now. The three assassination attempts and the chalet encounter. He probably hates you more than you can ever imagine."

"Ira, his hatred toward me is exactly what I am counting on."

After a long pause, Ira said, "Sam, please don't put yourself in harm's way again. I don't think my heart could survive another adventure like the ones you've put me through. Please don't."

"Ira, that's just so sweet. I love you so much."

"I love you too, Sam."

After they finished a very passionate kiss, Samantha said, "Ira, I have a feeling that our last attempt to make another set of twins didn't work. Are you ready to give it another try?"

"Sam, I thought you'd never ask."

CHAPTER 37
THE PLAN BEGINS

WHEN THE EIGHT WERE COMFORTABLY seated and drinking their coffee, Harlan stood up and announced, "Okay, everyone. Let's get started. As I said yesterday, since this is Samantha's idea, I think it is only right that she leads the meeting. Samantha, you've got the floor."

"Thanks, Harlan. But before we begin, I'd like to open in prayer."

But before she could begin, Admiral Roger Flaxon entered the room.

"Sorry everyone. Things kept coming up in DC, and I kept getting sidetracked putting out fires. Just go ahead. I'll try to catch up as we go."

"Hey, Roger. We haven't started yet. We were just about to open with a prayer. Would you accept the honor of leading us?"

"Samantha, it would be my joy to do so."

"Thank you, Roger."

Flaxon closed his eyes and bowed his head. He began, "Father in heaven. We thank you for the gift of this day. We thank you for this team of dedicated men and women you have put together to deal with this man who is possessed by demons so evil, we can't even imagine. Give us the wisdom and discernment to deal with this spawn of Satan. We know that we cannot deal with him on our own. We need you to guide us and show us the way so we will be able to carry the day. I know that all of us here thank you from the bottom of our hearts for all you do for us. We thank you and ask you for help in the name of your precious Son, our Savior and Lord, Jesus Christ." A chorus of amens followed.

Samantha said, "Thank you, Admiral. Well said. Let's begin. I think that the first order of business is how do we convince Jean that Anna is still aligned with and is sympathetic to her father. Any suggestions?"

Anna offered, "We could put on a charade for Jean. Make her think that you guys are trying to milk me for information on my dad. Information that you could use to capture him."

"Sounds good," said Matthias.

Rodrigo offered, "We could bring in a make-up artist to give Anna a look that we are mistreating her. You know, black eyes, bruises. Things like that."

"Also, I could look very tired and worn out."

"And very unhappy" added Josh.

Samantha said, "All good ideas. I think we should bring Jean in on what we are doing to Anna. Give her our intentions of getting Anna to talk against her father. I mean, we have to let her know eventually what our plans are so she can pass the information to the Ghost."

For the next two hours, the group offered suggestions as to how they could convince Jean that Anna felt that she was in a bad situation and wanted out.

Samantha eventually said, "Look. I think that we've got enough ideas on how to address this question. It's almost five o'clock. Let's reconvene tomorrow at nine o'clock and start talking about how we can get Jean and Anna working together to feed information to the Ghost. Once we've done that, we need to determine what our plan is to capture the Ghost and what information to feed to him so that he'll fall into our trap. Is there anything we should discuss before we break up for the day?"

No one raised an issue. "Okay, let me close in prayer, and we'll all get together tomorrow morning at nine."

When Samantha finished the prayer and was leaving the room, she noticed that Anna and Josh were talking intimately. They then cornered Harlan and began talking to him. Harlan nodded, took out his phone, and made a call.

Samantha smiled and said to Ira, "I think they want some alone time together, and they just asked Harlan if he could set up some safety precautions for them."

Ira responded, "I'm sure you are right, Sam." Then he added, "What do you say? Some clowning around for us tonight?"

"Why of course. I thought—"

"Don't say it, Sam. Don't say it."

They both laughed as they left the room holding hands.

The next two days were spent developing Samantha's plan. Samantha closed the final meeting with an announcement, "Okay, we all know the plan and what we have to do. We start tomorrow morning in Harlan's office. Any final questions or concerns? If there are, please bring them up now."

No one responded.

"Good. May the Lord be with us on this."

The next morning, Harlan walked into his outer office at eight o'clock.

"Jean, can you come into my office for a few minutes?"

"Yes, Harlan. Right away. What's going on?"

"I have to bring you up to speed as to what's been going on since Samantha and the boys got back from Switzerland."

"I'll be right in."

When Jean entered Harlan's office, he said, "Have a seat. Hopefully, this won't take very long."

When she was comfortably seated, Harlan said, "Jean, what

we discuss here today is to be held very close. Do you understand?"

"Yes, sir. I do."

"Good. As you know, our trap for the Ghost in Switzerland didn't work. He managed to escape again. You also know that we captured his daughter during the operation, and that Samantha was wounded in the left arm during their escape. By the way, she is recovering nicely from the wound."

"That's good to hear, Harlan."

"What you don't know, is that we thought we had convinced Anna that her father was a murderous psychopathic madman. We thought that we could use her to provide information on Yulov that we could use to lure him into a trap. Unfortunately, we were wrong."

"What do you mean?"

"She's clammed up. Changed her mind. Won't tell us anything of value. She maintains that she thought her life was in danger both from us and from her father. During the escape, she made the decision to feign helping us to buy her more time. She also had decided that we may have been the lesser of the two evils she faced."

"You mean that she thought her life was in greater danger from her father than from us?"

"Exactly. However, she's had a change of heart and refuses to cooperate with us. She's being very obstinate in not giving us anything useful. So, I'm giving you all this information because we are going to put the screws to her, and we are going to up the pressure and means of getting her to open up."

"Why don't you give her more evidence on who her father really is?"

"We've tried that, but she won't budge."

"What do you want me to do?"

"As I said earlier, keep everything you see or hear to yourself. Right now, we have been keeping her under house arrest at a safe house in Virginia Beach. Matthias and Joe Pinto have been her primary guards. Samantha has continued to try to give her confidence in us. You know, promise of a good life here in the States, a new identity, a job, stuff like that. But Anna just won't buy any of it. And I've got to tell you, Samantha's starting to get tired of trying to be friendly with Anna."

Jean nodded her head in understanding. She then said, "So, what's next?"

"Matthias and Joe are bringing Anna over here in a little bit. I'm going to play the Director of the CIA card and try to convince her that Samantha's proposal of a good life here is for real."

"What if she doesn't come around?"

"We go to plan B and up the pressure."

Jean then said, "Harlan, is it worth all of this? I mean, what could we get from her that would be of value?"

"That's a good question, Jean. But right now, she's all we've got. The Ghost is still the aggressor. We can't find him, and we are waiting for him to fire the next shot. He might not miss the next time, and Samantha will be history. Then it will be Bryan Boxer, and so on. Don't forget, I'm number thirteen, and I probably won't be the CIA director in a few months when the new president takes office. He's probably going to replace me. That's what new administrations do. And when that happens, I'll be more vulnerable then."

"You are right, Harlan. We have to get this guy."

Harlan thought, *And to think that I've trusted this woman for so many years. A friend of the family.*

At nine o'clock, Matthias escorted Anna into Jean's office. Joe Pinto was with them and remained outside the office guarding the door.

"Jean, tell Harlan I have Anna here to see him."

Jean announced to Harlan that Anna was here. He opened the door to his office and said in a very jovial tone, "Hi, Anna.

Come on in. It's great to see you. Coffee? Tea?"

Anna shook her head and silently went into Harlan's office.

Matthias remained in Jean's office and said, "Has Harlan briefed you on what's going on with Anna?"

"Yes, he has."

"I certainly hope this works and she comes around. She really seems like a nice girl, and I hate to be the one that has to be the brute with her."

After fifteen minutes of relative silence in Harlan's office, his voice elevated into what seemed like a yell. A few minutes later, his door opened, and he gently pushed Anna through the doorway. He said in a gruff voice, "Matthias, get her out of here, and take her back to the safe house. I'm through being nice. I want to talk to Samantha. Have Pinto drive Samantha back here when you have this woman secure."

"Yes, Mr. Bradbury." Matthias looked sadly at Jean as he escorted Anna out of her office.

The next day, Matthias again brought Anna into Jean's office. Only this time, he was less than gentle with her. He pushed rather than guided. When Jean looked at Anna's face, she gasped. One of her eyes was black, and she had red abrasions on both sides of her face. It also was clear that Anna had been crying. Her hair was badly disheveled and not in place as it had been a day earlier. Jean also noticed that Anna seemed very tired, as she shuffled her feet into Harlan's office. Pinto again stood guard outside Jean's office, and Matthias remained with Jean. He took a deep breath and shook his head sadly at Jean.

Five minutes later, Harlan brusquely pushed Anna out of his office and ordered her to sit down. He instructed Matthias to have Joe Pinto keep a watch on Anna, and he asked Matthias to come into his office. When Matthias was with Harlan, Anna looked directly into Jean's eyes. Joe was looking through the large glass window directly at Anna. Joe's phone chimed, and when he answered it, he looked away from Anna. Anna then looked at Jean and mouthed the words, "Help me. Help me, please." Jean just stared back at Anna deep in thought. She then nodded her head and softly said, "I'll try. What can I do?" When Joe had finished with his call, he once again began his vigil of Anna.

CHAPTER 38
CODED MESSAGES

"WELL, DO YOU THINK IT worked?" Samantha asked.

"We'll know when the Ghost and Jean talk. But their calls almost always last less than a minute. We can't trace them. Plus, the conversation is encrypted, and we only hear parts of what they are saying anyway. This guy has some very sophisticated technology at his disposal. Hopefully, we will be able to decipher the pieces in a day or two. The National Security Agency is working on it."

Anna said, "Jean really looked shocked when she saw my face. I think that she really believes that Matthias is getting rough with me."

"I hope so. It's critical that she believes that." Samantha looked at Harlan, Ira, Matthias, Joe, and Rodriguez and said, "Last night, Anna shared something with me that might help our plan. Anna, tell them what you told me."

"Sure. At the chalet, my dad used something that jiggled my memory banks. He set the lock combinations backward of what is normally used. It brought back memories of a game we used to play together when I was a young girl. When we were at a shopping mall, for example, my dad would say the name of some store backward, and I would try to find the store and say the name correctly. Well, we both got pretty good at this. My name was Voluy Anna, and his name was Voluy Notna. We got so good at this that we used to talk to each other backward. This would drive my mom nuts. I can still do it pretty well. Test me. Say a word or two to me. I'll say it backward."

Matthias said, "Yellow."

"Wolley."

Rodriguez said, "Rodriguez Ortiz."

"Zitro Zeugirdor."

Joe said, "Today is good."

"Doog si yadot," Anna fired back.

Samantha said, "Amazing, huh?"

Anna said, "Huh, gnizama."

"That's enough, Anna. We get the point. Quit showing off. Anyway, Anna and I think that this secret code might further convince Voluy, I mean Yulov, that Anna is really reaching out to him. What do you guys think?"

Ira said, "Seems a little hokie to me. But it could add a little intimacy between the two."

"That's what I think, Ira. I say we go with it."

"Fine by me," said Joe.

Matthias asked, "What are we going to tell him?"

"Anna and I are working on that now. Hopefully, tomorrow, Jean will tell Anna that she will try to help her. We've got a few schemes to try to get Anna and Jean alone so Anna can pass her a note. We'll put a few more bruises on Anna and make her look even more pathetic."

Anna said, "Josh is coming over for a little bit in about an hour. Can we be alone for a while?"

Samantha asked, "What's going on between you two? Something you want to tell us?"

"Josh is so cute. He's got a killer bod. His personality is amazing. He loves to ski. He's single. What's not to like? Joe, if you were a girl, you'd go after Josh, wouldn't you?"

"Whoa. Wait a minute. What kind of a loaded question is that?"

Samantha laughed and said, "Of course, we will let you guys be. But we don't want to hear you guys clowning around."

Everybody laughed. Even Anna.

The next morning in Harlan's office, an even more bruised up Anna was ushered into his office so that he could again try to reason with her. After thirty minutes, Harlan and Anna emerged from his office. He said, "Matthias, stay with Anna. Jean, come into my office for a minute."

When Jean went in, Harlan closed the door and said, "Anna has to go to the bathroom. I can't let her be alone, so I need for you to go with her. Matthias will escort the two of you there and remain outside the restroom. Watch Anna closely. Make sure she doesn't do anything unusual. If you are in there more than three minutes, I have authorized Matthias to go in and get you both out. I've told Anna this as well. Any questions?"

"No. I'll take care of it."

"Good."

When they reached the ladies room, Matthias said, "Three minutes. Understand?"

Both nodded their heads.

Once inside, Anna whispered, "Please help me, Jean. Matthias is hurting me. He's also told me that Pinto is a martial arts expert and can inflict pain much more than he can and not leave any visible signs when he's through. I can't take it anymore," she pleaded.

Jean said, "Why don't you cooperate with them? They can set you up pretty good anywhere in the States that you choose."

"I don't believe them, Jean. Plus, I'm afraid of my father. He will find me. My only chance is to convince my dad that I won't betray him, and that he will try to rescue me. I'm in a bind, Jean. What can I do? I'm caught between my father and the CIA."

Jean thought for a few seconds, then said, "I think I may be able to help you. I may be able to get word to your father that you need his help."

"You can do that? How?"

"When you work for the director of the CIA, you learn things. Things I can't talk about."

"Jean, you'd do this for me? I can't thank you enough."

"Anna, understand this, I can't guarantee you anything, but I'll try."

"Listen, we don't have much time." Anna said. "Tomorrow, I will pass you a note that will be in a special code. Relay the note to my dad or transcribe it exactly as I have written it and pass it to him. I will print it, so you won't make a mistake."

"Okay, I'll try."

"Jean, our three minutes are up. I'll figure out how to pass you the note. Thank you so much."

When they left the ladies room, Matthias said, "I was just about to go in there and get you."

Jean said, "Matthias, it takes a woman at least three minutes to pee, and unlike you men, we wash our hands. Give her a break."

Matthias just stared at Jean.

CHAPTER 39
ANNA AND JEAN TALK

THE NEXT MORNING, HARLAN ASKED Jean to come into his office.

"What's up, Harlan?"

"Jean, plan B isn't working with the Yulov girl. We've threatened her that we are going to let Joe Pinto take over for Matthias. But our threats are not working. She's a brave and stubborn girl. I actually admire her."

"What are you going to do?"

"Matthias and I have come up with a plan C, and it involves you."

"What is it?"

"Jean, you are my secretary, and what I'm going to ask you to do is not in your job description. You can refuse if you want to."

"Tell me."

"Threats and strongarm tactics are not working with her. We still feel offering her a good life and protection from her father is the best way to go. However, Samantha's attempts and my feeble try at this have failed. We believe that Anna is really scared. Scared of both her father and us. As far as she is concerned, we are both the enemy. Maybe if she heard our friendly case from you, she might be convinced."

"You want me to tell her that our offer is the best choice for her?"

"Exactly. You are a woman, not a CIA agent, and she may listen to you."

"But Samantha's a woman, and Anna won't listen to her."

"But to Anna, Samantha's a CIA spy. You are not. Look, Jean. It's worth a try."

"Okay, I'll do it. But how?"

"Today and tonight, we are going to ease up on her. Fix her up a lot so she doesn't look so mistreated. Have her hair done. Let her get a good night's sleep. Make it look like we are giving her more freedom."

"I don't think that she'll be fooled by all that."

"Probably not. But, as part of this nice-guy routine, we are going to allow her to have lunch with you in the cafeteria. That will be your chance to show her sympathy and, hopefully, to gain her trust. Convince her that we will keep her safe from her father. Tell her that, as part of your job of being my secretary, you have heard things about her father that makes your skin crawl. Tell her that also in your job, you have seen witness protection work all the time. Can you do that? Can you be convincing?"

"I don't know, Harlan. But I can give it a try."

The next day, Anna and Jean sat in the cafeteria eating their lunch. Anna said, "Jean, all this act of being nice to me is a lot of crap. I don't buy any of it."

"You are right. Harlan asked me to talk to you to convince you that if you cooperate with us, we can protect you from your father."

"Because of the way they've treated me, as far as I'm concerned, my father is my best hope."

"Do you still want me to try to get word from you to your father?"

"Yes, I do."

"What do you want me to say?"

"Drop your napkin onto the floor from the side of the table. I will pick it up for you and put a note in it. Get what's on the note to my father if you can."

"I'll do my best. I'll let you know how it goes tomorrow."

"Thanks, Jean. I'll never be able to repay you."

"That won't be necessary. Just remember, I am not guaranteeing that I can do this for you. I think I can, but I'm not sure."

"I understand. I thank you for trying."

CHAPTER 40
MANO A MANO

THAT EVENING, ANTON YULOV HUNG up the phone and looked at the cryptic message he had just received from Jean.

> EITEEWS, EVOL
>
> ?OD OT EM TNAW UOY OD TAHW. UOY PART MEHT PLEH OT EM TNAW YEHT. ESAELP EM PLEH, YDDAD

He read aloud the coded note. "Daddy, help me please. They want me to help them trap you. What do you want me to do? Love, Sweetie."

He thought, *They must think that I'm a total fool to believe that I could fall for something like this. Amateurs.*

Later that evening, Jean looked at the response from the Ghost.

> YDDAD, EVOL
>
> .NOOS UOY EUCSER LLIW I. THGIN TA SNOITATS RIEHT ?UOY DRAUG STNEGA YNAM WOH. ESU YEHT RAC FO RAEY DNA, ROLOC, LEDOM, EKAM. ESUOH EFAS FO SSERDDA DEEN I. EITEEWS

At lunch the next day, Jean secretly passed the Ghost's note to Anna. "What does all that mean, Anna?"

"Don't worry about it, Jean. It's a game my dad and I used to play. Just being able to contact him has made me feel so much better. My captors and I even played cards last night. All four of us. I'm not buying this goody, goody treatment. It'll probably turn to torture again soon. Or worse."

"What do you mean, Anna . . . or worse?"

"Jean, I'm afraid they may make me disappear. Permanently."

"My God, Anna. You're not serious, are you?"

"Hey, they are CIA, remember? I'm the daughter of a Russian assassin. Of course, I'm serious."

That evening at the safe house, Anna read the note to the others.

> SWEETIE, I NEED ADDRESS OF SAFE HOUSE. MAKE, MODEL, COLOR, AND YEAR OF CAR THEY USE. HOW MANY AGENTS GUARD YOU? THEIR STATIONS AT NIGHT. I WILL RESCUE YOU SOON. LOVE, DADDY

Samantha said, "He bit. We might have him."

Matthias said, "Well, let's give him what he wants. We'll be ready for him."

Samantha added, "There's something that bothers me about the Ghost's request for information."

"What's that, Samantha?"

"If we were truly holding Anna against her will, would we let her know the address of the safe house?"

"Hmmm. Good thought," said Josh.

"What do you think, Harlan?" asked Ira.

"Could go either way. I don't know."

Samantha added, "Why don't we leak the address to Jean and let her pass it to Yulov instead of Anna?"

Harlan asked, "Does anybody have a problem with that approach?"

Anna said, "I like it. That's the way I think we should go."

"Done," said Harlan.

Admiral Flaxon, who had joined the group at the safe house said, "Don't forget who we are dealing with here. We must not underestimate him."

Ira, who also was there said, "I don't want to put Samantha in any danger here. Or Anna. Are we sure that when he shows up, we'll capture him?"

"Look, Ira. We are never sure that these kinds of things will go as planned. Look what happened at the chalet. But we will have plenty of backup. We want to capture him alive, but we will kill him if we must. Samantha and Anna will be safe."

"I hope and pray that you are right, Harlan. God, I hope you are right."

That evening, Jean carefully spelled out Anna's message to Yulov. Before Yulov hung up the phone, he said to Jean, "Expect a call back from me later tonight."

Yulov read Anna's note and said to himself "Time to get busy. Four will die before this week is over. Such fun."

Just before midnight, Yulov called Jean and said, "Pass this on to my daughter."

.THGIN YADRUTAS

The next evening at the safe house, Anna said, "Saturday night."

Ira said, "That's three days from now. Will we be ready?"

Harlan answered, "Yes, we will. We will get him. Anna, are you okay with this? Your father could be killed if things don't go right."

Anna responded, "He killed my mother, my fiancée, and he wanted to kill me. I have no feelings for him except loathing."

The next day, Friday, Anna and Jean were having lunch in the cafeteria. Anna said, "Jean, I want to thank you so much for helping me."

"I'm just glad I could help. You looked so tortured. I felt sorry for you. But I have to ask you something in return."

"What's that, Jean? I'll certainly help you in any way I can."

"Please don't ever tell anyone what I have done here. It would cost me my job—or worse."

"Jean, I'll take care of you. Don't you worry."

When they were back at Jean's office, Harlan asked Anna

what she wanted to eat this evening. Anna responded, "Same as the other day. Pizza will be great."

Matthias said, "Joe, Anna wants pizza for tonight. Can you take care of that? Mr. Bradbury wants to see me and Anna in his office for a minute."

"Sure, Matthias."

When Matthias and Anna went into Harlan's office, Joe took out his phone and made a call.

"Domino's Pizza? I'd like to order two large pizzas for delivery at six o'clock tonight. One is a Hawaiian special, and the other is the Meat Lover's with a thin crust." After a pause, Joe said, "Yes, that's right. The name is Joe, and the address is 519 Twenty-Fourth Street in Virginia Beach."

Joe gave his credit card information. And he noticed that Jean was writing something down.

At mid-Friday afternoon, Jean passed the address to Yulov. When he hung up, he thought, *D-day. Time to take care of business so I can finally get to Master Chief Bryan Boxer.*

At five o'clock, Jean Barlow parked her car in her garage. When she got out of her car, she turned around and found herself standing face-to-face with the Ghost. "Who are you?" she asked with great fear in her voice, half-knowing who this man must be.

"We've never met in person, Ms. Barlow. But I'm sure you recognize my voice."

Jean screamed in terror. She continued to scream as Yulov tied her to the steering wheel, lowered the car windows, and started the car in the closed garage.

He said, "I've lost faith in you, my dear. You've been a big help to me, but I can't depend on you anymore. Sweet dreams."

When the Ghost was in his car, he thought, *Well, that's done.*

Now a relaxing three-hour drive to Virginia Beach, and I can finish my business for the evening. One down, three to go. I love my life.

At eleven o'clock that night, the Ghost watched two CIA agents relieve Joe Pinto of his duty of guarding Anna at the outside of the safe house. *Amateurs.* Yulov thought. *Did they really believe that I would think that the safe house address they gave me was the actual one they'd be staying at? It was so easy to follow their car to see where they really were staying. Well, Pinto, I'll take care of you later tonight when I'm finished with my fun here.*

Yulov avoided being seen by the relieving agents by parking on a side street and sneaking through a neighbor's backyard. He hugged the side of the safe house and made his way to the garage located on the side of the house and away from the street. He easily picked the lock to the garage's side door. Once in the garage, it was an easy matter to enter the house itself. He listened carefully for several minutes to be sure there was no one walking around. When he heard nothing, he quietly went down the hall to the bedrooms. He looked into the first bedroom and saw Samantha asleep. He quietly walked up to the bed, looked down at her, and saw that she was breathing deeply. He thought, *You look so peaceful, my dear. Just like you did when I was in your house the night before your wedding anniversary. You woke up the next morning then, but tomorrow morning you won't. I'll be back to see you in a few minutes.* He then went to the next bedroom and saw Matthias asleep. He thought, *Maybe I'll take out agent Roberts here instead of Pinto.* He then thought, *Nah. Doesn't fit. Too easy. Pinto is the secondary agent not Matthias. Got to keep to my signature.* The third bedroom had a light on. He carefully looked into the room and saw Anna sitting in a chair with her back to him and reading a book.

Well, my daughter, it looks like you are first. Then the bitch.

The Ghost took a garrote out of his pocket and stealthily

tip-toed toward Anna. *I sure wish I didn't have to do this.* He thought. Then he threw the garrote's wire around Anna's neck and tightened it. But something was wrong. There was no resistance to the wire from Anna's neck or from Anna herself. The wire cut through the neck easily, and the head fell into her lap.

"A dummy!" he exclaimed.

Then he heard, "Aren't you a little old to be playing with dolls, Yulov?"

Yulov spun around and saw Samantha standing in the room.

"You!" he yelled. He viciously threw the garrote at Samantha, and she easily moved her head to the side to avoid it.

"Well, you and me. We meet for the second time. The first was in the plane—remember that? Only then, I was tied to the copilot's chair and was quite helpless."

Yulov glared at her in disbelief.

"So, I'm not so helpless now. What are you going to do about it?"

Yulov took two steps toward her and said, "This wasn't part of my plan, bitch, but I'm going to kill you with my bare hands, and I'm going to love doing it."

"I can't wait. Give me your best shot, asshole."

Yulov charged toward her, jumped, spun, and threw a flying back kick toward her face with the heel of his foot. Samantha anticipated this move, and just before he reached her, she stepped to the side, turned her body slightly, and hit his outstretched leg with a well-placed hook punch using the fleshy side of her closed fist. Yulov grunted in pain, but he quickly regained his balance and charged toward her again. He was going for her neck by using a flick of his wrist.

Samantha dove to the floor and body-rolled under his legs. Yulov went sprawling forward to the floor and slid forward flat on his stomach. Samantha sprang to her feet in a flash and raced to the Ghost. He was trying to right himself and was on all fours trying to stand. Samantha put her right foot on the back of his neck and pushed Yulov until he was flat on his stomach again.

"Hey, asshole. Do you know what I could do to your neck right now, sweetie?" I could crush it like a bag of potato chips. It would probably sound the same too."

Yulov grunted in pain.

"You know, Yulov? I hear that you are very abusive to women. For a big, strong man like you, that is a very cowardly thing to do. Your wife and your daughter. Shame on you, you cowardly asshole. It seems that you are very experienced at hurting women. You can't let a weak innocent little girl like me get the best of you, can you? Here, let me help you up so you can try again."

She grabbed his hand and jerked him up onto his feet. Immediately, she planted her feet firmly to the floor, slightly turned her body away from him and delivered a hook punch into his side using the knuckles of her half-closed right hand. Yulov fell to his knees gasping for breath. She slapped him on each cheek with a spear-hand strike. His head spun to the side after each blow. She then hit him in the back of his head with the fleshy side of her open hand, sending him sprawling once again onto his stomach. She again pinned him to the floor by stepping on his neck.

"It doesn't look like you did much better that time, loser."

Samantha released her foot from Yulov's neck and offered him her hand.

He looked up at her and painfully growled through gritted teeth, "Who are you?"

"Come on, brave man, abuser of women, let me help you up. Want another try?".

She extended her hand to him even more. He remained on all fours gasping for breath. She then reached down, grabbed his wrist, pulled up hard, stepped over his body, and pulled again until he flipped over and was flat on his back. Still holding his arm up, she hit his forearm with a vicious hammer fist punch with her closed fist. The sound of his ulna and radius forearm bones fracturing was horrible to hear. Yulov screamed in excruciating pain, fell flat on his stomach, and began crying.

"Hi, Daddy. How does it feel to get beat up by a weak, tiny girl like her?" said Anna as she walked into the room. She looked at him and smiled. "Here, let me get you a tissue so you can wipe the tears from your crying eyes."

Harlan, Ira, Matthias, Jared, Josh, Joe, and Rodriquez walked into the room.

Samantha looked at Matthias and ordered, "Give it to him."

Matthias took the hypodermic needle he had in his hand, and he injected the fluid into Yulov's unbroken arm.

The last thing Yulov heard before he passed out was Joe Pinto saying, "Samantha, you are the best martial arts pupil I've ever had. I mean, your fight with Yulov was over before it even started. I sure wouldn't want to meet up with you in a dark alley."

Ira came up to Samantha and hugged her. "Sam, you're going to be the death of me yet. I don't know why I let you talk me into these hair-brained schemes of yours."

Ira then turned to Joe Pinto and said, "Joe, did you know that Samantha was the president of the karate club in high school?"

CHAPTER 41
SAMANTHA'S DEBRIEF

AT THAT TIME, THE TWO security guards that had relieved Joe Pinto came into the bedroom. One of them said, "Is this the piece of shit that Samantha was going to beat up? Oops! Sorry, ladies. Pardon my French."

"Don't worry about it. It's our opinion as well, and we've called him worse than that," said Samantha.

"Yes, it's him," said Harlan. Lock him up in the base brig and be sure that the MPs know how dangerous he is. He'll be unconscious for about eight hours. But keep an eye on him anyway."

"Yes, sir, Mr. Bradbury. We'll watch him ourselves just to be sure."

Samantha said, "Harlan, the Ghost needs a doctor to set the broken bones in his arm. Can we have Dr. Gunn take care of him?"

"Ira, here in Norfolk, this is more your jurisdiction. Can you handle that?"

"Sure, Harlan. I'll see if Gunner can look at Yulov in the morning."

Samantha asked, "What's next for the Ghost, Harlan?"

"The CIA jet is at Langley Air Force Base just a few miles from here. We'll fly him up to DC in the jet tomorrow and imprison him there. Then he'll be shipped off to our prison facility in

Guantanamo Bay, Cuba—a place no one wants to be. I'm not sure when that will be, but with the other coup leaders, it only took a week or two. Why do you ask?"

"Harlan, I have a special favor to ask of you."

"What is it?"

Samantha went over to Harlan and whispered in his ear. As she whispered, Harlan's eyes widened, and his jaw dropped.

"Samantha! Where do all these crazy ideas come from? What you want me to do breaks every rule and regulation that I'm sworn to follow and uphold. . . But, of course, I'll do it."

Everyone else in the room looked at one another in confusion. Finally, Ira asked, "What crazy thing does my wife want to do now? Harlan, what did she whisper in your ear?"

"She asked me to keep it a secret. I guess you'll find out tomorrow."

"No way," said Ira. He looked at Samantha and said, "Tell me and tell me now. What's going on?"

"Tomorrow, Admiral. Tomorrow."

The others kept looking at one another and shaking their heads.

Harlan laughed and said, "You guys are going to love this one." Harlan then changed the subject. "But on another matter, I want to have a short debriefing on what has happened over the last week. Tomorrow morning at nine o'clock. Ira, is it okay if we use your classified briefing room again?"

"Of course, Harlan."

Harlan said, "Great. Look, everyone, it is after midnight. Hopefully, we can all get some sleep. We had a hell of a day today, and we have a busy day tomorrow. I also got word earlier that if everything went well tonight, President Milsap wants to see us in the Oval Office at one o'clock tomorrow afternoon. Tomorrow morning's debrief will help me give a summary to the president. Good job, everyone."

At nine o'clock the next morning, Harlan opened the meeting.

"Okay, Samantha. Tell us how you put all this together and pulled off a capture the CIA hasn't been able to accomplish in almost two years."

Samantha stood up and said, "First of all, I want to thank everyone here, especially Anna, for being such convincing actors. Fooling Jean was critical to making this plan work. The most important thing for me was trying to put myself into the head of the Ghost. I learned this from Ira during our mission in the Sea of Okhotsk. To defeat the Russian submarine commanders, he had to anticipate or figure out what they would do. You know, get into their heads. He was able to do this to perfection. I must admit, that trying to do that with an insane person is difficult and scary. But I've been studying and dealing with this guy for quite some time now, and I felt I could figure out how he thinks and what he might do. I just knew that his king-sized ego would convince him that he had figured out that we were using Anna to trap him. I'm positive that he does care for Anna, but loyalty and usefulness to him are more important than mere caring. Even more than love. He killed his wife, Rhetta, and was about to kill Anna for this very reason. I'm sure that he knew it was Anna shooting at him from the helicopter during our escape from the chalet. So, I asked myself *what would I do if I were him*? First, I would know that the CIA would try to lure me into a trap at the safe house. Second, and this is important, I would be sure that Anna and I would be somewhere else and not at the safe house. When the Ghost asked Anna for the address of the safe house and information on our shuttle car, I was sure that I was right. He would follow our car to see where we were really staying. I also did not believe that Saturday was his actual assassination day. He passed Saturday to us through Anna so we would be setting things up for him on Saturday, when in reality, he would hit us on Friday when we weren't expecting it. Well, we were expecting it on Friday, and voila. We have him in custody."

Josh asked, "How did you know the Ghost wouldn't kill Matthias or you first while you were in your beds?"

"First—Matthias. In all three assassination attempts on me, Yulov killed the secondary or junior agent. Not the primary. Bartholomew Frampton, Nathaniel Breakstone, and Simon Prather were all the junior bodyguards. I felt that this was Yulov's so-called signature. Kill the junior agent. I also thought of another possibility, but I am not sure if I am correct. The senior agents are all Black. The junior agents were all white. James Breland, Matthias, and Big John were the senior agents guarding me, and they are all Black. If this was part of the Ghost's signature, Matthias being Black, would not fit. Joe Pinto is the junior agent, and he is White. Joe would be the Ghost's target. And don't forget, Josh, I had you hiding in Matthias's bedroom closet and Jared in my closet in case I was wrong. Second—me. I believe that the Ghost wanted to kill Anna first, then kill me. Remember, at the chalet, he tied up Anna in a chair. He could have killed her then. Instead, he came to get me so he could make me watch as he killed his daughter. Unbelievable! What an animal he is. Actually, animal is too nice a name. Monster is closer to the truth. In any event, I was pretty sure that he would go after Anna before me. Also, we had Anna's bedroom light on, and I was counting on Yulov seeing this. He'd have to see if she was awake before he tried to kill me."

Jared asked, "How did you know you could take the Ghost down in a fight? My God, Anna. You were shot in the arm less than two weeks ago."

"Jared, I didn't know if I could. All I do know is that Joe and I have had my arm's wound in consideration during our training. He taught me how to protect it and not leave it vulnerable to attack. And despite the tender arm, I have been able to best Joe during our daily taekwondo lessons. At least it seemed like I was besting him."

"You did," confirmed Joe. "I can't beat you."

Ira looked back and forth between Samantha and Pinto with his eyes as wide as saucers.

Samantha continued, "Besides, I had Jared, Josh, Matthias, Joe, and Rod standing at the ready if I got into trouble. I was also counting on Yulov's age to slow him down a bit—he has more than twenty years on me. But to tell you the truth, I wanted to beat the shit out of that scumbag so bad, I could taste it. I had to give it a go."

"Well, that you did, Samantha," said Rodrigo.

Harlan asked, "The Ghost went after Jean. What about her? How did you figure that out?"

"It was clear to me that Jean's reliability had worn away. The Ghost couldn't depend on her anymore. The scheme we implemented by using the three possible relocation cities had to shake Yulov's confidence in Jean. She was now in the liability stage. Not a good place to be when it comes to him. From the Ghost's point-of-view, she had to go. I wasn't sure when he would do it, but I felt it had to be sooner rather than later. That's why I recommended that we have Big John watch her house. Sure enough, Yulov tried to put her to rest with carbon monoxide, but the big guy was there to rescue her after the Ghost left."

Harlan added, "We have Jean in custody now. She'll be tried for treason." He added, "Any other questions for Samantha?"

Ira raised his hand and asked, "Yes, Harlan. How did my wife talk you into letting her fight Yulov with her bare hands? And why didn't anyone tell me about this?"

"Listen, Ira. I opposed her fighting Yulov tooth and nail. But you know her. She had her mind made up. She even threatened to show her taekwondo skills on me. But like she said, Joe was confident in her, and we had several trained experts to intervene if necessary. We didn't want to worry you, Ira."

Ira grunted and shook his head in disapproval.

"Anything else? Okay, let's get everyone and the Ghost to Langley Air Force Base and fly to DC."

Ira said, "Wait! One other thing. What's this secret that my wife over here whispered in your ear yesterday?"

"Patience, Ira. All in due time."

"This is ridiculous. I'm an admiral in the US Navy. I demand an answer."

"In a few hours you'll know, husband dear."

CHAPTER 41
THE EGO HAS FALLEN

AT LANGLEY AIR FORCE BASE near Norfolk, the CIA jet was warmed up and ready to go. At eleven o'clock, a prison transport van drove up to the aircraft. Four armed guards escorted the Ghost from the van to the jet. He needed help getting up the jetway ladder because he was still groggy from the drug that Matthias had injected into him, his left arm was in a sling, and he had only one useful arm.

As he was being secured in his seat, Samantha sat facing him. She said in a loving voice, "Hi, Yulov. Hope you slept well." She smiled at him then said, "Sorry about your arm. But it looks like Dr. Gunn did a nice job fixing you up. Dr. Gunn is the best, and we want nothing but the best for you."

Yulov glared at Samantha with clear hatred in his eyes.

"What's the matter, asshole. Cat got your tongue?"

He growled at her, "Who the hell are you?"

"I'm a nobody, Yulov. Just like you. I'm a physical scientist, and I work at the Naval Research Laboratory in Washington, DC. You know, just an average female trying to make a living." Samantha smiled at him and said, "But I know who you are." She paused. "You're a loser," she said with contempt. "And in a few minutes, you are going to get what's coming to you. What you deserve. In just a few short minutes," she repeated.

For the next fifteen minutes, Samantha looked at Yulov and smiled. Then she looked at Harlan, nodded her head, and said, "It's time."

Harlan stood up and announced, "Like the lady said, it's time. Open the door."

Jared opened the plane's door, and a whoosh of air rocked the cabin as the air pressure changed.

Samantha smiled even broader at Yulov, and then the smile disappeared from her face, and she said in a gruff voice, "Get this asshole on his feet."

Ira asked in a worried voice, "What are you people doing?"

Samantha said, "Why, Ira. We are going to throw this bag of shit out of the airplane. It's starting to smell in here."

Yulov's eyes widened in horror. Rodrigo and Jared unbuckled the Ghost and began dragging him toward the open door. The look of terror on his face was clear.

Anna spoke up. "Wait! You can't do that. He's my father." Then she thought for a moment as she looked up toward the cabin's ceiling and said, "But then again, he murdered my mother and my fiancée, and he tried to cut my neck with a piano wire last night. Can I be the one that pushes his sorry ass out the door?"

"No, Anna. He tried to kill me three or four times, and he tried to kill my infant babies. I'm the one that should kick him out."

Jared said, "What about me and Josh? He sent two German trained killers after us. Maybe we could all push him out at the same time."

Ira yelled out, "You people can't do this! It's not right! Harlan, stop them!"

"I don't think so, Ira. I know it's not right. But he has killed three of my best field agents. The way I look at it is that by jettisoning him out of the plane, we save fuel and taxpayer's money. I think I'll help them push that cockroach out."

"Harlan, you can't be serious! Stop them!"

Samantha looked at the Ghost, who was gasping uncontrollably, and said, "The last time we were in a plane together, you jumped out of it with a parachute. You did great. You landed right on the fantail of your yacht. Let's see how you do this time. Oops. We don't have a parachute, and I forgot to arrange for a yacht for you to land on. My bad."

With terror in his voice, he begged, "No, you can't. You don't have the right to just kill me. Please don't do this."

"Let me think." She paused for a moment and said, "Nah. You're going out the door. But it was nice playing games with you. It was actually fun." She turned to Jared, Josh, and Anna and ordered, "Get this scumbag loser off our airplane."

Yulov started screaming, "Please! Please don't do this! I'm sorry! I was just doing my job! Anna, Sweetie, please, don't let them do this!"

"Bye, daddy. Have a pleasant flight down. If you flap your arms really really fast, you might slow yourself down. Oops. I forgot; you only have one useable arm. That won't work. Sorry."

When Yulov was at the edge of the door, and he was screaming for mercy, Samantha said, "Wait! Wait! I have a better idea. Put him back in his seat."

Yulov's eyes were bulging out of their sockets, and he was looking at Samantha in terror.

When he was buckled back in his seat. Samantha said, "Stop your pathetic mewling. You're sobbing like a little baby. Matthias, give it to him. Shut this crybaby up."

Matthias injected another shot into Yulov's good arm.

Ira realized that he was the only one not in on the charade the gang pulled on Yulov. Yet, he breathed a sigh of relief and said, "Thank God." Then he asked, "Was I the only one that wasn't in on this secret Samantha whispered to Harlan?"

Samantha said, "Ira, I knew that you would strongly oppose

what I wanted to do to the Ghost. You are a truly good person. That's who you are. I just wanted to have Yulov experience some of the terror he has brought on others."

"You are right, Samantha. I would have really opposed what you just did. I'm just glad that it is over."

"Well, Ira, as they say in so many of those infomercials, 'But wait! There's *more!*'"

"What do you mean?"

Samantha just smiled, looked at Harlan, and nodded her head.

Harlan then passed the word to the pilot to return to Langley Air Force Base.

Four hours later, Anton Yulov started waking up from a cloudy sleep, the vision of the nightmare on the plane still in his mind. He felt cold and wet. In fact, he was freezing. When he tried to move, he couldn't budge an inch. In his foggy condition, he couldn't focus his eyes on anything. He felt a sharp pain in his left forearm when he tried to move, then, his memory started coming back to him. He remembered that he was just about to be thrown out of an airplane. The vision of falling thousands of feet into the ocean was horrible to him. He gasped at the thought. The feeling of cold and wetness remained. Gradually, his eyes began to focus on his surroundings. He could see two indistinct shadows, one to the right of him and the other to his left. As the shadows gradually came into focus, he could see that there were two women sitting in aluminum beach chairs facing him. He had to look up to see them. It was then that the realization of his situation hit him. Samantha was in a chair to his right, and Anna was in a chair to his left, and he was buried up to his neck in wet beach sand. Wet, very cold November beach sand.

"Hi, shitface. I thought you'd never wake up. I was afraid you were going to miss the fun."

Yulov stared at Samantha with hatred in his eyes. He tried to struggle, but the pain in his broken arm was excruciating.

"Hi, Daddy. Remember me, your daughter, *sweetie*? I know that I'm supposed to be dead by now. Sorry to disappoint you."

Samantha said, "Anna, here, confided in me that you have a horrible fear of drowning. I remembered this on the plane a few hours ago. Then I thought, pushing your sorry ass out of a plane was too good for you. Over too quick, you know?"

Yulov looked back and forth between Samantha and Anna with horror in his eyes.

Samantha said, "Look dung-heap, as you said to me on that airplane when you tried to kill me. Here's your situation. As you can tell, you're buried up to your smelly neck on a beautiful beach in Virginia Beach. The tide is coming in. At high tide, which is in about an hour, actually a little less, the water will be up to here." Samantha stood up and pointed to her mid-thigh. "As you can see, that's well over your head. About two hours later, the tide will have receded back to where it is now. Can you hold your breath for that long? Probably not but give it a try. I also hear that the blue crab population is high on this beach, and the crabs will probably pluck your eyes out before the water recedes back to where it is now."

Just then, an advancing flow of ocean water stopped just short of the Ghost's chin. Panic struck him, and he tried to wiggle himself free. He could only groan with pain.

"No, please! Don't let me drown! I don't want to drown! I'll do anything you want!"

"Why, Daddy. You're begging for mercy. Did any of your victims beg for mercy? If they did, I'm sure it didn't do them any good. Did it? Well, it's not going to do you any good either."

The advancing water reached his chin. He looked at Samantha, then Anna in complete terror.

"Please! Please! I'm begging you!" he cried.

"Sorry, you pathetic, miserable excuse for a man. You abuser of women. You killer of innocent babies. You have no regard for human life. Why should we care about yours? Come on, Anna. Let's get out of here. I'm tired of this asshole begging for mercy. So pathetic."

Anna and Samantha stood up and nonchalantly washed the sand from their beach chairs by the next wave coming in, which hit Yulov in the face and caused him to spit out and swallow the sandy salty ocean water.

"Bye, Daddy. Just think, you're going to be roasting in hell in just a few minutes."

"He doesn't believe in such things, Anna. He told me that on the plane when he tried to kill me. He also told me that he was having so much fun while he was alive. I guess the fun's just about over for you, Yulov."

"Speaking of fun, Samantha, you promised me we'd go skiing in Maine as soon as we finished with this loser."

"I did. How about next week?" They both laughed as they walked away holding hands.

The small waves were now breaking onto Yulov's face. He screamed between the swallows of salty water, and he continued to shout for mercy.

As they walked away, Samantha ordered the men standing behind Yulov to dig him out of his sandy prison. The men raced to Yulov and began extricating him from the sand.

Samantha said to Anna, "For a man that has no regard for human life, he sure begged hard for his."

Anna said, "The Ghost is too nice a name for him, Samantha. What if we rename him the Coward?"

CHAPTER 42
THE PRESIDENT'S BARBECUE

AN HOUR LATER, THEY WERE on the CIA jet heading for Washington, DC. Harlan said, "The president agreed to postpone his meeting with us. He suggested that we have dinner with him at the White House at eight o'clock. Should I tell him it's a yes?"

Anna said, "Harlan, Samantha and I aren't dressed properly to have dinner with the president. I mean, look at us. We're sandy from the beach, our hair is all wind-blown, we have on the same casual clothes we've been wearing all day."

"Don't worry about it Anna. Milsap will understand. I'll tell him the situation."

"Samantha! He's the president of the United States! We can't go there looking like this!"

Samantha chuckled. "Men just don't understand these things, Anna. They are so crude. But don't worry about it. Harlan, instead of having a formal dinner, can we ask Milsap if we can have a barbecue with beer? Lots of beer?"

"I'll check with him. If I know Milsap, he will prefer that. Especially if there's lots of beer."

At 7:45 that evening, the limo dropped off the nine passengers, and they were escorted to the Rose Garden. On the way, they could smell the hamburgers cooking on the grill. When they entered the

Rose Garden, Big John confronted Samantha and said, "Samantha, I'm going to have to pat you down to be sure you're not packing."

"Big John, touch me, and you'll wish you were the Ghost."

They both laughed and hugged each other tightly.

"God, Big John, I love you. I only wish I could get my arms all the way around you so I could give you a real hug."

James Milsap came up to the couple and gave Big John a beer and said, "Big man, take this beer to Anna Yulov."

"Yes, sir, Mr. President."

"I don't know how many times I've said this to you, Samantha, but it's so great to see you alive."

"James, it's good to be alive so I can enjoy a hug from you."

"I thought you'd never ask."

Samantha laughed, and as she was giving Milsap a hug, she said, "You've been talking to my husband too much."

"Samantha, I could hold you like this all night, but I've got a Ukrainian girl I have to meet and hug."

Milsap went up to Anna and said, "So you're the beautiful and brave Ukrainian girl that Samantha and Harlan have said so much about."

"Mr. President?" Anna asked in awe.

As Milsap put his arms around Anna, her eyes got wide, her jaw dropped to the ground, and she dropped her can of beer.

He said in her ear, "I know that I speak for all the people of the United States, Anna. Thank you for what you've done. You are a courageous woman. I will never be able to thank you enough."

Milsap then turned around to Big John and said, "Get Anna another beer, Big John. I just knocked the one she had out of her hand."

The barbecue went on until almost midnight. During that time, Milsap thanked each one of the nine personally for their service in capturing one of the most dangerous and evil men the world has ever seen.

After he thanked everyone, he announced, "Gather around here everyone. I've got something important to tell you."

They formed a small semi-circle around the president, and all had curious looks on their faces.

"I've thanked you all for your service to the United States. But there is one more thing that I'd like to share with you. Samantha, can you please come here beside me?"

Samantha moved her head backward, crinkled her eyes, pointed to herself, and mouthed "me?"

"Yes, you. Come here. Please."

Samantha looked around to everyone with a confused look on her face as she walked up to Milsap. He smiled at her, looked at the others, then looked directly at Samantha.

"Samantha, on behalf of the people of the United States of America, I am proud to present to you for your outstanding service and sacrifice for your country, the Defense of Freedom medal."

Samantha stood there with her mouth agape as President Milsap pinned the medal on her blouse.

"Samantha? Anything to say to your friends here?"

Samantha cupped her hands around her mouth and nose and looked at her husband, her friends, and the president's ever-present entourage.

After about thirty seconds of just looking at everyone's smiling faces, she said, "The president had threatened to embarrass me with this award, but I was hoping that he would forget about it. Obviously, he didn't. All I can say here is that if I could break this medal into a bunch of pieces, I would share it with all of you who were by my side the whole way. This was a perfect example of a team effort. Every one of you were critical in catching that madman. I can't thank you all enough."

Josh leaned over to Anna and whispered in her ear, "That's typical Samantha. She always passes the credit to others."

President said, "Thank you, Samantha for a job well done."

Everyone there erupted into loud cheers and began clapping vigorously. The applause lasted for over a minute. Samantha smiled broadly and continuously shook her head with her hands clasped over her heart.

When the applause died down, Milsap said, "Samantha, while you are up here, I want to ask you a question that I know everyone here is dying to ask."

"What's that, James?"

The president smiled at Samantha's use of his first name. He nodded his head in approval. He then said, "I know I speak for everyone here, Samantha, so let me ask you this. How did you know that you were going to have to fly that helicopter to escape from the chalet?"

Samantha's eyes widened, and she looked at Milsap in surprise at his question. She looked at the crowd and asked, "You're *all* wondering this?"

In almost perfect unison, they shouted "YES!"

She thought for a moment then took a deep breath. Finally, she said, "When Anna first showed me the helicopter, my first thought was that I had to disable it so Yulov could not use it to escape. I could have disabled it in many ways, but after some thought, I wanted to disable the helicopter yet have it appear flyable so he would try to fly it. I thought that this might delay him even more and increase our chances of capturing him. I had no idea as to how to do this. My faith has taught me to pray for all things and not rely on my own wits to solve problems. So that's what I did the night Anna and I stayed overnight at the chalet. I asked for wisdom to disable the helicopter. That night, I woke up, and I realized that I had been dreaming. In that dream, I was flying that helicopter. This kind of thing has happened to me before. You know, dreams answering my prayers. I knew that I should take this dream seriously. I thought about it for a long time that night. In the morning, I texted Harlan and asked him if he could locate any videos on how to fly that particular make and model of helicopter. He sent me three videos to look at. I spent the last afternoon studying those videos in my hotel room. At the time, I had no idea that I would be flying the copter that night. My plan A was to set fire to the cockpit using the can of charcoal lighter that Yulov had in the hanger. Instead, I used the lighter to burn his prized bows just to tick him off."

Samantha looked at the crowd for a few seconds and said, "That's it. I prayed, and my prayers were answered. Simple as that."

Everyone there just stood in silence, staring in awe at Samantha. Finally, Ira began a slow clap, which gradually increased in speed and loudness, as everyone added to the applause. Even President Milsap and his entourage were clapping vigorously. Before the clapping had even ended, Samantha's friends were coming up to her for a hug. Tears were flowing from everyone's eyes, especially Samantha's.

Everyone was trying to get some of Samantha's time to congratulate her on her award. However, President Milsap cornered Harlan and said gruffly, "Bradbury, we have to talk. Come with me."

When they were out of earshot, Milsap said, "Why in God's name did you decide to put Samantha in such danger by having her fight Yulov mano a mano?"

"I knew that you'd be upset over that, Mr. President."

"Upset isn't the word for it. She isn't a CIA agent, for crying out loud. Yet you have her take on a task that would be highly dangerous even for our most skilled agents. And to top it all off, she had a two-week-old gunshot wound in her arm. Harlan, what were you thinking?"

"Mr. President, you know Samantha and how she is. Yulov has put her through so much pain and anguish. Heaven knows she is a very loving person. But with Yulov, I clearly saw hate in her eyes and in her voice. She wanted to torment him. Belittle him. Bring him down from that high horse he was on. She's a very humble woman, and she has a difficult time dealing with people that have super big egos, like Yulov. Plus—and in my mind, this is the biggest factor—Yulov almost killed her twins. Mr. President, I've never seen anyone so motivated to develop martial art skills as Samantha. She wore poor Joe Pinto out with her desire to hone her hand-to-hand fighting skills. Her plan to capture the Ghost was built around her meeting him face-to-face and humiliating him. And like I just said, you know Samantha. And when she has her mind made up, no one is going to change it."

"What about her arm? You've conveniently ignored my question about that."

"Mr. President, I argued with her continuously about her arm putting her in a disadvantageous position against Yulov. But, as we've seen before, she is a quick healer. Her arm was tender, for sure, but Pinto assured me that she would be able to protect it in a fight. He told me that he went for the arm numerous times in their training sessions, and she easily deflected his attacks every time.

Milsap thought for a moment, then said, "I understand what you are telling me, Harlan. But what would you have done if Yulov got the best of her and seriously injured her?"

"Sir, I had two Navy SEALs and three trained field agents ready to step in instantly. Fortunately, they weren't needed. Samantha made a pathetic fool out of Yulov."

"What are you two guys whispering about all alone?" asked Samantha as she walked up to them.

"We were actually talking about you."

"Oh? I hope it was good."

"It was." Said Milsap. "We are in awe of how brave you were to take on Yulov like you did."

"Well, if you want to know the truth James, I was scared to death."

CHAPTER 43
SAMANTHA'S GIFT

ONE WEEK LATER, IRA SAID to Samantha, "Sam, Harlan just called and told me that tomorrow morning they are shipping Yulov off to Gitmo."

"Ira, can we go to DC? I want to see him off."

"I'll ask Harlan. I'm sure he will allow that."

"That would be great."

"Sam, in the last week, I haven't mentioned anything about the Ghost. I wanted to just forget about the whole thing for a while."

"Me too, Ira. That last week or so—especially my time in Switzerland—was very stressful for me, and I wanted to chill out for a while myself. I'm glad you felt the same way."

"Are you ready to confront Yulov again tomorrow?"

"I think so. I've calmed down quite a bit in the last week."

"Sam, if that's the case, can I ask you something?"

"Sure. What is it?"

"Please be truthful."

"Okay."

"What you did to Yulov after we captured him was so out of character for you. You know, threatening to push him out of the plane and making him think that you were going to let him drown. I could never imagine you doing something like that to anybody. And your language. I've never heard you use such foul language before. Calling him all those filthy names. I know that you hate Yulov. But we had him in custody. He will get what he deserves. Why did you do that to him?"

"Ira, I've asked myself the same thing many times. How could I have done such cruel things to another human being? My language? I know the words, Ira. I just never think of using them. That is until I met this evil man. The names I've called him just seemed so appropriate. I know that seeking retribution from Yulov was wrong. In Colossians 3, we are reminded that God has forgiven us of our sins and that we should do the same to those that wrong us. Also, I've been taught in my faith not to judge anyone. That's the Lord's job. But with Yulov, I saw pure evil. He has no conscience. No regard for human life. In fact, what he did to people was fun for him. Can you believe it? Fun! Plus, he is so full of himself. He feels that he is superior to everyone else. It's disgusting. Ira, he put me through so much anguish for so many months. He took my life away from me. You. My infant babies. Everything. Because of him, I've got physical scars on my body that I will have for the rest of my life. Scars that will remind me of what he put me through. And it's not just me, Ira. Look at what he did to other innocent people. The high school archery boys and the four innocent people that died with them. His wife was going to marry another man, so he killed her fiancée. He killed his innocent wife, Rhetta. My God, Ira. She may have revealed critical state secrets about the SOOF to Mr. and Mrs. Smith. But Yulov is the one who gave the secrets to her even though she didn't have a need to know. He was the guilty one, not her. In reality, he should have assassinated himself. He killed Anna's boyfriend so they wouldn't get married. Imagine that! What about his political opponent? He discredits him so he will win the election, then he murders him anyway. Mary Graham and her husband. My three Secret Service bodyguards.

The innocent fake flight attendant in Gulfport. He murdered Irina when he didn't have to. Then we find out that he killed the hotel maid and an innocent elderly couple in Grindelwald. He tried to kill his only daughter. My God, Ira, what kind of a man considers the killing of two infant babies as mere collateral damage? There may be others we don't even know about. Ira, I hated this man with a passion, and I wanted to torment him so badly. To bring him down from his high horse. To belittle and humiliate him. To make him feel the fear he put me through. I know I was wrong to hate him, Ira, but I am human, and I sinned. However, I've repented, and I will try to never do that again."

"Wow, Sam! This whole thing with the Ghost has really affected you. I knew it had, but I didn't know how much."

"I'm over it now, Ira. I believe that in my heart, I have forgiven him. He is possessed by the devil or is insane. Maybe both. Either way, I feel sorry for him. Not hatred as I did before. I want to put this to a test tomorrow. I want to see if this hatred is still in me. I won't really know until I'm standing directly in front of him and looking into his eyes."

Ira nodded his head in understanding.

The next day, Samantha and Ira were waiting at the prison to see Yulov. A short time later, they saw Yulov being escorted to a waiting transportation van. His head was down, and he looked dejected as he shuffled his chained feet.

"Hi, Yulov. How have you been? Have they been treating you well?" she asked as he was passing by.

When Yulov saw Samantha, he glared at her with hatred in his eyes. "What are you doing here? You come to gloat?" he growled through gritted teeth.

"On the contrary. I just wanted to wish you well. I see that you don't need an arm sling anymore. Just a cast. That's good."

Yulov continued to glare at her.

"You know, Yulov, my faith demands that we should forgive

one another. I want you to know that I truly forgive you for what you did to me and to others I know and love—you know, trying to kill me and my babies, putting me in the hospital several times, stuff like that. I do forgive you in my heart. And I hope that you forgive me for what I did to you. I know that I made a complete fool out of you. I outsmarted you, turned your daughter against you, stole your money, put you in jail for the rest of your life, and best of all, I kicked the crap out of you with my bare hands. Do you have it in your heart to forgive me for all that?"

Yulov continued to stare at her with hatred.

"I thought not, Mr. Yulov. It seems that you are beyond help, and you will burn in hell and be tormented by your boss, Satan, for eternity.

"Who are you?" he growled.

"I told you a few weeks ago who I am. Just a normal, everyday person. Still, there is always hope. I mean, Jesus saved one of the thieves on a cross moments before he died. I'm certain that the prison where you'll be living the rest of your life has an extensive library. I recommend that you locate and check out the best self-help book ever written. It's called the Bible. You've probably heard of it. I suggest that you make sure that you get a study guide version. The footnotes will help you to understand what the Bible is trying to teach you. Start with the Gospel of John and go from there. Mr. Yulov, if you do this, I'm sure you will be glad you did."

Samantha turned to leave, then back toward the Ghost. "Oh, one other thing. I know where you are going before you check into hell for eternity. There will be some very big men there in your Cuban prison. Some very, very big men, if you catch my drift. Because of that, I brought you a little gift that might come in handy."

Samantha reached into her purse and took out a small package wrapped exactly like the gift Yulov had secretly left for her at her first wedding anniversary barbecue a year and a half before. It was wrapped in purple foil and had a yellow bow on top.

She handed the gift to Yulov and said, "This is just a little token from me to show that I have truly forgiven you. Enjoy."

The guards then brusquely pushed Yulov into the transportation van for the first leg of his trip to Cuba.

As Ira and Samantha were walking back to their car, Ira said, "That was very nice of you to forgive him and to suggest that he read the Bible. You never know. By the way, it was very thoughtful of you to give him a gift, Sam. What did you give him?"

Samantha said with an evil grin on her face, "A tube of KY Lubricating Jelly."

Ira said in disbelief, "Sam!"

EPILOGUE

TWO MONTHS LATER

"IRA, YOU'VE BEEN TELLING ME that you have a special day set up for us tomorrow. When are you going to tell me what we will be doing? I'm so excited about this."

"Okay, I've been keeping it a secret from you, but I can't hold it in any longer. In the morning, we will go to church like we do every Sunday. We will have lunch at the Ocean View Golf Club. Then, I've reserved a one o'clock tee time at the club's golf course. I'm finally going to do what I've wanted to do for a long time: teach you how to play golf. But, Sam, don't worry about it too much. I'm an excellent golfer, and I can teach you the basics. It's easy to learn how to play golf. It's just hard to get good at it. You'll have fun. I promise."

"Sounds great so far."

Then, I've arranged to have a candlelight dinner catered by the O 'Club right here in our home."

"Wow! Ira, that sounds great. I can't wait. Then what?" she asked with a lascivious grin.

"Then I'm going to teach you how to play chess," Ira said with a triumphant smile.

Samantha's evil grin disappeared from her face. "Aren't we going to go to bed and clown around?"

"After chess."

Samantha shook her head.

The next day, on the first tee, Ira showed Samantha the proper golf grip and how to swing the club to make good contact with the ball.

Four hours later, when they were walking off the eighteenth green to their golf cart, Ira said, "You beat me by four strokes, Sam. Why didn't you tell me that you were the captain of the ladies golf team at Oregon State?"

"You never asked."

"Well, this was very embarrassing. You even let me give you some basic lessons on the first tee. And right in front of that couple we were paired with. Why did you do that?"

"Ira, you said that you were an excellent golfer. I was hoping to learn something new from you."

"You could have told me. It was humiliating."

"What is it with men?" she muttered under her breath.

Later that night, after the O' Club caterers had taken away all the dishes and left, Samantha and Ira were alone. Ira broke out the chess board and chessmen. He meticulously placed the pieces in their proper positions on the board.

Samantha sat opposite him staring at the board.

"Okay, now I am going to show you how each piece can be moved."

Samantha said, "Let's skip that part, Ira. You're playing white. White always moves first."

Ira glared at the smiling Samantha and exclaimed, "No, no, no, Sam!"

"Yup. Chess club. Middle school. President."

ACKNOWLEDGMENTS

AS MOST AUTHORS KNOW, WRITING a fiction novel requires the utmost in support from the family. This is so true for me. My wife, Sylvia, has supported and encouraged me from start to finish. My two daughters, Monica Tooma Smoot and Stephanie Tooma Sturm have provided me guidance from countless manuscript reviews and numerous discussions. The suggestions, ideas, and critical reviews from these three women have been a blessing to me, and for that, I am eternally grateful. I also wish to thank Dr. Timothy Scharold for his review of the medical situations depicted in *Assassins Revenge*. He has helped me avoid foolish mistakes in my discussions of medical treatments, terminology, and affects resulting from the injuries my characters received during the story. Thank you all.

CPSIA information can be obtained
at www.ICGtesting.com
Printed in the USA
LVHW100705071022
730138LV00004BA/67